INVASION!

Selected Borgo Press Books by ROBERT REGINALD

Academentia: A Future Dystopia
Ancestral Voices: An Anthology of Early Science Fiction
Ancient Hauntings (ed. with Douglas Menville)
The Attempted Assassination of John F. Kennedy
BP 300: A Bibliography of the Borgo Press, 1976-1998
Choice Words: Writers Writing About Writing (editor)
Classics of Fantastic Literature (with Douglas Menville)
Codex Derynianus III (with Katherine Kurtz)
The Dark-Haired Man; or, The Hieromonk's Tale (NE #1)
Dreamers of Dreams (ed. with Douglas Menville)
The Exiled Prince; or, The Archquisitor's Tale (NE #2)
Forgotten Fantasy: Issues #1-5 (ed. with Douglas Menville)
The Fourth Elephant's Egg; or, The Hypatomancer's Tale (#4)
"A Glorious Death": The Human-Knacker War, Book Three
The House of the Burgesses (with Mary A. Burgess)
If J.F.K. Had Lived (with Jeffrey M. Elliot)
Invasion! Earth vs. the Aliens (War of Two Worlds #1)
The Judgment of the Gods and Other Verdicts of History
King Solomon's Children (ed. with Douglas Menville)
Knack' Attack: A Tale of the Human-Knacker War (Book Two)
The Martians Strike Back! (War of Two Worlds #3)
The Nasty Gnomes: A Novel of the Phantom Detective—#2
Operation Crimson Storm (War of Two Worlds #2)
The Paperback Show Murders
Phantasmagoria (ed. with Douglas Menville)
The Phantom's Phantom: A Novel of the Phantom Detective—#1
Quæstiones; or, The Protopresbyter's Tale (Nova Europa #3)
R.I.P. (ed. with Douglas Menville)
The Spectre Bridegroom and Other Horrors (ed. with Menville)
They (ed. with Douglas Menville)
Trilobite Dreams; or, The Autodidact's Tale: An Autobiography
Worlds of Never (ed. with Douglas Menville)
Xenograffiti: Essays on Fantastic Literature

INVASION! EARTH VS. THE ALIENS

WAR OF TWO WORLDS, BOOK ONE

ROBERT REGINALD

THE BORGO PRESS

MMXI

INVASION! EARTH VS. THE ALIENS

Copyright © 2007, 2011 by Robert Reginald

FIRST BORGO PRESS EDITION

Published by Wildside Press LLC

www.wildsidebooks.com

DEDICATION

To the Memory of

Major Roy Walter Burgess, U.S.A.F.

(4 July 1922 - 16 February 1998)
Pilot and Veteran of World War II and Korea

and

Carpenter's Mate First Class
Frank Joseph Kapel

(5 December 1913 - 26 April 2006)
Seabee and Veteran of World War II

and for

H. G. Wells and Tim Underwood

Who inspired it!

AUTHOR'S NOTE

Despite the plethora of indications to the contrary on the Internet, this Borgo Press edition is the first separate publication of this novel, which has only previously been issued as part of the omnibus edition, *Invasion! Earth vs. the Aliens* (2007). The novel was announced for publication by Underwood Books in the Fall of 2005 under two titles, *War of the Worlds* and *War of Two Worlds*, the latter of which has now become the series title for this new edition; covers were created for same, and orders were solicited, but for a variety of reasons beyond the publisher's control, the book never actually appeared then. Ironically, if *War of Two Worlds* and its sequel, *Operation Crimson Storm*, *had* appeared on schedule, the third book in the trilogy, *The Martians Strike Back!*, might never have been written, since its fate was dependent on sales of the first two volumes. And so it goes!

—Robert Reginald
16 January 2011

CONTENTS

PART ONE: THE EARTH IN FLAMES

PART ONE
THE EARTH IN FLAMES

I am a man.
I consider nothing human alien to me.
—Terence

But who may actually live *on*
These worlds if they're inhabited?
—Johannes Kepler

PROLOGUE
BANG! BANG! YOU'RE DEAD!

You Only Live Twice.

—Ian Fleming

ALEX SMITH, 29 DECEMBER, MARS YEAR I
MARIN COUNTY, CALIFORNIA, PLANET EARTH

I don't know why I lived while so many others died.

I should have been killed.

I was chased and bruised and bent and broken and twisted every which way—and still I survived.

Why?

Why did I live while so many others died?

There has to be a reason.

* * * * * * *

The blast rolled me into a ditch, along with the tattered jigsaw pieces of my late comrades-in-arms.

I remember hearing two successive explosions—*blam! blat!*—and being covered with dirt and leaves and branches and half an arm, leaving only my eyes and nose exposed. Then I watched the clouds scudding by above me, interspersed with wisps of green-and-black smoke, in a world made dim and deaf by the thunder of war. It was almost scary in a way.

But I wasn't scared! I don't think I really understood what

was happening. My ears were ringing with the effects of the after-blast, but despite my temporary deafness, I could feel the rumble of something very large approaching.

Thud!

The ground belched and bolted and raised itself up. At first I thought "earthquake," but then I figured it out: one of the alien monstrosities was striding boldly over the landscape towards me. I couldn't see it and I couldn't hear it, but I knew it was there nonetheless. I tried to move, but my limbs seemed paralyzed. My breath caught in my throat.

Thud! Thud!

The zap-zit of a death-ray flashed over my head and incinerated one of the trees down the road, making it a Roman candle of instant flame.

Thud! Thud! Thud!

Closer and closer the machine strode. I thought I could hear someone crying in the distance, but I couldn't have, could I?

"Help!" he screamed. "Help me!"

It might have been Mayer. It might have been Stromwick. Whoever it was, I couldn't save them.

Thud! Thud! THUUUD!

A great metal pad splattered right down on top of me, straddling my narrow reserve. I could see the cross-pattern, the stitchery, if you will, of its fabric hanging right above my face. It paused for a moment to release another great *zzzappp!*—and someone from our squad replied in turn, the RPG striking twenty feet away. But the shadow of alien machine's foot protected me, saving me from myself. I could feel the vibration of the metal fragments rattling off its armor.

And then it was gone, just like that!

I was free.

But still I couldn't move.

I felt a pressure on my chest, as if the Martian were yet perched there, squeezing the life out of me, sucking it from my very heart. I'll never forget that moment, however long I live.

Bang! Bang! You're dead!

Thud! Thud! Thud! Thud!
Was it me who was rumbling and rambling—or the alien?
Was I dead—or just barely alive?
Why did I live while so many others died?
Why?
I wish the bloody hell I knew.

CHAPTER ONE
"THE MAN IN THE MARS"

Ours is the invading army.
—Henry David Thoreau

ALEX SMITH, 21 JUNE, MARS YEAR I
NOVATO, CALIFORNIA, PLANET EARTH

Call me Alex.

I want to tell you a story.

"Once upon a time…."

Well, I guess you've heard that one before.

No, *my* story is about life and death and war and peace and all those good and ugly things.

I could tell you that we won every fight and killed every alien and drove the dirty buggers right back into space, but it wouldn't be true.

I have quite another tale to tell, of terror and temerity and tremulousness.

It goes something like this:

In the early years of the twenty-first century, no one would have believed that our world had become the target of extraterrestrial intelligences vastly older and greater than our own.

We'd sent probes to the furthest reaches of the Solar System, and they confirmed the utter deadness of the deeps. SETI, that grand experiment to identify intelligent life "out there," failed to produce even one "peep" of nonsense. We carefully measured craters and rocks and gas. We found no life, none at all.

The machines told us that Mars once had oceans and rivers and lakes—just like Earth. Where did the water go? Underground or into the sky, our scientists said, leaving few traces of its presence in that world's barren fields and stony red hills.

Life on Mars, we all said, is certainly gone and dead—if it was ever there at all.

We were wrong.

We just hadn't read the signs right.

Our robots woke the monsters from their long, leisurely sleep. We gained their sudden attention. We aroused their interest or suspicion or who the hell knows what.

I saw it all first-hand.

I was there when it started.

I was there when it ended.

This is the tale of the War of Two Worlds.

* * * * * * *

That was the Year we later called Mars One.

I decided to take a sabbatical from the college. I'd had enough of the academic rat race to last me a lifetime. I would have been happy never to have seen Dean Broker's pinched face or my sad-eyed students ever again. The Dean wanted more students—the students wanted more jobs. The serious discussion of history and philosophy, of why and how and for what reason, was somehow lost in the shuffle.

"The problem with philosophy," one of my coeds joked, "is that it Kant make up its mind!"

"History is dead," said another, "so why don't we give it a decent burial?"

Ahem and amen. For a few months, at least, I had a book to write and grass to grow under my feet. It felt pretty damned good.

Then CNN reported a series of green flashes on the Red Planet. At the same time, our satellites around Mars suddenly went dead. The coincidence of the two events was much commented upon in the media. Carl Rover assured the press that the President had been briefed and knew what was happening, although she couldn't tell the American public—for national security reasons, of course. Fox News thought this was another liberal conspiracy, and undoubtedly it was so.

Some scientists questioned the existence of the phenomena, treating the sparks of light like some UFO sighting. "Transient radiation," a few said. Others thought that it was the interplanetary equivalent of "marsh gas."

If I hadn't bumped into Mindon at the market, I wouldn't have known much more than the other boobs. Dr. Min was an eccentric colleague and part-time lecturer who specialized in astronomy and Native American studies, and claimed some small percentage of Indian blood himself, enough to qualify him for membership in the Moroño Tribe. He looked more like a washed-up hippie than a teacher, always sporting turquoise bolo ties and rings and beads over rather garish, unbuttoned Hawaiian sports shirts—"gotta rent the rug!" he'd say. He kept a reflecting telescope in a cabin he owned a half-mile west of his house, where he sometimes practiced his flute and smoked some Humboldt hash while instructing the local damsels-in-distress in the ways of AmerIndian love songs. I'd known him for years.

"Man, you just gotta see this!" he said, leaning on a cart filled with Dos Equis, low-salt, low-fat corn chips, kosher wieners, turkey burger patties, plus more beer. "It's like Fourth of July up there. All these green and red lights popping out. I've invited Barbi and Bonni and Jillie and Stassi and Lissie and Evie and Frannie and Ollie…of course, you and Becky have *got* to come. Plenty to eat and drink."

* * * * * * *

It was getting dark by the time Rebecca and I reached Min's hideaway. He'd already fired up the barbecue, and the 'scope was set on the concrete patio, outlined against the darkening sky like some praying mantis ready to pounce. I still remember that night: the small light glowing behind us against the garage, the near-burnt odor of hotdogs and chicken and burgers searing over charcoal briskets, the murmur of voices undercut by the rasping of crows and the twittering of crickets, and the smooth ratcheting of the telescope gears as the instrument was calibrated and pointed toward Mars.

Mindon moved about like some ancient wizard, barely visible in the failing twilight, somehow keeping his beard from dipping into the fire.

"Hey, Mindon!" One of the girls giggled. "What's your *first* name?"

"That *is* my first name," he said, and went back to work.

Then he called me over to the lens, shushing everyone up. I peered into the aperture, and could suddenly see the tiny, rust-colored planet swimming in the field. It was such a bitty thing, so bright and small and still, faintly marked with transverse stripes, white at the poles and slightly flattened at top and bottom, silvery warm, a pinhead of reddish light. It quivered in the Earth's atmosphere.

As I watched, Mars seemed to grow larger and smaller, to advance and recede, but that was just my eyes growing tired. The planet was millions of miles distant, separated from us by an immensity of near-empty space.

A flash of brilliant green light shot from the planet's surface, just for a second.

"Oh my God!" I said, "What's *that?*"

"Something I've never seen before."

"But there's no life there. Everyone knows that."

"Then what *is* it?"

Of course, I couldn't respond, because I didn't know, and I didn't want to *admit* that I didn't know.

"It's the Man in the Mars," one of the girls said, and everyone laughed out loud, a nervous, tittery, twitchy sort of thing, a hollow hitching sound without much mirth to it.

The evening was unseasonably warm and I was seasonably

dry, so I left the 'scope to someone else and went looking for another cold brewski. Mindon took his turn showing the lassies just how to view the night sky.

"Ohhh, Min!" one of them said. The orbs Min was staring at weren't anywhere near the sky!

I sat on a wooden bench in the dimming light, patches of green and crimson swimming before my eyes. I hadn't smoked in years, but I suddenly wanted a cigar so bad I could taste it. That wasn't the kind of smoke that Mindon stocked in his rural retreat, however. We kept watching for another hour before finally giving up. Becky and I drove slowly downhill back to town.

"What do *you* think it is?" she asked.

"Probably nothing," I said, "just the Martian equivalent of farting."

I chuckled at my witticism, but she didn't think it was funny. Marriage is often like that: it survives (or not) based on the efficacy of one's humor, good or ill.

The next day, the *Chronicle* ran a long story on the Martian lights, eventually concluding that the phenomenon was indeed some vast geological outgassing. After all, volcanism was common on the other planets within the Solar System, and we'd seen signs that Mars had had its share of eruptions in the past. Why not now? We knew so little about the planet, really, that anything was possible.

Truer words were never thought.

That evening I walked downtown with Becky by my side. I pointed out the twelve signs of the Zodiac, showing off, as academic men like to do, my accumulated superficiality of knowledge. Then I identified Mars, a dull red hostile eye hanging low in the evening sky.

"It's beautiful," she said.

"The Roman God of War," I said. "It was he who brought death and destruction and chaos to the ancient world. Only Janus, the two-faced God of Peace, could stare him down."

"Only a man can start a war," she said, once again showing

a wisdom that seemed beyond anything I could comprehend, "and only a woman can end one."

"Yes, but...." I rambled on and on with my philosophical meanderings.

But peace was demonstrated on this summer's eve with ice cream and chocolate and some gentle conversation, and gradually the rabid beast was stilled within. On our way home, we passed several groups of young people, energized by their noisy boom boxes and singing off-key in accompaniment.

"Were we ever so foolish?" I said.

"Oh, I think we were, Alex."

"I'd almost forgotten."

I sighed for all the years lost.

And I noticed, as we strode quietly towards home, the lights beginning to dim in the windows around us, blinking out one by one.

It was the end of day.

It was the beginning of night.

And there were only fifty million shopping days left until Christmas.

It was the last time that any of us really felt safe.

CHAPTER TWO
WISH UPON A FALLING STAR

If wishes were horses, beggars might ride.
—John Ray

ALEX SMITH & MINDON MIN, 23 DECEMBER, MARS YEAR I
NOVATO, CALIFORNIA, PLANET EARTH

But nothing actually happened for another six months. I got further into my book and further away from academe. I found that I didn't miss the classroom at all, and I'm sure the randy little buggers didn't miss me. I was quite content to putter around with my book and my wife, and she didn't seem to mind my presence either.

The first meteor was spotted in late December, scudding through the atmosphere over Hawaii. It shot by Mendocino, leaving a bright green trail in its wake, pieces of it flaking off as it dove headlong towards the Earth. Despite the hour, thousands witnessed its passage and took it for an ordinary shooting star.

Dr. Dylan Gregory, a well-known tele-astronomer, was quoted on CNN as saying, "This one was *really* big! Maybe it *hit* something! Ha, ha, ha!" He urged residents of Marin County to be especially vigilant at this rare opportunity of discovering a freshly-deposited meteorite.

I was ensconced in my home office late that evening; and although the blind on my west-facing French windows were open (I loved to look at the night sky), I somehow missed the object's passing. The phenomenon was visible as far south as San Francisco and as far east as Berkeley. Some observers described a hissing sound, others a kind of crackling in the atmosphere. But I was buried deep in my new book, contemplating the future of civilization (which actually had less of a future than I supposed), and couldn't be bothered with anything "real."

If wishes were horses, then beggars might ride.

* * * * * * *

But Min had actually seen the falling star, as he told me later, and was convinced that it had landed somewhere up in the hills west of Novato. He drove out of town as far as he could, and then set off across the countryside on foot, taking with him a couple of flashlights and some extra batteries. He would have included his female understudies if any had been available.

After meandering through the woods and being attacked by giant mosquitoes, he stumbled across an open sandy field just after dawn, a few miles west of State Highway 101. There an enormous hole had been carved by the impact of the falling star, with sand and gravel heaped all around it. Some dried shrubs had burned at the edge of the site, and he could see a thin line of blue-green smoke rising against the new-born sun.

The thing was almost entirely buried, surrounded by shattered splinters of pulverized trees. The uncovered section was thirty or forty yards wide, and had the appearance of a huge egg caked with reddish mud and earth, its outline softened by thick, scaly, iron-colored encrustations.

Min carefully approached the site, surprised at the size and shape of the object, since most meteorites appear as melted chunks of bare rock; but the metal casing was still so hot that he had to keep his distance. He could hear a kind of grinding noise inside, but assumed it was being generated by the gradual cooling of the thing beneath the earth's surface.

He realized, of course, that this was a major find! The

"Mindon Meteorite" would make his reputation, if only he could devise some way of removing the artifact without actually destroying it.

He stood there at the edge of the pit, gazing down at the steaming thing, and then, as the light began to grow, noticed that it had an odd symmetry. Maybe, he thought to himself, just maybe this would *more* than make his reputation. If this was a machine of sorts, or even a Martian probe sent to explore *our* world....

The morning was wonderfully still. He wiped an unnatural sweat from his brow. Then he noticed that the winter birds had gone completely quiet. The only sound that he could hear was the faint crackling emanating from within the cindery ship.

Some of the crusty ash that covered the protruding end began flaking away in rusty scabs and raining down upon the sand, where it shattered into small bits. A large piece dropped off with an audible pop that brought his heart into his mouth.

Although the thing continued to radiate heat, he was finally able to scramble into the pit to view the rock more clearly. There was something about the structure of the meteorite that was profoundly disturbing, even artificial. This just didn't look like anything that he'd seen in the museums.

Then he realized that, very slowly, the top of the thing had begun rotating. It was such a gradual thing that he discovered it quite by accident, noticing that a black mark that had been close to him a few minutes earlier was now positioned on the opposite side of the meteorite. He watched it more closely, and was able to see it slide forward an inch or so. Understanding came in a flash. Yes! The thing was artificial! It was hollow, in fact, with an obvious hatch that could be unfastened! Something inside was trying to get out!

"I'll be damned!" he said to himself. "I was right! It's a probe from outer space! I'm rich!"

The thought of his soon-to-be-famous visage appearing on *O-rah-rah* nearly overwhelmed him, causing him to lose his balance. Fortunately, he caught himself before actually touching the hot, glowing metal, which would have burned him terribly. He had to do something quickly, and he obviously needed help. He scrambled out of the hole and ran as fast as he could back towards Novato. This was around eight in the morning.

He'd completely forgotten where he'd left his car. He stopped a passing vehicle, trying to make the driver understand; but his story and appearance were so bizarre that the man simply drove on. He was equally unsuccessful with a restaurateur who was just unlocking the doors of a local café, Zee's Zippy Zone. "Zee" was inarticulate on the best of occasions, and didn't fare well under pressure (Mindon had once criticized his *bœuf latté*), so he threatened to knock Min down if he didn't get out of his way.

That sobered my friend long enough to think clearly for the first time since his grand discovery; and when he spotted Owen M. Owen, a writer for the *Pac-Sun*, seated at his desk in the newspaper office, he calmed down and tried to make himself understood.

"'O'!" he said, "you hear about that meteor last night?"

"Yeah?" said Owen.

"…it's landed west of town."

"Good!" The man was a bit deaf and had left his hearing aid off, so what he heard was: "…sanded the western down," which made no sense at all.

"It's some kind of ship! There's something inside it."

Owen cupped his hand to one ear while continuing to work. "What?"

Mindon reiterated him what he'd seen.

"You're kidding, right?"

"Swear to God," Mindon said.

Owen grabbed his jacket and hearing aid and got his car; they picked up a spade at his house on the way out of town. The two men then hurried back to the site, but the noises within the meteorite had ceased. Small circles of bright metal now showed around the top surface of the thing. Air was either entering or escaping the ship with a high, thin, whistling sound.

They listened closely and "O" rapped on the singed casing with his shovel. Nothing happened.

"Gotta be a probe of some kind," Min said.

"Maybe we should contact the authorities. Also, I need to check with my paper."

"Just so long as you spell my name right: it's the 'Mindon Meteorite,' OK? M-I-N-D-O-N."

"Yeah, yeah, sure," Owen said, pulling out his cell phone and ringing his office as they drove back towards town.

They ran up Main Street in the bright sunlight as the stores were opening their doors for business. Owen stepped into a nearby coffee shop, the Green Tiger, and after taking time to call the police, sat down and e-mailed his paper, quickly putting together a story that would be circulated nationwide within the hour.

By mid-morning a few folks were wandering back into the hills to see the "Ship from Mars" for themselves. Mindon called me as I was finishing a late breakfast. I was excited at the prospect of viewing the artifact for myself, so I grabbed Becky and drove as close as I could to the site. We then started hiking westward.

It was Christmas Eve.

It was the *last* day that we would ever think of ourselves as alone in the universe.

CHAPTER THREE
AFRAID TO GO HOME
IN THE DARK

I'm afraid to go home in the dark.
—Harry H. Williams

ALEX SMITH, 24 DECEMBER, MARS YEAR I
NOVATO, CALIFORNIA, PLANET EARTH

By the time we reached the site, forty of the locals had arrived ahead of us, with more on their way. We gathered 'round a huge hole in which the alien ship was embedded upright in the ground. The gravel on either side of the opening had been charred black by the impact of the landing, although the vessel itself no longer radiated any heat. "O" and Min still hadn't returned yet.

Four or five teens were dangling their feet over the edge of the pit, amusing themselves by throwing stones at the bloody thing.

"Stop that!" I said, but they just laughed. Kids!

When I looked around at the bystanders, I recognized a couple of folks with their bikes, among them my yard man, a woman with a stroller, a store owner and his son, and two or three others who nodded back at me.

There wasn't a lot of conversation. I mean, what could you say?

Most of the people were just staring quietly at the large,

egg-shaped end of the ship. After awhile, when nothing else happened, some of them left while others took their place. Even Becky began pestering me to go home. I finally told her to take the car, that I'd join her later for lunch. She reminded me that we'd planned to go shopping that afternoon. After she left, I climbed down into the pit to examine the thing more closely, and thought I heard a movement somewhere inside. But if the top had shifted before, it'd stopped by now.

At first glance the oval just seemed like a large lump of charred rock, but on closer examination I noticed some thin, wavy lines, almost cracks, that permeated the top third of the visible portion of the artifact. The scales that flaked off left a sheen of shiny, unscarred metal underneath. I'm no scientist; I didn't recognize the yellowish-white surface that gleamed at me in the sunlight, reflecting a glare that almost blinded the onlookers. Even the crack around the lid had an unfamiliar color and texture. Obviously, the probe would have to be examined more closely by our scientists.

And it was pretty clear in my own mind that this *was* a probe, likely sent from Mars in response to our own explorations on the Red Planet. I didn't even consider the possibility that the meteorite was natural. The unscrewing of the top, if that's what it'd been, was similar to the way our rovers had prepared themselves for their journeys across the Martian terrain. I wondered if the artifact might have some message for us, some offering of peace and a sharing of the benefits of our respective civilizations, and speculated on the translation difficulties that might occur. This was the greatest thing that had ever happened to mankind—and I was part of it! I was impatient to see something further, but nothing more actually happened then. About noon I too wandered back to my two-story home on Olivet Avenue.

The Internet was already blaring the news:

THE METEORITE—
MENACE OR MESSAGE FROM MARS?

NON NEWS FROM NOVATO!

ALIENS AMONG US!?

HAS ELVIS RETURNED?

UFOs Attack California!

MARIN MIRAGE—LIBERAL CONSPIRACY?

and so on, getting progressively more lurid with each new rendition.

Mindon had phoned several observatories in the western US, and CNN had already sent a reporter up from San Francisco to provide an "objective" story on the event. Fox hadn't even bothered, simply announcing that another "Kooky Kalifornia Komedy" was unfolding among the "marinated minds of Marin County." I flipped through the TV channels, getting progressively more disgusted by the lack of serious coverage.

"It's as if we didn't exist," I told Becky.

"It doesn't matter, Alex," she said, putting down her book. "They'll find out soon enough."

Once again, I wish in retrospect that I'd paid more attention to my wife's prescience.

"What are you reading?"

She showed me the garish cover: *What the Future Holds!— and What You Can Do About It!!!* by Madame Stavroula.

"You remember her," she said. "She was the one who told your fortune at the Renaissance Fair last year."

"Oh, yeah."

I *did* remember, all too well. She'd been dressed in some kind of *faux* medieval garb (she looked like a washer woman, to tell you the truth), and she'd suddenly grabbed my hand and wouldn't let it go, oohing and ahing over the lines in my palm.

"*Nai!*" she'd said, her voice warbling as it deepened (they're always so cheery, these soothsayers), "Such interesting intersections thou hast here, such curious crossings. *Malista*, thou art, how do you say? *Moiraios*, the destined one, thou art…." Then she'd looked at me as if she were seeing me for the first time, her black eyes growing very large and very wide, and she'd suddenly released me, pulling back with a flutter. "I…no! Here! You take back your money. Go away from me!"

She'd thrown some bills on the table, more actually than Becky had paid her, and gathering her skirts together, had pushed her chair aside and bolted the room. Harrumph indeed!

"Well, I'll be," Becky'd said.

Suddenly I came back to myself.

"You *do* remember her," she said, tilting her head.

"How could I ever forget?" I sighed.

"Anyway, she sent me this book, inscribed 'To the one who showed me the way,' so I'm just getting around to reading it now. It's really not bad. I don't believe all of it, of course, but it sure does make you think."

"*I* think I'm going back to the landing site," I said. "Want to join me?"

"No, I probably need to uncover our joint destiny."

I was laughing along with her as I exited the door.

When I returned to the field that afternoon, I couldn't park anywhere near the pit. Dozens of cars now lined the shoulder of the dirt path closest to the impact site, and the road had now been cordoned off by the local police. Since this was Marin County, a fair number of motorcycles and bicycles were also in evidence. The crowd numbered, I suppose, several hundred individuals, including some young women, whom I thanked under my breath for decorating the scenery. Mindon waved at me from the other side of the hole, one arm wrapped around a delicate delight. I joined him.

"This is, uh, Barbie," he said, introducing his companion.

"Hiiii!" came the girlish gurgle.

"Hi yourself," I said. "What's happening, Mindon-Man?"

(I was one of the very few individuals in the whole wide world who knew that Mindon had adopted his name from a nineteenth-century Burmese king, Mindon Min. His real name was Gorace Alonzo Styles, Ph.D.—and he hated it, he absolutely despised it, he utterly loathed his name. I asked him once why he'd never changed it legally, and he said something about an inheritance owed him by his Great-Uncle Gorace—"Liz"—who was rich and stuffy and would cut him off immediately without a red cent if he ever dared such a step. He wanted the money, honey, and that's the whole truth of it.)

"Not a hell of a lot," he said.

It was almost hot for December. Not a cloud in the sky, not a hint of wind. The only shade was provided by a few scattered pine and live-oak trees. The burnt brush had blackened the field for several hundred yards in either direction, and was still giving off occasional puffs of smoke where embers had nested in some downed tree limbs. One of the ever-present Chicano vendor-vans was selling ice cream bars and soda and hotdogs and chips off to one side, making, I'm certain, a whole week's worth of income in just one day, and playing a tinny version of "Für Elise" over and over again. I could have strangled him.

What a reception for the Martian probe! All the worst elements of humanity were represented here—and perhaps even a few of its best.

The rim was the domain of Owen, Mindon, and a tall, blond, middle-aged fellow with glasses whom I learned afterwards was Hastings Johnson-Carson, an astronomer at Berkeley. He had several workers with him armed with spades and picks. J.C., as we called him, stood on the end of the ship like a naval captain, imperiously giving orders in his nasally, needling voice, his pudgy crimson face streaming with perspiration. All he lacked was a sailor's cap. Something seemed to be irritating him, and it was probably Mindon, who was still claiming the meteorite as his own, and that he should therefore be the only person consulted concerning its disposition.

A large portion of the artifact had now been uncovered, but

its lower section yet remained buried in the soil. Mindon pulled me aside and asked me to get help from City Hall.

"Look, that damned interloper is going to steal this thing from me. We're within the Novato city limits. The Mayor has authority over the site, if he chooses to exercise it. See if you can get him to intervene, OK?"

I promised to do what I could.

Min wanted a rail erected to keep the people back, and especially to remove "certain" individuals from the site. He said that he could still hear noises within the probe, but no one had been able to break the thing open yet, thank God! The casing seemed impervious to ordinary tools.

It was a little past four, and I knew City Hall closed at five. I walked to my car and drove to the Art Deco-style building that had housed the facility since the 1940s. I asked to see Mayor Cory.

"What do ya want, Smith?" the man said, chewing on a pretzel stick like some old cigar.

I told him that there was a safety issue involved: with all the people milling around the pit, that someone might get hurt, and that he didn't want the city to be sued for lack of proper preventive measures on the part of the local government.

That got his attention.

He immediately phoned the Chief of Police, and ordered him to restore order to the site, pushing back everyone to a safe distance.

Then I went home to Becky and shared a dinner of cold sandwiches and canned fruit, before returning to the place that marked the beginning of the Martian hegemony on Earth.

CHAPTER FOUR
O SUCH COMPANIONS

O heaven! That such companions thou'dst unfold.
—William Shakespeare

ALEX SMITH, 24 DECEMBER, MARS YEAR I
NOVATO, CALIFORNIA, PLANET EARTH

By the time we reached the site again, the sun was starting to set. The crowd was larger now. The police were trying to bring some order to the situation, but they were too few to control the area effectively. Something was beginning to happen in and around the landing site itself.

Then I heard J.C.'s voice booming: "Back! Come on, get back, folks! Officer, push these people out of the way!"

But the cops had no more effect than anyone else.

Then someone came running towards me.

"It's *moving!*" he shouted as he ran by. "Hey, people, it's moving!"

We tried to get a better view, but there were too many onlookers in the way.

"Someone fell in the pit!" a man shouted.

"C'mon, watch out!"

"What's happening out there?"

"Jesus H. Christ!"

The crowd ebbed and swayed a bit and somehow Becky and I managed to elbow through. I heard a peculiar humming sound emanating from the hole.

"Alex!" Min said when he saw me. "Keep these blasted idiots out of the way. We don't know what's inside the damned thing yet."

A young woman wearing cut-off jeans—no one I recognized—stood on top of the ship and then tried to climb her way out.

But the "egg" suddenly began separating from its shell, peeling away from itself at the top, and then unfolding section by section into the protective lid that covered the thing. Someone banged against me and I almost fell forward into the hole. As I cursed the slob who'd rammed me in the back with his elbow, the canopy caromed off with a clunk. Becky grabbed my waist.

"Alex?!" she half screamed.

I looked down into the heart of darkness.

For a moment the cavity seemed perfectly black, particularly with the setting sun glaring in my eyes. Then I saw something stir within the shadows, swishing around in the liquid interior with a soft, almost billowy movement, wave after wave. Two luminous disk-like eyes abruptly popped out of the goop, staring at me. Something that looked like a squid's tentacle, as thick as a baseball bat, rose out of the aperture and wriggled towards us—followed immediately by another, and then another.

Oh, the horror! The horror!

Becky shrieked. I, brave soul that I was, couldn't even move, I was so scared. It was as if that thing, that creature, whatever the hell it was, had impaled me there on a needle, pinioned beneath its imperious gaze and waving arms.

"Alex!" Becky yelled again.

More tentacles were now creeping out of the cavity. I pushed Becky away from the thing, and slowly moved back, keeping myself between her and the horror rising up behind us. Everyone was screaming and running and clawing, trying to get away from that terrible place. The stench of the creature almost overpowered my senses. Even Dr. Johnson-Carson—well, all of them, really—were affected by the same gut-wrenching disgust and distaste and dislike, and were falling all over themselves trying to be the first ones to escape. I saw people trampled beneath the feet of men and women whom I would have called "friends" earlier that day. Terror gripped my soul and squeezed it into a little black stone. I had to force myself finally to move.

A great gray bulk the size of a dolphin was prying itself slowly, even painfully out of the ship, dripping mossy red fluid from its hide. It looked like a piece of well-worn canvas as it bulged up on the edge and caught the last of the sunlight, glistening like wet leather. It slowly positioned itself above the gaping entrance to the spaceship.

Two large, black-rimmed eyes regarded me dispassionately. That it saw me I have no doubt whatsoever, because it followed my movements as I retreated backwards, step by stumbling step. That it regarded me as an enemy I understood instinctively, as a mouse trembles before the cat.

The head of the thing had sort of a hump on top. Its face, if you could call it that, occupied one side of the leathery gray body. Beneath the oversized eyes was scratched a broad mouth, its vee-shaped brim quivering and panting with its exertions. Ruby fluid of some kind drooled and dripped to the surface below. It had no obvious nose, but the whole creature was heaving convulsively with its breaths, obviously burdened by the immense gravity of Earth as compared with that of Mars. Two of its tentacles gripped the edge of the ship, securing its body, while a third swayed in the air.

Those who've never experienced a living Martian in the flesh, so to speak, can't really imagine the sudden impact of a first encounter on one's senses. It wasn't just the odor, similar to decaying flesh, that bothered me, but the peculiar vee-shaped mouth with its pointed upper lip, the absence of brow ridges or chin beneath its wedge-like lower lip, the constant quivering of the opening, the Gorgon-like groups of the short feelers surrounding the orifice, the constant huffing and puffing of its lungs struggling to inhale our thick, humid atmosphere, the heavy and painfully slow movements of its body, and the dozen or more tentacles protruding from its base.

More than anything else, I found disquieting the intense gaze of those large, inhuman eyes, monstrous and cold—oh, so frigid—as they watched and waited and weighed us, and found us wanting in the balance. The oily, brown-gray skin looked almost slimy in the bright light, and there was something very mean and nasty in the clumsy deliberation of the alien's movements.

I had no illusions at all about the thing: this was a monster! It was never going to be a friend to mankind. It was always going to be "Us vs. Them." There was no compromise possible with those pitiless orbs.

Of course, all this was just my first take on the creatures, and as with so many other things, eventually proved to be, well, inaccurate, to say the least.

Suddenly the creature vanished, toppling into the pit below with a dull thud, like the thump of a huge whale stranded on a sandy beach. I heard a peculiar cry, something like *"Hah-hoo!,"* and then another alien appeared, hovering in the shadows of the exit portal, ready to step out into our world, ready to assume its crown of leadership.

I was very, very frightened—I'm not a brave man. I grabbed Becky's arm, turned, and ran like hell, making for a grove of trees a hundred yards away, stumbling and looking back as I pushed her forward in front of me.

When we reached the oaks, we were panting heavily. I had to hold Becky to keep her from falling, she was so exhausted. We were surrounded by people staring in half-fascinated terror at the pile of dirt marking the hole.

And then I saw the "jeans" girl bobbing up and down on the rim, like a little dark toy outlined against the setting sun. She managed to get her shoulder and knee up over the lip, then slipped back again until just her head showed. Suddenly I heard a faint shriek and she vanished for good. I wanted to go back and help her, but I couldn't, I just couldn't, and Becky wouldn't have let me anyway.

Our little drama was being obscured by the onset of darkness. Anyone driving along the road from Novato would have been stunned at the sight of a hundred folks scurrying around, trying to hide in ditches, crouching behind bushes and trees, hardly speaking to each other except in short, excited bursts, and staring, staring, *staring* at the heaps of sand piled around the pit. But there was nothing more to be seen.

The wiser ones, the ones with any sense at all, fled for home. A few vehicles stood nearby, abandoned and derelict, outlined against the declining pastels of pink and orange that signaled the end of another day.

It was the end of *our* day, all right.

It was the end of man's rule on Earth.

CHAPTER FIVE
STING-RAY

Float like a butterfly, sting like a bee.
—Muhammad Ali

ALEX SMITH, 24 DECEMBER, MARS YEAR I
NOVATO, CALIFORNIA, PLANET EARTH

After my first *tête-à-tête* with the Martians, something made me stay close to the action. Becky was begging me to leave, but I had to see it through. I wanted to know what was happening. I kept staring at the mound that hid the aliens. I wavered between fear and curiosity—and curiosity "killed the cat," as they say.

Of course, I wasn't foolish enough actually to venture any closer to the damned thing. I hid myself in the brush, and Becky finally stopped tugging at me.

"What is it about men, anyway," she muttered under her breath, "that makes them do such stupid things?"

What indeed?

But, the fact remains that I wanted to experience the outcome of our little adventure. This was the most exciting thing that had ever happened to me. I'd become a spectator of our first encounter with a species from another world. However it came out, this meeting was the most important event in human history. We were no longer alone in the universe!

I tried to find some better vantage point, dragging Becky along behind me. I almost climbed a tree. Suddenly I saw several black whips, like the arms of an octopus, flash against the darkening sky. Then a thin rod was pushed out of the pit, joint by joint; it had a circular disk at the top rotating in a wobbling motion. It reminded me of a juggler balancing a plate on a stick. What the hell were they doing over there?

Most of the onlookers were wandering their way back to Novato. I recognized Frank Somebody-or-Other. I don't recall his name now.

"Goddam slimy critters!" he was saying to anyone who'd listen. "Gotta kill 'em all!" He repeated this refrain over and over again.

"What do you see?" I asked, but he paid no attention to me, just moseyed on by. Although the crowd had largely dissipated, a few diehards gathered together in a group. I could hear their occasional murmurs in the background.

After awhile sheer boredom brought some of the people back again, including new arrivals from town. As the light dimmed, I could see the reestablished crowd jerking forward back towards the alien craft. They spread out in a thin, irregular crescent to the right and left. I followed their lead, moving slowly out of the cover provided by our trees, but telling Becky to stay where she was.

"Wait!" she said, but I was already moving; of course, she trailed along right behind me, silly woman.

Then I noticed several men standing in front of the mound marking the spaceship; one of them was waving a white flag made from his undershirt. They were too far away for me to recognize anyone, but afterwards I heard (although I could never confirm) that Min, J.C., and "O" were among those trying to communicate with the buggers.

Suddenly, a bright green flash slashed through the night, and then again! and again! in three distinct jabs of lightning, sizzling—*zap, zap, zap!*—and highlighting everything before me.

Briefly I saw the little group of folks with their pitiful white flag as their faces turned a pale green and just faded away. I heard their flesh boiling and smelled the odor of roasting pork. Becky was violently sick behind me. The hissing slowly mutated into a bass humming, and then became a long, loud, almost droning sound. Slowly a great humped shape rose out of the pit, highlighted by a ghost of pale green light that seemed to flicker within.

More flashes of green fire stabbed through the night, their brilliant glare jumping from one individual to another, turning each man and woman into a pillar of emerald light.

By the glow of these human torches I could see individuals staggering and falling and trying to run away, but always too late, always too goddamned late.

"Oh, the people!" Becky said, choking on her vomit, "oh dear God, the poor people!"

I just stood there agape, not yet realizing what was happening here. *Zap!* came the lightning, and another man fell forward onto the earth; and, as the shafts of light and heat passed over and through them, the live-oaks surrounding the basin suddenly burst into flame, together with any unburned bushes and brush surrounding them. As far south as Terra Linda I could see trees and shrubs and buildings suddenly coming alight. For a moment, I thought I was seeing some kind of Christmas display, and then realized that everything was tinged with a sickly green.

My God, I thought, *what kind of range does this sting-ray have?*

Back and forth it swept, this flaming agent of death, this invisible sword of heat and light, back and forth, seeking anything that moved and much that didn't. I saw it drifting back towards me, and I was a dead man for sure, until Becky grabbed my chest and pulled me to the ground beside her, sheltering us both in a natural hollow. I was too astonished even to protest. I heard the crackling of fire around the pit and a sharp, quick scream that was suddenly choked off in mid-voice. Along a curving green line beyond the hole the ground smoked and sparkled and spit, and oh, oh God, did it ever burn! Something fell with a crash far away to the left, where the road from Novato parallels the fields. Then the hissing and humming ceased, and the black, domelike object sank slowly back out of sight.

We were alive! Becky's quick action and the luck of geography had saved us when nothing else could. It's better to be lucky than smart, I discovered, and I remembered that lesson in later days.

Everything had happened so quickly that I was still dumbfounded and dazzled by the residual flashes of light. They seemed burned into my retina, the odd shapes that still floated there. If the sting-ray had swept around again, well, I probably would have died with the others. But it didn't, and once more I was reminded how much my existence depended on the quirkiness of fate. Call it God, call it what you will, but I lived when so many others died. Even so, the night had become dark and unfamiliar and terrible to me.

"Let's get the hell out of here," I whispered to my dear wife. I should have spoken those words "years" earlier.

The world had declined to near-black. Our road to safety lay gray and pale under the deep ebony sky. The field was nearly deserted. Overhead the stars were beginning to appear, but in the west a small crescent of sky was still tinged almost greenish blue. I could see the tops of a few surviving trees and the distant buildings of the suburbs against the fading dusk.

The Martians and their weapon were gone now, save for one thin black line that continued to move up and down like a metronome. Everything around us stank of destruction. A few houses on the outskirts of town were still spurting spires of spindly flame into the stillness of the evening sky. I could hear the squeaky sirens of the fire engines responding. "Ooh-lah," they said, "ooh-lah."

The people were gone. Most of those killed probably didn't realize what was happening to them. Some had had sense enough to hit the ground, as we had, and one of these, I discovered later, was my friend Min.

But right now we were helpless, unprotected, and alone.

"Quiet!" I hissed.

We turned and began a stumbling, shuffling run back through the smoldering brush.

Our fear turned to panic and terror, not just of the Martians, but of everything around us. We ran quicker and quicker the further away we got. I started weeping underneath my heaving breath; I just couldn't help myself. We'd lost something out there that could never be recovered. Neither of us dared to look back.

I suddenly got the idea that we were being toyed with, that, just before we reached safety, something would rise up and strike us both dead.

Mercifully or mercilessly, whichever you prefer, we reached our home again within the hour. But we both knew in our heart of hearts that we'd never feel safe—anywhere, anytime, anyplace.

"What do we do now, Alex?" Becky asked.

"I don't know," I said. "I just don't know."

Even to this day, the question is the same.

Even to this day, the answer is the same.

CHAPTER SIX
MERRY CHRISTMAS, NEW NOVATO!

Heap on more wood!—the wind is chill;
But let it whistle as it will,
We'll keep our Christmas merry still.
—Sir Walter Scott

ALEX SMITH, 25 DECEMBER, MARS YEAR I
NOVATO, CALIFORNIA, PLANET EARTH

But where were the media?

Some forty bodies lay sprawled around the pit, charred and distorted beyond recognition in grotesque parodies of slumbering sleepers. A few of those killed had been completely or partially vaporized by the sting-ray, leaving just a shoe or watch or leg or arm or...whatever. All during the night the hills west of Novato and south towards Woodacre continued to burn, lighting up the sky with their flames.

What we didn't know is that the second and third and fourth ships had already impacted on other parts of the Bay Area, one falling on Mountain Court in Walnut Creek to the east, another striking Windswept Lane in Bodega Bay to the northwest, still another crashing into an apartment complex on Fredonia Avenue in Mountain View to the south. News coverage converged on these areas as the alien capsules began to open and their inhabitants emerged, with results similar to those in Novato.

Another Martian ship landed at San Bernardino in Southern California, smashing onto the campus of some university there. I watched the news reports on CNN showing the administration building in flames, men and women running around outside and screaming their heads off, completely without direction or purpose. More impacts occurred over the next week in the Los Angeles metropolitan area, including Maiden Lane in North Hollywood, Santa Avelina Alley in Santa Monica, Wendigo Avenue in Aliso Viejo, El Borgo Boulevard in San Bernardino, Citrón Avenue in Redlands, and near the Hollywood sign in the hills over Los Angeles.

More vessels fell just outside Nevada City near Squirrelly Drive and into the Pacific Ocean west of the Farallones Islands; this was seemingly confirmed by a small tsunami ten to twenty feet high that swept certain south-facing beaches later that day.

The aliens appeared to be intent on occupying the major population centers of California and destroying pieces of the physical infrastructure, to some purpose yet unknown.

Our efforts to communicate with the invaders were rebuffed. I saw several reports on MSNBC of peace delegations being wiped out to a man, just as they'd been during our own encounter with the Martians.

Word of the so-called "Novato Massacre" was initially reported as a California wildfire tragedy, one of a series of such events that we'd been experiencing throughout a very dry year. By the time anyone realized what was actually happening, no one was much interested in Marin County; too many other things were going on.

The next morning was Christmas Day. In Novato the stores were mostly closed, save for a few restaurants and fast food outlets serving breakfast. A number of folks took advantage of the cool morning weather to walk west along Novato Boulevard (it'd been closed to through traffic during the night), just to see what had burned. Clouds of gray-brown smoke indicated several active fire zones, and the police directed the people away from these areas. But the excitement of a disaster and the clear weather still brought the crowds out to watch, despite the holiday.

Few folks in Novato knew anything at all about the Martian ship. The stories in our newspaper were mostly dismissed as a hoax; and nothing further had happened in any case, save for the fires, which were thought to be the work of arsonists. Those missing had been reported to the local police, but they too were believed victims of the smoke and flames of the previous evening. As the authorities began recovering the bodies, all of which showed evidence of charring, the remains seemed to confirm these theories.

The pit had covered itself during the night, leaving no sign of the aliens.

As people wandered in twos and threes into the open fields west of town, they found little knots of survivors talking about the "spinning mirror" and the flashes of green lightning. But there was nothing left to prove these wild tales.

I returned to the site alone at midday, much to Becky's chagrin. We'd opened our few presents that morning, and then shared a quiet breakfast together, before getting into another argument.

"I wouldn't go back to that place for anything in the world," she said. "Not even for you, Alex. We need to get some supplies together and evacuate."

"Evacuate?" I said. "But we still don't know...."

"We know enough! We've seen enough. What more do you want? Do you *really* think they're going to stay up there? I don't believe that and neither do you. They'll move into town as soon as they can, and then we're dead or worse. We need to go, Alex, while we still can."

"I just want to see what's happening. I'll be back in time for dinner."

She shook her head at my stubbornness, but she couldn't stop me. No one could. She was putting together some clothes when I left.

* * * * * *

When I returned to the pit, the whole place had changed.

The trees were mostly gone, burned down or at least sheared of their leaves. The hole had become a mound, completely filled in, even covering the spaceship. The bodies of the dead had been removed by the authorities.

I saw Chief Conger directing operations.

"Did you find Mindon?" I asked.

"Oh, it's you, Smith. God, what a mess!" He gestured out at the field. "No, didn't see him. Owen was out there, what was left of him, and a number of others I recognized, but not Min. 'Course, some of the bodies will have to be ID'd through DNA. You here last night?"

"Yeah."

"What happened?"

I told him what I'd seen.

"You're shittin' me, right?"

I shook my head.

"Well, where is it *now?*"

"Somewhere beneath that pile of sand," I said. "I sure as hell wouldn't go poking around in there, though."

"We're almost done here, I think."

He ordered his men to cordon off the area with yellow police tape attached to the bare stumps of the remaining trees. While they were working, I felt rather than heard a rumbling somewhere underneath me, and I yelled as loud as I could, "Get to cover!" before running for the tree line and throwing myself into a hollow.

Conger, however, just stood his ground and pulled out his pistol, dropping into the classic shooting stance. The sand began to fall away in sheets as something very large and metallic poked its way up out of the mound.

"Down!" I shouted at the Chief, but he ignored me.

Instead, he fired one-two-three-four-five shots in a row. I could hear the slugs ricocheting off the carapace of the Martian machine, and something breaking, like the tinkle of shattered glass, and then a hooting sound ("*Ooh-meh!*") from the alien.

"Got one of 'em!" the Chief screamed.

Six-seven-eight-nine-ten came the retorts. Then a long *zzzttt* as the sting-ray reached out its bright green tongue and licked the man away, leaving his upright shoes, with smoking feet and ankles still attached. The machine rose up higher, ten or twenty feet or more, and began seeking out the remaining cops, who returned fire with their primitive pea shooters and bows and arrows (which they might as well have been, for all the effect they had), until they too were obliterated.

"*Hoo-teh!*" bleated the Martian, in what I interpreted as a cry of victory, or maybe a call for assistance, I didn't know which.

Then it levitated even higher, coming up right out of the hole to stand sentinel by the side of the ship, as several other machines began to join it, clickety-click, clickety-clack.

I crawled down the trace of the hollow, keeping my head really low, until it entered a ravine; and then carefully and quietly crept away from that hell-hole, hearing behind me the ratcheting of the Martian implements, as they began to assemble more of the tools with which they intended to smash mankind.

This was war, I now knew. People had to be warned. We had to fight back—while we still could!

CHAPTER SEVEN
HOME AGAIN, HOME AGAIN

To market, to market, to buy a fat pig,
Home again, home again, jiggety-jig.
—Anonymous

ALEX SMITH, 25 DECEMBER, MARS YEAR I
NOVATO, CALIFORNIA, PLANET EARTH

I remember very little of my escape except blundering through the trees and stumbling around the brush. I found the road again just outside of Novato, but I was so exhausted that I had to sit down for awhile.

I remained there for quite some time. Then I saw an ant tugging the dead carcass of a beetle three times its size, struggling to maneuver the body over the rough earth, taking the food to its nest. If I reached down my finger and crushed the insect, would it understand? Could I stop its frenetic activity by reasoning with it? Maybe convince it to become a vegetarian? In spite of everything, I chuckled out loud.

Then I stood up and began walking unsteadily towards town. Home again, home again!

I suffer from this strange sense of detachment, both from myself and from the world around me. I watch everything from the outside in, so to speak, from out of time, from out of space, from beyond the stress and the tragedy of it all. That's why I'd gone back to the pit. I had to see it all for myself. That's what

Becky never really understood about me.

Yes, of course I was scared, just like everyone else. Yes, I understood the risks. But it just didn't matter: I still had to eyeball everything first-hand.

But I suddenly understood the distant discontinuity between our local, small-town community and the death and destruction that had occurred just a few miles away. People were still having lunch in the local cafés, or strolling through the downtown section of Novato, enjoying the afternoon sunshine—and the Martian invasion was a non-event. It was something that happened to *other* people, not to them.

"What's happening?" I asked one young couple.

"You mean the fire?" the man said.

"Have they got it under control?" the woman asked.

"You didn't hear about the landing?" I said. "You know, the aliens?"

"Oh, yeah, sure!" The woman laughed out loud.

I was suddenly angry at my inability to communicate what I'd seen—but also for their blind stupidity.

"Get out while you can!" I yelled back at them.

The man was shaking his head at the old fart who'd gone crazy.

"Home again, home again, jiggety-jig."

* * * * * * *

My haggard appearance startled my wife. I squatted in my favorite chair, sipped some Pinot Noir that she brought me, and as soon as I could collect myself, told her what I'd seen. She'd just begun putting out dinner, which turned cold on the table while I related my story.

"The one thing in our favor," I said, "is that they're the slowest damned things I've ever seen. They're so sluggish that they can barely get around on their own. Sure, they can hold onto that pit forever if they really want to, and kill anyone who comes near it, but I doubt they're going to be able to move very far from their base. The army'll stop them as soon as they get here. I sure wish Min had survived, though."

"He's in the guest room."

"What?!"

"He came staggering in an hour after you left. I guess he'd spent the whole night wandering through the hills. I gave him some food, and he just collapsed into bed."

I heard a noise in the hallway, and there he was, *sans* undershirt, but still as "raggedy a man as ever man can."

"Gotta get out of here, man," he said, belching. "They'll be coming for us soon. Got any more of that wine, Becky?"

"But where do we go?" I asked, handing him the bottle.

He began chugging it straight down. Nothing refined about Min.

"Damn, that *does* taste good. North to Sonoma or Santa Rosa or even Willits. Eureka or Coos Bay or Medford or...." His voice trailed off.

"But you said the Martians weren't a threat."

"I said a lot of things, Alex. I've always been so full of shit. You know that."

"You told me that Earth's gravity is three times that of Mars. And you could see for yourself how they struggled to get up, to breathe, to do anything at all."

I was in fine academic form indeed.

"Yeah, and I also saw them take us out with that ray-thingie of theirs," Mindon said, wiping his mouth with the back of his hairy hand. "Look, man, they've got machines, just like we do. There are a lot of animals out there who're stronger than man, or bigger, or faster. We've beaten them all. That's because *we've* got machines. And if the Martian machines are better than *our* machines—it sure looks that way to me—we're dead ducks. So let's get movin' and groovin'."

"That's what I've been saying all along," my dear wife said. "I've put some things together, Alex. We should leave immediately."

"Wait a second," I said, fingering my wineglass. "They just

landed. We don't know anything about them, really. Sure, they might be dangerous, but maybe they're just as afraid of us as we are of them. Maybe they didn't expect to find anybody here, certainly no one intelligent."

"I don't believe that for a minute," Mindon said. "They came for a reason. We may not understand that reason yet, but it's there. Believe me, Alex, it's there."

"Yes, but the military'll be here soon, certainly by tomorrow. They'll force the aliens to negotiate—or they'll wipe them out. The buggers've only had to face popguns so far. There's no way they'll be able to withstand our artillery shells and bombs."

"You don't think so?" Mindon shook his head. "You don't know, my friend. You're just guessing again. But I've seen enough. I'm leaving. My ancestors went through all this shit, and look what it got them: the Last Stand and Wounded Knee and all those other 'victories' of Indian manhood. Yeah, we won so damned many battles that there aren't any of us left anymore. *This* Indian has had enough excitement for one lifetime. He's going to keep his scalp intact. I'm leaving, folks. Take my advice, Alex: protect that pretty lady of yours and get the hell out of Dodge while you can."

But I didn't, of course. I couldn't, not while things were still "happening" out there.

The events of the last day had scrambled my brains. All I could think about was that *this* was it!—the most historic moment in my life. I wanted to be there, to bear witness to the first encounter between man and an alien species.

Well, I encountered them, all right. I wish to God now that I hadn't. I don't know where my common sense went, and I sure as hell wouldn't listen to anyone else.

"To market, to market, to buy a fat pig!"

But I do recall with some pleasure that small Christmas dinner, just the three of us eating cold, simple fare, washed down with plenty of Pinot Noir. I remember that evening with an extraordinary clarity even today. Becky's beautiful anxious face, her dark hair gracefully framing her cheeks, gazed at me intently, while Mindon discoursed on the tragedy of mankind and the tragedy of the Martians. The white table cloth, the fine cups and silverware and good china, the crimson-purple wine swirling in my glass, all are distinctly etched in my memory. At the end of the meal I sat there sadly regretting Min's perversity, and denouncing the cowardice of the Martian race.

"Why don't they come out and fight us like men?"

"Because they're *not* men, Alex," Mindon said. "They're *not* men, and we shouldn't make the mistake of giving them human motivations.

"Look, my friend, I've really got to go. I've rented an SUV, and I'm going to walk over to the Boulevard now to pick it up. No, I don't want a lift. You guys"—he shook his head again—"you guys take real good care of yourselves, and maybe we'll see each other again in some other life."

If only he'd known.

We were like the dodos, those nice, big, plump, juicy, stupid birds on the island of Mauritius, discussing the arrival of a ship full of pitiless sailors who were looking for fresh meat, and saying to each other, "Why, we'll just go peck them to death tomorrow, my dears."

I didn't know it, but that was the last civilized meal that I would enjoy for many strange and terrible days.

I burped.

I farted.

I belched.

Merry Christmas, New Novato.

CHAPTER EIGHT
STURM UND DRANG

Sturm und Drang (Storm and Stress)
—Friedrich von Klinger

ALEX SMITH, 25 DECEMBER, MARS YEAR I
NOVATO, CALIFORNIA, PLANET EARTH

Owen's e-mail describing the ship's arrival was initially judged a hoax, until the other alien vessels starting plopping down all over the California coastline. Even many of those living in Novato dismissed the rumors initially. Nothing could be confirmed on the web, so it just wasn't real. They continued going about their lives on an ordinary Christmas Day, visiting church to celebrate the Prince of Peace, organizing family get-togethers, eating dinner, watching a few football games on TV. Fires were such a normal risk in California that no one gave them much thought.

After dinner, I scoured the news channels on cable, while Becky checked the Internet. It was all the same old holiday crap, recycled from last year. It's a wonderful life, indeed!

"There's nothing about the landing, nothing at all," she said. "Where *is* everyone?"

"Well, it's Christmas!" I said. "They never give Novato much coverage anyway."

It was about that time, I later learned, that another capsule smashed into Nevada City, flattening a home business there.

The few survivors from the previous night's escapade mostly weren't believed. The local police had been decimated, but the appropriate reports had certainly been filed by next morning with the appropriate state and federal agencies. However, the sleepy-headed politicos in Sacramento and Washington were slow on the uptake, particularly in D.C., just dismissing the messages as "Kooky Kalifornia Krap."

None of the other ships had received much attention yet. The Martians initially stayed very close to their landing sites. Buses were operating as usual across the Golden Gate Bridge, the ferry from San Francisco to Sausalito and Larkspur kept dropping batches of revelers on the docks of those towns, and Highway 101 was crammed with thousands of folks heading back home from their weekend gatherings somewhere else.

Gradually, though, the news began filtering out of Novato. Even though the fires were largely under control, the clouds of ash were still very noticeable that afternoon. Folks on the Tiburon Ferry could look northwest across the Bay as the light began to fail and spot several thick plumes of brown smoke.

Half a dozen homes had burned on the western edge of Novato. Communications had been seriously disrupted after the incident at the pit, and it took some time for the police to regroup. The Chief was missing and couldn't be raised by pager or cell phone. All this activity kept the inhabitants of the west side of town awake through much of the night.

After the Chief had been killed, local firemen and police were ordered to avoid the pit entirely. Radiation, it was said, had spread from the wreckage of an experimental aircraft that had gone down in the hills. Dozens, even hundreds of people had died from exposure to the stuff, and until the appropriate hazmat teams could be mustered, all official personnel would maintain a respectful distance and establish a perimeter around the affected area. This had supposedly been ordered by the Mayor in consultation with the Board of Supervisors of Marin County. In fact, no one actually knew what was happening. As a precaution, Lieutenant Governor Willa Lambert ordered the National Guard out to restore order, since Governor Jay Banisoff was visiting relatives in West Virginia.

The first troops arrived early the next day, on the feast of St. Stephen the First Martyr in the Catholic Church.

The crowds surrounding the pit had dispersed by then. There was nothing to be seen except the mound of sand covering the craft. Meanwhile, more officers, including a few state police, were busily scurrying about, setting up new barriers. One or two unlucky souls had snuck near the ship during the night, but they never returned and their bodies were never found. We didn't learn why until much later.

Except for that, the fields were silent and desolate at first light. A few charred, "irradiated" bodies and pieces of bodies lay prostrate in front of the mound. A faint pounding noise emanated now and again from the direction of the pit, but the sound could only be heard by the nearby security personnel who were manning the roped-off perimeter fence.

At home, though, things seemed pretty normal, at least until Becky and I had our little discussion just after dawn.

"I'm leaving, Alex," she said. "I'm taking the car, with or without you, and I'm going to stay with Aunt Anita. I already called her."

"Not the *bird lady!* Jeez, Becky, she *talks* to her tweeties all the time! She's *crazy*—I'd say as a loon, but you know what I mean. And that laugh of hers, it's like a hyena's. You've got to be kidding."

"I'm not kidding. It's too dangerous to stay here any longer, and I'm going. I hope you'll come with me, but if you don't...."

"But we...."

"I've seen enough, Alex. I saw what they were like. They almost killed you. You're just fooling yourself if you think those, those...things are going to stop coming. They're evil. They'll kill us all if they can."

"Look, I've got to see this out, Becky, I've just got to," I said. "Tell you what, though, I'll drive you there myself this afternoon—that way I'll have the car—and I'll join you again in a day or two, when everything is over. I'll be fine here for a few days. Nothing's going to happen. Now that they have the army coming, that'll be the end of it. You'll see."

And that's where we left it. She wouldn't touch me at first, but then she embraced me and hugged me close. Maybe it was just fear, but I'd like to think, particularly considering what happened afterwards, that it meant something more to her. It sure as hell did to me, especially later.

About eight that morning, while we were having a light breakfast, I heard a convoy of trucks rolling down Novato Boulevard, and I rushed out in my robe to see what I could see; but my vantage point on Olivet Avenue just gave me a glimpse of the camouflaged military vehicles as they rumbled by. I thought I spotted a couple of half-tracks, a few artillery pieces, and some transport trucks littered among the Humvees. I quickly got dressed, gave Becky a peck on the cheek, and told her I'd be back for lunch.

Half an hour later, a second convoy of National Guardsmen deployed north of the impact area, together with some state police and a representative from the Governor's Office. The new landings of Martian ships in the Bay Area had finally alerted the authorities to the seriousness of the situation, and similar responses were already being initiated at the sites where the capsules hadn't yet unfolded.

Somebody yelled and pointed at the sky. I saw a long streak of green stretching its way from the western horizon towards us, finally disappearing eastward with a loud, single clap of thunder, like a sonic boom.

Another alien ship had just planted itself in good California soil.

CHAPTER NINE
INTERPLANETARY WAR

Be not disturbed by planetary war.
—Elinor Wylie

ALEX SMITH, 26 DECEMBER, MARS YEAR I
NOVATO, CALIFORNIA, PLANET EARTH

After throwing on some old clothes, I hurried down Novato Boulevard, following the traffic and hordes of people to where the military was. Some of the locals were carrying lawn chairs and picnic lunches and ice chests filled with drinks. Blasting the aliens—or whatever they were—had become almost a town party.

The National Guard had established two emplacements, one to the north of the pit and one to the south, both in non-populated areas. The police had been moved away from the perimeter and ordered to keep the lookie-loos from interfering with the military. There were maybe a hundred Guardsmen at each camp, and more were arriving all the time in small convoys.

The funny thing was, nobody seemed much concerned about the situation, either soldiers or civilians. I saw a vending truck selling sandwiches, beer, soft drinks, and other snacks. With the weather so unseasonably warm for winter, people spread out blankets on the hills surrounding the pit, picking out the best spots to view the coming action while munching nattily on their Nachos. The Guardsmen began moving very slowly and methodically to position their mobile cannons and half-tracks where they could cover each other.

I saw my next-door neighbor, Brice Boston, sitting on one of those portable lawn stools, the canvass kind, drinking a Coors Light, and holding a portable radio in his lap, earplugs already strapped over his patriotic NRA cap. Brice was a strong supporter of the current Governor, a real horror show.

He popped his plugs and said: "Hey, man, it's all over but the shouting. The Guard'll cut 'em to shreds in two minutes, if they actually start something. Want a brewski?"

He held out a Quatro Equis, but I passed. A bit early in the day, if you know what I mean—and in any case, I never understood what the additional X's meant.

"What we really oughta be worried about," he said, "is the goddamned Liberals. They'll probably want us to hold off or somethin', so we can analyze the little buggers to death. I say kill 'em all before they kill us!"

Brice was a practical kind of guy. He had an old-fashioned revolver stuck in a holster right there in his lunch box. The permit was taped on the top for everyone to read, assuming that they could. No way *he* was going to let the aliens get away!

"I thought we had this Alien Registration Act," he said in his whiny little voice. "When are those goddamned Congressmen going to do something right for a change? There oughta be a law."

Still, I suggested, it might be best to move a little further away from the possible action.

"Naaah, I mean, what are they going to do, man?" Brice said. "Piss on us? Hey, I want to see everything."

"They say Nevada City's burning," someone said. "One of those things crashed there. The fire companies are just going crazy."

I bought a turkey sandwich from a mobile van, together with some cold bottled water, and then thought about Min while I munched away on the miserable mystery meat. I wondered where he'd gotten himself to by now—I hoped somewhere cool and pleasant and safe. I managed to eat about half of my snack before throwing the rest away. Then I decided to mosey on down towards the landing site.

Under the Novato Creek Bridge I found the first group of soldiers. They told me no one was allowed past the stream; looking down along the road, I saw one of the men standing sentinel there. I talked with them for half an hour, and told them what I'd seen the previous night. None of them had glimpsed the Martians themselves, so they were very curious.

But I was startled to find that the Guardsmen really didn't know all that much about their situation, or even what their commanders intended to do. They were as ignorant of the aliens and their war machines as the townspeople. I described the sting-ray weapon to them.

"Hey, we'll just hunker down and rush 'em," a Private named Mayer said.

"Yeah, piece o' cake," another soldier said. "Our guns'll knock 'em out for sure."

And so on.

One of them wanted to know what the Martians looked like, so I gave them a general description.

"Squids," Mayer said, "that's how I see 'em. Well, one tentacle or ten, they're going down when the bullets start flyin' 'round here."

"You bet," another said, "friggin' freaks of nature. We're goin' on safari, guys."

That got a big laugh all around, but they didn't have any idea of what they were talking about. I'd seen the aliens in action; they hadn't.

"Big game huntin'!" Mayer said, jerking his head at the black guy, "Hey, we're headin' for the Serengeti, and Larrah here's our 'Bush' Man."

They all laughed again, until Sergeant Larrah lunged forward and knocked the man's helmet off.

"Don't try droppin' any of that racist shit on me," the noncom said. "I'll boot your ass all the way back to 'Frisco."

"Didn't mean nothing by it," the first man said, backing away and holding up his hands. "Talkin' about the President, you know?

"Hey," one of his companions said, "why don't we just shell the damn things and be done with it?"

"This is the Army, boys," the black man said. "We don't do nothin' without 'due consideration.' We move when we get orders to move."

"Shit," they all said together, and added the soldiers' standard refrain: "It's all FUBAR."

They were still discussing the situation, waiting for orders from their absent officers, when I left. I couldn't get close enough to the landing site to see anything else. The surrounding hills didn't provide enough elevation to observe more than the mound itself, and the troops that I talked to in both camps didn't have any hard information. The officers were mysteriously absent, apparently consulting with *their* superiors. People from town were feeling secure again for the first time in several days. I overheard Jan Alexander, manager of the local Ralf's market, say that her son Benedict was among those missing from the previous day. The police were evacuating people from the western sections of Novato, forcing them to abandon their homes.

I returned for a late lunch a little after one, feeling very tired. The day already seemed dull, filled with that yellow atmosphere that drew the energy right out of your bones. I tried waking up by taking a cold shower. Becky wanted me to drive her to Sonoma and Aunt Anita right away, but I managed to put her off, saying I was too beat to do anything. About half past two I checked the news again, because the early reports had only given a sketchy and inaccurate description of the multiple landings of the Martians around California.

But there was little in the evening editions that I didn't already know. The Martians hadn't shown themselves anywhere since last night: they were all still buttoned up in their respective ships, doing whatever they were doing. They seemed to be very busy at *something*, hammering and creaking and pounding very loudly for extended periods of time. Every so often the microphones on these sites would record the sounds of sloshing and what appeared to be Martian "conversation," the "oohs" and "aahs" that they made seemingly at random. No one could make any sense of it. The pits themselves were sealed up, possibly as a defensive mechanism, but issued an almost continuous stream of gray-green smoke.

The wire services and the Internet and CNN all reported "Fresh Attempts at Communication" with the aliens, but most of the time the invaders didn't even bother to zap the groups trying to reach them. Only when individuals approached the pits within a perimeter of, say, fifteen or twenty yards, crossing some invisible line in the sand, did the Martians respond immediately with a vile and vicious attack, wiping out everyone and everything within range, even those beyond the "border" area.

One small group of officials tried to get around this by waving an American flag on a long pole, as if they were actors in some old '50s flick. The Martians took about as much notice of this as we might of cows mooing in the pasture. I had the impression that they didn't really regard us as intelligent, although why this should be so I couldn't possibly imagine. I mean, the signs of our highly-developed civilization were evident everywhere around them.

About three o'clock I heard the dull thud of a big gun firing at measured intervals from the northern military camp. The Martians didn't respond. I hurried to the battle site, as close as I dared approach, and used a pair of old binoculars to peer through the haze. I couldn't see much, even with the increased magnification. Becky had remained at home, refusing to join me.

About five I heard another muffled detonation from the north camp, and immediately afterwards a burst of firing in very rapid succession, like machine-guns or small-arms fire— rat-a-tat-tat! I was near the southern emplacement, which was closer to Novato proper. A violent boom suddenly shook the earth. The high school behind me burst into smoky red flame, and the tower of the First Baptist Church came crashing down beside it. When the smoke cleared, I could see that the cross on the pinnacle of the church had vanished, and the roof line of the school looked as if a hundred-ton woodpecker had been gouging away at it.

This was getting way too close for comfort! I retreated from the base as half-tracks began moving forward and unleashing their weapons. The Martian response was immediate: one of the vehicles exploded in a cacophony of flame and bursting shells, while a second partially melted sidewise into the ground. It just missed me.

I ran away, I'm ashamed to admit. I wasn't a soldier, and I couldn't face death straight-on.

Our house stood near the apex of a small hill in Novato, just off the main drag. As I ran home, I could just see the roof as I came down our street. A stray shot had cracked our chimney open, and knocked a piece of it down into the yard.

"I'm sorry!" I shouted to Becky, who was standing on the front porch. "We can't possibly stay any longer. The Martians are breaking out. I should have.... Forgive me?"

I held her close for just a moment.

"Come on," she said, pushing me away. "Time enough for that later. We've got to get out of here. Everything's packed and ready to go."

I backed the car out of the garage. People were screaming and running up the street behind me.

"They're coming!" one man was shouting.

"101?" Becky asked over the din.

"No," I said. "Everybody'll be heading for the freeway, and it's too close to the danger zone anyway. 37 will do."

State Highway 37 was a four-lane road that slanted northeast from Novato towards Vallejo.

"I thought we were going to Sonoma."

"We'll take 37 to 121 north. Maybe we should go even further, I don't know."

"I'll call Anita and tell her we're on the way."

Down the hill I saw a truck full of soldiers pull to a stop by the bridge over Novato Creek; they began running from house to house, yelling at the occupants to get the hell out. The sun dimmed suddenly, obscured by the smoke rising from the burning trees and structures; the blood-red light threw a lurid slant upon the scene.

A policeman was directing traffic at the intersection.

"What's happening?" I yelled out the window.

He turned, stared at me, and shouted something about "a thing like a dish cover," before I lost him in the rearview mirror. In another minute we were out of the smoke and noise and heading across town.

Even on 37 it took us forever to get out of Novato, or at least it seemed that way, although Becky assured me later that it was just fifteen minutes to the junction. Before us stretched a vista of serene, sunny suburban landscapes, filled with houses and stores and restaurants and sanity. Behind us in the mirror I could see thick streams of black smoke shot through with threads of red fire driving shafts into the still air, throwing dark shadows upon the green-black treetops to the west. The cloud already extended a great distance into the sky, almost like a thunderhead—maybe as far north as the pinewoods outside of town, and running towards Stafford Lake on the west. Everywhere people were scattering like ants from a stirred-up nest, not knowing what to do or where to go.

And very faintly now, but very distinctly through the warm, quiet air, I could hear the rattling of a machine gun and the crackling of small arms fire. Then it all stopped, just like that. Apparently the Martians were destroying everything with their sting-ray.

It took all my concentration to avoid running someone down. Just before we turned onto State Highway 121, I glanced back at downtown Novato, but it was completely hidden behind a pall of black smoke. From there we drove north to the town of Sonoma, a little more than twenty miles from Novato.

The trip took us forever and a day, and it seemed almost like another world when we finally stopped.

Anita, I thought to myself when she appeared at her front doorstep, a crazy bright orange shawl wrapped over her head like a turban, *you just laugh your funny laugh all you want*. I stepped forward and enthusiastically embraced her. I never saw a more surprised person in all my life.

CHAPTER TEN

THE MARTIAN SCEPTER

Night, sable goddess! from her ebon throne,
In rayless majesty, now stretches forth
Her leaden scepter o'er a slumbering world.

—Edward Young

ALEX SMITH, 26 DECEMBER, MARS YEAR I
SONOMA COUNTY, CALIFORNIA, PLANET EARTH

Sonoma lies northeast of Novato. It's ensconced within a beautiful green countryside sprinkled with patches of woods, fields, vineyards, houses, and farms, although the latter are rapidly being developed out of existence. The heavy firing from Novato ceased as suddenly as it had begun, leaving the evening peaceful and still and mercifully cool. We reached the town without incident just after dark. Anita had saved us a cold dinner, which we gulped down like the starving refugees we were.

"What have you heard?" she asked.

I told her about our journey.

"There's absolutely nothing on the news," Anita said.

Becky had been curiously silent throughout our drive. I pointed out to her again that the Martians were certainly tied to their pits by Earth's gravity and by their sheer bulk, but I didn't really believe what I was saying, not after seeing what we had seen in Novato.

She answered me in monotones.

After we'd filled our bellies, she turned to me and said, "You're *not* going back, Alex."

By then, though, my perversity of curiosity had once more supplanted my better sense.

"I've got to, Becky," I said.

"Why, Alex? *Why?*"

"I just want to see this through. Nothing's ever really happened to me, nothing like this anyway. I've had an easy, complacent life, pontificating to my students and planting my nose firmly in my books. I'm not complaining, mind, but I've never really done or experienced anything truly big. This is my great chance, Becky. It's an opportunity for me to see history in the making, and then to report back to the world what's actually occurring here."

"What if they reach Sonoma? What then, Alex?"

"Even if they beat us, which I don't believe, they're going to be heading south towards the big city"—I was talking about San Francisco—"not this way. You'll be perfectly safe here."

"You don't know anything about them. You really don't. You think you do, but what you're seeing is your own image reflected back at yourself. Don't leave me alone, Alex. Please don't abandon me."

"You'll be in good hands with Anita and Dave."

Dave Bol Kwon was Anita's current "live-in," whom I'd just met for the first time an hour earlier. Old Dave was a nice enough guy, I suppose, but a bit stodgy for my tastes. I doubt if he'd cracked a book since high school. Still, salt of the earth and all that.

"Listen, I'll be fine," I said. "I'm just going back for a day or two, and then I'll return."

"*Please*, Alex, listen to me."

"I have to go," I said.

Then I kissed her once, and once again. My heart was a lump of lead in my chest, but that wasn't enough to deter me. Nothing was, not fear, not loss, nothing! There was a fire in my soul that drove me forward. God Himself couldn't have stopped me.

Becky's face, I remember, was a pale white mask in the darkness. It watched me sadly as I drove away, and then turned and went back into Anita's house.

But I was excited at the prospect of experiencing war up close again. I forgot my fear. I could see myself writing a book, being interviewed by Carson "Nuts" Davis or one of the other "regulars" on CNN. Oh yes!

By the time I returned to Novato late that evening—and it was a lot easier coming than going, let me tell you—I was even afraid that the silence that greeted me meant that I had missed the main event between Earth and Mars. I wanted to be in at the death! I wanted to see blood!

It was eleven o'clock when I reached town. The night was pockmarked with occasional streetlights, but many of them had been knocked out. I knew nothing of what'd happened in the ensuing hours. The radio was full of wild reports, as usual, but they didn't convey all that much hard information. I suspected that the authorities were already censoring the news, trying to keep it both from us and from the enemy. What a dumb idea that seems in retrospect.

I didn't even know what'd precipitated the initial conflict between our forces and theirs. It was just boom, boom, boom, rattle, rattle, rattle, *zzzttt, zzzttt, zzzttt,* and that was that. Wham, bam, thank you, ma'am. As I entered the outskirts of Novato, I could see along the western horizon a blood-red glow. As I drove ever nearer, it crept slowly upward in the sky. The clouds of the gathering storm mingled there with masses of black and red smoke.

Quartermass Street was deserted, and except for a lighted window or two, showed no signs of life whatever. I narrowly escaped hitting a multi-car pileup at the corner of Glass Road and Niswander Lane, where a small group had collected on one of the corners. They eyed me suspiciously as I edged past the tangled wreckage. From Niswander I partially followed Novato Creek into the small downtown area. As I ascended the little hill beyond St. Katherine's Church, I could see signs of fire again.

The nearby trees shivered in the fresh breeze. The rooftops were silhouetted black and sharp against the red-tinged clouds.

Suddenly a bright green flash illuminated the road around me, and I heard a very loud roaring noise pass over my head. It was a falling star—and a close one too. Another Martian ship was landing. I almost laughed out loud. When would it end? How many more were coming?

As I drove up Novato Boulevard, I could see the wreck of an Army transport hanging over a ditch off one side of the road, somewhere near Schweitzer Street. I passed Sargent's Pepper Pot and Zee's Zippy Zone, both closed and locked up tight. Even the KFC outlet had been abandoned, and the twenty-four-hour sign at McDonald's, with its echo of Carl Sagan's "billions and billions," was turned off for the very first time that I could recall. I guess they didn't serve Martians.

Because of the abandoned vehicles littering the street and the garbage strewn everywhere, I had to keep my eyes on the road. Then my attention suddenly wavered. Something was moving rapidly down one of the side streets. I couldn't make it out at first. The light reflected off its dome in a flickering fashion unlike anything I'd ever seen. For a moment, I thought it was one of ours, some bizarre Army vehicle sent by the National Guard to defend the town. And then the thing shot forth its searchlight of destruction, illuminating the surrounding territory and its own immense body in pale emerald light.

How can I describe something so bizarre, so inhuman? It took the shape of a great tripod, twice as high as the houses around it, towering over most of the trees; and it strode down the street swaggering from side to side with imperial potency, smashing anything that got in its way, a walking, wobbling, withering engine of glossy, glittering metal, with long, articulate, almost animate ropes of some whitish alloy writhing beneath it. The clattering tumult of its passage intermingled with the riot of the flames and the revving of its weapon of mass destruction. Another immense flash, and then it abruptly heeled over on one foot, two of its supports waving in the air, and changed direction in mid-stride, moving down towards me on Kurtzoff Avenue, vanishing and reappearing almost instantaneously with each flash of its lightning-like weapon.

I've heard young people use the word "awesome" to describe just about everything that amazes them (which is just about everything in the world!); but I'd never been so surprised by anything in all my life. "Awesome" indeed!

The trees lining the street a block ahead of me parted like the Red Sea. The brittle reeds that were trunks snapped before Moses's imperious command. A second tripod appeared, rushing headlong towards me. It must have been a hundred feet high, even larger than the first death-machine. And I was driving right at it down the middle of the main street in town! I slammed on my brakes, swung the car around, the tires protesting this unwanted exertion, and floored the gas pedal. The sting-ray touched the trunk of my vehicle, and I slewed sideways into a ditch filled with shallow water.

I unbuckled my belt and crawled out, almost immediately falling into the muck, just a second before another blast seared the top of the car, scorching me with its heat. Only the cool water saved me from being fried along with my vehicle. I scurried away as fast as I could, keeping my head down. The gas tank exploded behind me, showering me with metal debris. I looked back: one of the car's burning wheels was still spinning slowly in the wind. Then I heard a clanking sound, and I pressed myself deep into the mud. The colossal mechanism went striding right by me, evidently satisfied that it had crushed the vermin menace. It ran up the avenue towards its brother.

Seen from behind, the thing was unbelievably large and strange. I had the distinct impression that it was somehow more than a gadget, more than just an odd collection of nuts and bolts, more than the classic robot warrior depicted in the old "B" films of the 1950s. There were plenty of mechanical parts, to be sure, and some kind of greenish alloy had been layered over the carapace and legs; but the long, flexible, glittering tentacles that dangled beneath the thing one of them gripping a tree trunk, swung and rattled against its shiny body. I spied an occasional glistening of gleaming flesh amidst the metal sheen.

The huge machine picked up its pace as it strode along, proud and arrogant and utterly without fear. The brazen hood that surmounted the thing moved to and fro, back and forth, like a giant mantis head looking for some new prey. Slung behind the main body was a basket of white metal that looked similar to a fisherman's creel. Puffs of green smoke squirted randomly from the monster's body as it swept by.

And then, in an instant, it was gone.

As it passed it began warbling a defiant, deafening howl that drowned out everything else:

"Ah-loo!" It screamed to the æther. *"Ah-loo!"*

In another minute it had joined its companion half a mile away, and then both of them moved on, stooping over something cached in the open field. I have no doubt that this was another of the alien ships dispatched from Mars.

"Ah-loo!" came the call once again. I thought of a pack of wolves baying to the stars.

I didn't—and don't—know what any of it meant, or if, indeed, the ululation meant anything at all. Maybe it was just the Martians' cry of exultation.

I lay there in the mud for some time, wet and weary, watching the flashes of intermittent light and the monstrous metal gods bobbing in the distance under the skeletons of the few remaining trees. Their figures sometimes grew misty within the clouds of smoke, and then would suddenly flash again into sharp clarity. Occasionally the night swallowed them up altogether.

I was soaked through, but it was some time before my senses allowed me to struggle back up the bank to a dry spot on the asphalt. I'd been a fool, once again! I never seemed to learn.

I could see Min's old observatory-*cum*-garage a few hundred yards distant. I made a run for it and hammered at the door, but no one answered (Mindon himself, of course, was long gone). I thought about breaking the glass, but decided that I really needed to get away from here altogether before the striders returned.

After awhile I succeeded in crawling home unobserved by the monstrous machines, heading back towards the residential area of Novato.

I pushed on, wet and shivering, towards my own house. It was very dark indeed on the back roads. The streetlights were now out completely.

If I'd had any sense at all, I would have tried to rejoin my wife in Sonoma. But the shock of that night, and my physical weakness, prevented me from thinking clearly. I was bruised, I was weary, I was wet to the skin, and I was really, really dumb.

I blundered into a man in the darkness. He cried out in sheer terror, as did I, and then sprang sideways, rushing pell-mell down the street before I could gather my wits sufficiently to speak to him. I stayed close to the fence line, where I could keep my bearings, and worked my way down the street, yard by yard.

Near the intersection with Brea, I stumbled onto something soft and large, and was able to feel around enough with my feet to realize that I was touching the broken, bloody body of a man. A flash of light in the distance gave me just enough illumination to see that it was Brice Boston, his head bent down at an awkward angle, the rest of his body crumpled up on the sidewalk, as if he'd been flung there from on high. There was no sign of his weapon.

I felt for a pulse, but he was quite, quite dead. He'd owned a bar in town, the Shawnee Shack on Joseph McCarthy Boulevard; its walls had been littered with short snippets of really weird verse and prose poems, so his death was a kind of poetic justice, in a way. I had to stop myself from breaking out in hysterical laughter at the thought.

I stepped around the body and pushed on. The police station was abandoned and burned out. My own home, though, was still intact, save for the cracked chimney, and most of my neighbors' dwellings seemed to have come through the conflagration relatively undamaged.

Down the road towards the bridge I could hear distant voices and the occasional sound of rushing feet, but I didn't have the courage or energy to investigate. I just wanted to be left alone.

I let myself in, closed and locked and bolted the door, staggered to the foot of the staircase, and sat down, appalled by what had happened to me. All I could think of was the striding metal monsters, like something out of A. Merritt, and the dead body of my neighbor smashed against the walkway, unloved and unmourned and unparsed.

I crouched there on the stairs with my back pressed against the railing, shivering violently, sick and empty and filled with dread. I had no idea what to do or where to go. I knew nothing. That terrible night seemed to last forever, and I knew what my fellow citizens were feeling, each and every one—in Novato, in California, in the grand old U.S. of A., even in the world.

The age of man had ended.

CHAPTER ELEVEN
I WILL FIGHT NO MORE FOREVER

Our chiefs are killed, the old men are all dead.
The little children are freezing to death.
My people have run away to the hills.
I will fight no more forever.

—Chief Joseph

ALEX SMITH, 26 DECEMBER, MARS YEAR I
NOVATO, CALIFORNIA, PLANET EARTH

After awhile I came to my senses. I was cold and wet. Little pools of water were dripping from my clothes onto the stairs. I got up and went into the living room. By feeling my way along the side of the room, I found a bottle of whiskey and fixed myself a sloppy drink. Then I crept upstairs to change my clothes.

I felt better afterwards, and went into my office, the window of which looks west towards the original Martian landing site. St. Katherine's Tower and the trees surrounding it were gone. This opened up the view so much that I could see, very far away and backlit by a vivid red glare, the field surrounding the sand pit. Etched against the light were the huge black shapes of the Martian machines, grotesque and cartoonish, busily moving back and forth, up and down, and doing…something.

It seemed as if the whole countryside was on fire. The hills were crawling with tongues of flame, the brush in the open fields were burning fiercely, trees were going up one by one like Roman candles, swaying and writhing with the gusts of the night wind, and throwing a ruby reflection upon the clouds of smoke scudding overhead. I couldn't see what the machines were doing or clearly identify the large black objects that they were manipulating. Neither could I determine exactly where the fires were burning, except that the nearest was located in one of the residential areas on the west side of town. The reflections of the flames danced up the walls and ceilings of my home. I could smell the sharp, biting tang of the smoke.

I crept closer to the open window. I could now see a charred and blackened zone of mixed pines and expensive homes in the Santana District, a relatively new development southwest of Novato. Many of the houses along the far end of Novato Boulevard had been reduced to glowing ruins. The light reflecting from the area surrounding the high school puzzled me at first, with its row of yellow oblong objects, but then I realized that these were the wrecked and abandoned carcasses of school buses. Some of them appeared to have burned.

Here and there I could see irregular patches of darkness scattered amidst the dimly glowing ground. There was no sign whatever of any attempt by "Official Novato" to contain the damage. The electricity was completely out by this point. I'd tried earlier to use my computer, but it was dead, along with everything else. I still had my laptop and cell phone, of course, for however long their batteries held out; but when I tried calling my wife a few minutes later, I couldn't get a signal. Nothing else would connect, either.

It was as if my brief departure from town earlier in the evening had drawn a curtain over the city, shutting down all life and activity save that of the aliens. I had this weird sense of empowerment; it almost seemed to me as if I was somehow responsible for everything that had happened.

I didn't see any signs of human life at first, but as I watched the *tableaux* unfold over the next hour, I was able to distinguish a number of small black figures scurrying from one side of the street to the other, keeping to the shadows, looking like bugs dodging for cover after a rock has been lifted from their hidey-holes.

This was my secure little world of the past five years. What had happened these last few days seemed unbelievable to me. Why had the Martians invaded Earth? What was their goal? I scarcely knew or understood, and even today many of their motivations are unclear. But as I continued to gaze out my window, I could see three gigantic black tripods striding to and fro in the glare from the landing site.

These machines never stopped except to "retool," so to speak. I wondered if they were intelligent in themselves, or whether they were directed, personally or at a distance, by Martian controllers, using the artifacts as extensions of their own consciousnesses. I tried to imagine how an automobile or airplane might appear to dogs, if they'd been intelligent enough to understand such things.

Someone scrambled into my garden just below me with a slight scraping of the fence, and I roused myself from my lethargy. I could just make him out clambering over the stakes. I quietly leaned over the sill.

"Hssst!" I whispered.

He stopped, one leg poised over the barrier. Then he hopped into the yard and ran across the lawn to the corner of the house.

"Who's there?" he asked, keeping his voice low. He stood under the window peering up at me.

"What are you doing?" I said.

"Trying to survive."

"I'll let you into the house."

I went down and opened the door and then relocked behind him, for all the good that would do. I couldn't see his face, but he was wearing some kind of uniform.

A flash of green light revealed his features.

It was Private Mayer.

"What happened?" I asked.

"What hasn't?" he said. "They wiped us out—just plain wiped us out." He kept repeating the phrase over and over again.

"Here," I said, handing him the bottle of whiskey. I didn't bother with a glass.

He chugged down several swallows before gasping as the liquor hit the back of his throat. Then he sat down by the table, put his head on his arms, and began crying like a boy. It was a long time before he could answer my questions, and then only very haltingly.

He'd been a transport driver for the National Guard. The Martians had emerged from their pit about the time I was driving Becky to Aunt Anita's. When the engagement started, they'd fired several rounds into the enemy camp, but seemed to cause little if any damage. The aliens had begun crawling slowly towards them under the cover of some kind of metal shield.

Then this canopy had somehow risen up on three legs and become the first of the great fighting-machines. Mayer'd taken over one of the half-tracks when its driver had been killed, and had driven it around in circles for several minutes until it'd stalled in the sand. He'd just gone out to free the vehicle, when it'd taken a direct hit from one of the striders. He'd been thrown by the explosion into a hollow, which had saved his life, but the half-track had been destroyed. He'd been unconscious for a few minutes. When he awoke, he found dead bodies all around him.

"I used 'em as cover," he said. "I was scared to death. Far as I could tell, my company'd been wiped out except for me. The smell was awful, like charred meat! Something had fallen across my back, probably a piece of the half-track, so I lay there until I felt better.

"They wiped us out!" he said again.

He'd remained there among the dead for some time, occasionally peering out to see what was happening. The Guardsmen from the northern camp had tried rushing the pit, keeping low, but the killing-machine had suddenly risen to its feet and begun striding back and forth across the field, its diamond-shaped hood methodically sweeping left and right like the head of a cowled monk. One of its many "arms" had carried a metallic case of some kind that had generated the sting-ray. Up close it looked very much like a green laser beam.

Within a few minutes there hadn't been a living soul left on the field, and every remaining bush and tree (and there weren't many by this time) had been reduced to blackened skeletons. There'd been other groups of soldiers somewhere beyond one of the hills—he had no idea what'd become of them. Our boys had exchanged fire with the enemy for at least another hour, and then everything had gone quiet again.

"Like the grave!" he said.

After that the great striding machine had then walked away across the landscape, apparently seeking out another Martian landing site somewhere close by. It'd been gone an hour or two, and then had returned with a second fighting-machine even larger than the first.

"Why didn't you run away?" I asked.

"Where would I've gone?" Mayer said. "I didn't know what was happening or where my friends were. I'd been told to stay put at the camp until I received orders to the contrary, so I did."

"What happened then?"

"Well, the buggers came back to the first pit, gathered up some equipment or supplies or something—I'm not sure what—and then left again. This time I had the feeling that they'd gone for good. Not that I was going to crawl over there to find out, mind! But finally I needed to take a dump, and so I headed off into the brush. And afterwards, I waited as long as I could, but when none of the other guys showed up, I decided to return to Novato."

I questioned him about what he'd seen along the way.

"Man, there's just nothing left," he said, "nothing. The people are either gone or dead. Some of the houses were burned by the fires. The roads're all jammed—I could see that the 101 was packed bumper-to-bumper north and south, but the cars are mostly empty. I only spotted a few folks still alive, and they hid whenever they saw me."

And then he told me something that chilled my very soul.

"They were harvesting the people!" he said. "The machines,

I mean. I saw them doin' it out near the freeway. Some they killed, some they took prisoner, stashing 'em in a kind of webbed basket.

"I gotta get to Frisco, man. There's gotta be someone left down there. I've gotta find an officer. I've gotta get my orders. See?"

Mayer had eaten nothing other than a few crackers, so I found some meat and bread in the fridge, which was still holding its temperature pretty well, and would for another day or so. I also had some candles, but we dared not light them for fear of attracting the Martians, so we did everything by touch. He rambled on for a bit before dozing off. I couldn't sleep, so I waited in that godawful dungeon until things began to emerge again from the shadows, and the trampled bushes and broken roses beneath my second-story window grew more distinct. I could now see his face quite clearly, blackened and lined; mine probably wasn't much different.

When we'd finished our early breakfast, we snuck softly upstairs to my office, and I looked out again over the western part of the valley. In one night, just one, everything had become a vale of ashes, everything but our street and a good part of Novato Boulevard. The fires had dwindled now, although I could still see occasional gusts of smoke. The ruins of the shattered, gutted houses and the blasted, blackened trees that the night had hidden now emerged gaunt and terrible in the pitiless light of dawn.

Here and there some object or building had escaped the devastation—a house, a business, a church standing out white and fresh amidst the wreckage. In the distance, sparkling brightly in the growing light of the sun, were three of the great metal giants, standing sentinel around one of the newest of the Martian landing sites, their cowls rotating constantly as though surveying all the desolation that they'd made.

It seemed to me that this new pit was larger than the original, and that the aliens were building something there. I could see puffs of green vapor streaming from the site towards the brightening dawn, jumping up and around in playful patterns until they vanished into the haze. Even at this distance, I could hear a low boom-boom-boom sound emanating from the pit. It reminded me of hip-hop music.

It was now the Twenty-Seventh.

I knew we had to leave Novato, but there was no place to go.

CHAPTER TWELVE
THE METEOR FLAG

The meteor flag of England shall yet terrific burn.
—Thomas Campbell

ALEX SMITH, 27 DECEMBER, MARS YEAR I
NOVATO, CALIFORNIA, PLANET EARTH

As the rosy-fingered dawn began to brighten our small world, we withdrew from my office window and pattered very quietly downstairs.

Mayer agreed with me that the house wasn't safe anymore. He wanted to go to San Francisco to find any military units that remained. I wanted to find my wife in Sonoma, and then evacuate with her and her cousin to somewhere in the north or east, if those areas were more secure. I already knew that the Bay Area in general must inevitably be the scene of some final battle between the Martians and our military for the control of Northern California, and that San Francisco would ultimately be the focal point of that encounter.

Between Novato and Sonoma to the north, however, one or more new Martian landing sites had now been established, and were guarded by their companions, the death-machines. I wasn't sure where any of these were located specifically, other than the one just north of town. If I'd been unmarried, I think I'd have taken my chances and headed cross-country on foot; but Mayer said something at that juncture that I later thought very wise: "It's no kindness to make someone a widow. My wife died a year ago, and there hasn't been a day since that I haven't missed her."

Thus far there was no indication that the invaders had occupied any territory to the south of us, so in the end I agreed to accompany the Guardsman on at least part of the journey, until we'd passed through the danger zone. Then I'd try to find some way to slip by the striders to the east or west.

I'd have started immediately, but my companion had a bit more sense.

"Look," he said, "an army marches on its stomach. We need to carry some rations with us. There aren't going to be any fast-food joints open along the way, and we can't count on the water somewhere else being drinkable."

He still had part of his kit left, including his canteen. I found several backpacks that Becky and I had used in our younger days, and a couple of large plastic bottles. The water was still running, amazingly, although the pressure was low. I packed some protein bars, crackers, soup, canned fruit, apples, half a loaf of bread, and some meat, which wouldn't last long, but could be kept cool for a day with a few blue ice packs that I retrieved from the freezer.

"What about transportation?" I asked.

"We don't want anything that makes noise," he said. "They'll attract too much attention from the buggers. No, bicycles would be much better."

I knew of a shop down on Citrus, if it was still there.

We crept out of the house, and ran as quickly as we could along Olivet Avenue. The dwellings on our street seemed deserted. Two blocks on I saw three charred bodies sprawled close together, struck dead by the sting-ray; and here and there were things that the evacuees had dropped in their flight—a Rolex, a slipper, a wallet, a torn doll, a skateboard, and other detritus. At the corner in front of the post office I saw a child's cart filled with toys and cookie boxes; it'd overturned near the body of the woman who'd been pulling it. Someone had left a small stack of rubber-banded one-dollar bills in the ditch. All junk now!

None of the structures here had suffered much damage. The fires obviously hadn't spread to this neighborhood. I didn't see a living soul anywhere. The inhabitants who survived must have escaped, I supposed, along the highways exiting the east or south parts of town.

"Kinda quiet," Mayer whispered in my ear.

"Too damned quiet," I said.

Other than the distant booming and hooting of the Martians, I could hear nothing. Even the birds seem to have forsaken the sky.

Then we both turned at the same moment, as a jet came roaring out of the southeast, flying just above the treetops. As it passed over us, it unleashed a missile from under one wing, obviously aimed at the new Martian pit north of town. But the weapon had hardly cleared the aircraft before the green finger of a sting-ray blasted both it and the fighter right out of the sky. We heard the fragments of the plane crashing into a field on the other side of Kendall Street.

"Jeez!" The Guardsman ducked his head.

"I guess we know what happened to the Air Force," I said.

"If the Army's no good and the Air Force's no good, how do we survive?" Mayer asked.

"Right now," I said, "we'll do exactly what we'd planned to do."

I led the way to Briskette's Bicycle Shop on Citrus, which was still intact. We pried open the back door without making too much racket, and picked out a couple of sturdy mountain bikes. We strapped our packs on the back, and then made our way through the city streets, generally heading southeast towards San Rafael. The damage to the structures and houses became progressively less the further we traveled, although we did encounter the body of a man in black slumped by the side of the road in Hillside Park; it looked as if he'd been shot in the back by a small-caliber gun. We stopped frequently to listen for the alien machines, but heard and saw nothing. South of Hillside we headed east to the Redwood Highway, also called the 101 Freeway. It was the easiest route to get through, even though we felt very nervous about being so much in the open.

There wasn't a breath of wind that morning, and everything was strangely hushed. As we hurried along between the wrecked and abandoned vehicles, the Guardsman and I talked back and forth in whispers and looked over our shoulders constantly. We stopped every mile or so to rest and watch.

We exited at Marinwood, just north of San Rafael, and there we encountered a Humvee with an Army lieutenant and several privates. They were the first living souls we'd seen all morning. We hailed the vehicle, and they halted while we peddled towards them.

"Identify yourselves!" the officer ordered, while one of his men manned a machine gun mounted on the rear.

"Private First Class Oliver W. Mayer, sir!" the Guardsman said, saluting his superior; he then recited the name and number of his devastated unit, neither of which I now recall.

I added my own name, and would have included my rank and serial number, except that I didn't have any. The officer wasn't interested in me, though.

"What happened to you, soldier?"

"Sir, we engaged the enemy, sir, but were driven back."

"And the rest of your men?"

"All dead or dispersed, sir."

Then he told his story in more detail, and I corroborated what I'd seen myself.

"Where's the enemy now?"

"You'll see the Martians five or ten miles up this road, sir, or maybe sooner. But you don't really want to see them," Mayer said.

"Why not? We're supposed to be scouting this area."

"Well, sir, with all respect, sir, if they see *you*, you're dead!"

The officer wanted a description.

"Giants in armor, sir, a hundred feet high at least, with three legs and a body like steel and aluminum, and a great head in a hood, sir."

"Oh, come on, Private!"

"Really, sir! They carry a kind of weapon, sir, that shoots fire and strikes you dead."

"You mean a laser?"

"Not exactly, sir," and the artilleryman began a vivid account of his encounters with the sting-ray. Halfway through, the lieutenant interrupted the soldier and looked at me.

"It's all perfectly true," I said, nodding my head.

"Well," said the officer, "I suppose I'll have to see for myself. We've had very few accounts from the front. Private, you'll report immediately to General Harroll at HQ near San Rafael, and tell him everything you know. He's somewhere near the freeway a few miles south, around Los Ranchitos. Just ask the men you meet."

"Yes, sir," Mayer said.

Then the officer drove on, and we never saw any of them again.

Later we encountered a group of three women and two children, trying to clear a path through the wreckage. They had a little pick-up with a few belongings piled in the back. We stopped and gave them a hand.

"Where are you ladies heading?" I asked.

"North," one of them said. "We walked across the Richmond Bridge yesterday, and found this truck. The Martians are all over the East Bay now."

I told them that they really didn't want to go north, since the aliens were already there, and that it was impassible anyway; they might be better off heading west to someplace like Woodacre.

We finally reached San Rafael, but the place seemed deserted, although relatively intact save for occasional looting. We were far beyond the range of the sting-ray here, and if it hadn't been for the complete absence of traffic and people, the day would have seemed much like any other.

When we couldn't find the Army HQ at Los Ranchitos, Mayer suggested that we move further southwest towards San Anselmo. At the edge of town we came upon another emplacement of half-tracks and artillery pieces. They looked like regular Army to the Guardsman. We checked with the soldiers, and they said that General Headquarters were now located further west. So we moved on.

As we neared the small town of Fairfax, California, we saw increasing signs of a military buildup, including a group of MP's blocking the road.

We told them our business, and were conveyed to a vacant house that was being used as temporary HQ. There we repeated our story to General Harroll.

"Well," he finally said, "the Martians haven't faced the real army yet, or any real weapons either. We've got some really big guns here."

"Yes, sir," Mayer said. "With respect, sir, you haven't seen the Martians yet."

"No, son, I haven't, but I certainly will, and very soon, from what I hear. There're supposed to be one or more of the fighting-machines heading towards us. I don't know when they'll get here, but we'll have to stop them when they do."

The Guardsman was ordered to refresh himself and report later in the day to a recon unit.

"Smith, I'm sorry, but you'll have to stick around for awhile," Harroll said. "I'd suggest staying close to Private Mayer."

We headed for the temporary mess hall in a local school, where we finally got a hot lunch and some cold drinks; and then tried to find the company where Mayer was supposed to report.

We noticed a number of officers periodically staring over the treetops towards the northwest (and *not* towards Novato); many of the soldiers were engaged in the age-old military tradition of digging ditches.

Fairfax proper was being evacuated. It had apparently served as a processing center for refugees, and the military was determined to get the civilians out of the area, ferrying them south to the coast. I saw a makeshift ambulance rush by, large red crosses painted on its sides. The roads were being kept open by the MP's. Heavy equipment was pushing stalled or wrecked vehicles off the roads, and at least one bulldozer was clearing away the brush.

Of course, some of the locals didn't want to leave, but they were picked up and forcibly loaded onto trucks when they refused. After asking around, we finally located the recon company to which Mayer had been detached, and received orders to take our bikes and peddle four or fives miles out along San Pedro Road to where it overlooks San Pablo Bay. Apparently, they were afraid that there might be an enemy attack from El Cerrito and Richmond, which were now overrun with the great striders.

We reached San Rafael again in ten minutes. This section of the town showed more life than the northern part had, although the place was in such turmoil that no one seemed to know anything about anything. I saw refugees from other cities trying to find somewhere to go with their families, plus long convoys of military trucks and transports and half-tracks and Humvees—and even a few tanks. Everywhere I encountered chaos and disorder. Mayer had to threaten several people to get us through.

We finally found the camp where the recon squad was located, and Mayer reported to the noncom there. I could see a fair distance in every direction, so I decided to remain awhile.

The Bay was filled with small boats as people tried to flee variously perceived perils to the east and west. Some of them were so packed with refugees that they sank under their own weight, but there was nothing we could do for them. Around us an excited and noisy crowd of fugitives was trying to escape inland. Several times the squad leader, Sergeant Antonio Vásquez Caballero, had to warn people away with his rifle.

I talked with one old couple who'd rowed from San Pablo to Barbier Memorial Park that morning. They lived on San Carlito Avenue in El Cerrito. Apparently, a Martian machine had come west from Walnut Creek, and another had followed the coast down from Vallejo. Together they'd destroyed the big refinery at Richmond. We could easily see the flames still burning there.

I don't know where these people eventually went. I suspect a great many of them just died over the next few days. There wasn't any place left that was safe from alien incursion. Some folks had the idea that the Martians were simply human beings from some other country. They couldn't accept the idea of an attack from outer space.

Except where the boats were landing and the people were milling, everything else seemed pretty quiet. The folks who were decamping on the beach headed away from the shore fairly quickly, particularly once they understood that we couldn't share our provisions. One tried to pull a pistol on us, and Vásquez Caballero shot him in the face. I could see a large ferryboat beached a few miles south of us, but it had long since emptied out. Three or four soldiers were standing around doing nothing.

"What's that?" one of the refugees said when a big boom echoed in the distance.

Then the sound came again, this time from the direction of Fairfax, a deep, muffled thud, the throaty exhalation of a very large gun.

The fighting was beginning again. God, I'd already seen enough of the war to last me all my days. Almost immediately, the unseen batteries across the Bay took up the chorus, firing one after the other. A woman screamed down on the beach. Everyone stood around, not knowing what to do or where to go. We could see nothing of the Martians.

"The Army'll stop 'em," one woman said, but she didn't sound too sure of herself.

Then explosions came seemingly from everywhere, left and right and all around, and the air began filling with clouds of smoke and dust and signs of fires burning in some of the houses in San Rafael. I could now hear the unique *zzzttt* of the weapons used by the great metal striders.

"HQ, HQ!" Vásquez Caballero shouted into his radio, "Cease fire! You're firing on us!"

"Here they come!" one of the soldiers said.

Across the Bay near the Richmond Bridge they appeared, one tripod striding after the other. One, two, three, four of the armored machines advanced through the city of Richmond, looking like miniature Eiffel Towers in the distance. I could see the squirts of green fire emanating from under their hoods.

A fifth strider materialized further north in San Pablo, its glittering body shimmering in the afternoon sun as it swept forward, destroying the gun emplacements there. One of the aliens in Richmond aimed a shot at the Richmond-San Rafael Bridge, damaging it. A second bolt accidentally breached the walls of San Quentin Prison; God knows what happened to the men sequestered there.

At the sight of these terrible machines the crowd of refugees near the water's edge seemed struck mute by horror and dismay. They could only stand there, mouths agape and faces stricken, shocked silent by the approaching danger. There was no screaming or shouting—not yet anyway!

Two of the Martian tripods entered the water, and began heading across the Bay towards San Rafael.

"Get out of here!" I shouted to the masses, but they needed no urging from me. They rushed west into the park and then into the streets of the city. But where could they go?

As I turned around again to face the Bay, I realized that the fifth machine was coming right across the water to Peacock Gap, where we were standing. Then I broke and ran, not waiting for Mayer or anyone else. The approaching fighting-machine rushed right up the gravel beach towards us. The recon site was blasted out of existence with one shot. One of the boatloads of fugitives was swamped by a huge wave when the tripod's foot splashed into the water nearby. The stones under my feet were muddy and slick. Then, as the Martian machine towered overhead just a couple of hundred yards away, zapping some target off in the distance, I flung myself forward into a depression in the ground, and put my hands over my head.

But the strider took no more notice of the people running

from it than a man would of a bunch of ants in a nest that his foot had disturbed. The machine's hood pointed at the batteries that were still firing near Fairfax and let loose a mighty blast. Most of the guns went silent.

However, the Army had hidden a couple of camouflaged tanks in a nearby residential section. Two or three of these weapons now opened fire at close range. The sudden near concussion, the last one close upon the first, made my heart jump. The monster was already raising its sting-ray when the first shell burst just six yards from its cowl. Simultaneously, two other shells exploded in the air near its body, slewing it around—and then a fourth shell impacted directly on the hood. The strider's carapace bulged, flashed green and red, and disintegrated into a thousand tattered fragments of ruby flesh and glittering metal.

The refugees uttered a collective cry somewhere between a scream and a cheer.

Amazingly, the decapitated colossus didn't topple. It must have had some automatic stabilizer that restored its balance, because it started walking forward in a straight line into the city, obviously without direction, crushing cars, people, and even houses beneath its huge pads. It smashed forward until it hit the brick *façade* of St. Gandalf's Church, which it demolished in the act of destroying itself. There was a muffled explosion that sent pieces of the machine in all directions, but the greater part of it was still intact, although crumpled on its side.

I ran the several city blocks to the wreck.

Thick clouds of smoke were pouring from the downed strider, and through the whirling wisps I could see its giant limbs churning the soil and flinging a spray of dirt into the air. The tentacles swayed and struck out like living arms, maiming anything they encountered. It was as if some great wounded thing was struggling for its life. Enormous quantities of a reddish-brown fluid were spurting in noisy jets out of the machine in all directions. I didn't know whether it was blood or oil or some combination thereof.

Two other machines responded immediately to the plight of

their brother, heading in our direction, advancing with gigantic strides from the beach. As soon as they were in range, the tanks opened up again.

I ran a half block and hit the ground once more. I could hear the shells whistling over my head and impacting on the Point, and the returning zaps of the Martian weapons. The noise was deafening. Then I saw them again, those twin towers of gray, as they attacked and destroyed the tanks. They'd passed me by somehow, and were now stooping over the still-spurting remains of their comrade.

A third and fourth machine now appeared, zapping their sting-rays in every direction. I heard rather than saw a flight of jets high above me, but they either quickly passed by or were blasted out of the sky, because they were only evident for a short period of time. The whine of shells, the crackling hiss of the Martian beams, the crashing of the houses, the screaming of the people, the burning of the fires, all mingled together to form the cacophony of battle.

I wanted to hide.

I wanted to run away.

I had no idea where to go.

Clouds of dense black smoke obscured the city and San Pablo Bay, limiting my vision on those occasions when I was able to raise my head. I knew that the tanks were out of action, because the distinctive whoof-swish sound of their shells had vanished.

I stood up, finally, to see what was going on. Through the fog of war I could spy some of the refugees, still trying to find some hole in which to hide. In the distance they looked like little frogs leap-hopping through the grass, running back and forth in dismay.

Then the sting-ray was back again, its emerald lance poking ever closer to me. The nearest row of houses caved in as it dissolved with the touch, sending flames of despair into the sky; the trees in the park caught fire with a roar of protest. And still the green light flickered up and down, here and there, licking up the people, and coming within fifty yards of where I stood.

I screamed out loud, and staggered through the leaping, hissing earth back towards the beach. Had my foot stumbled, that would have been the end of me. I ran helplessly away in full sight of the Martians.

I expected to die.

I have this dim memory of a great Martian foot coming down within yards of my body, driving straight into the loose gravel, whirling its way forward and lifting again. Then the four remaining machines strode away from me and gathered around their fallen brother. They picked up the shattered remains, and gently carried the debris of their comrade between them back across the Bay to Richmond. I thought of a baby rocking in its cradle.

Slowly, then, so very slowly, I realized that by some miracle I had once again escaped the touch of death.

CHAPTER THIRTEEN
THE MINISTER'S LAMENT

*Ministers who spoke of God as if
they enjoyed a monopoly of the subject.*
—Henry David Thoreau

ALEX SMITH, 27 DECEMBER, MARS YEAR I
MARIN COUNTY, CALIFORNIA, PLANET EARTH

The Martians then retreated back across the Bay to their major base at Richmond. Had they just pushed on immediately towards San Francisco, there would have been nothing to stop their advance south of San Rafael other than a few scattered tanks and half-tracks. Most of our forces had been knocked out already, apparently including the military headquarters at Fairfax.

But the aliens seemed in no hurry to redeploy. If anything marks the Martian invasion of Earth, it was their slow but steady plodding as they moved from one place to another. "One small step for Mars, one giant step for Marskind!"

Spaceships were landing in North America every few hours, adding to the alien forces. And not just on the West Coast, either: I heard later that capsules had fallen near Jackson Hole, Wyoming; Grand Forks, British Columbia; Chinook, Montana; Wichita, Kansas; Craig, Missouri, and many other locations, mostly west of the Mississippi. No one knows why these towns were picked, or whether the targeting was random.

Meanwhile, our military command was now fully aware of the power and potency of the enemy, and worked furiously to target the new landing sites. A few of these were actually destroyed, I later understood; but any that managed to assemble a fighting-machine quickly became invulnerable. Every minute counted when countering the Martian threat.

In the Bay Area fresh troops and equipment were airlifted to the San Joaquin Valley, since Sacramento and the big cities had already been compromised. The Air Force tried bombing several of the alien landing pits with Stealth aircraft, but they weren't stealthy enough, apparently, at least after their first run. One 500-pounder did manage to cripple a Martian tripod, which was, however, soon rebuilt; but all of the other jets that approached the pits thereafter were shot out of the sky before they could even come within range. The buggers learned very quickly indeed.

A similar pattern was repeated when the military tried deploying cruise missiles: the first one was effective, the others almost wholly *ineffective*. The aliens seemed able to communicate almost instantaneously—as we now know, their ability was telepathic in nature.

The digging-machines began clearing away all of the vegetation surrounding their pits, preventing anyone from approaching closer than about three-quarters of a mile. As our forces began employing larger, more effective weaponry, the aliens became more attentive to even minor incursions by our soldiers.

Gradually, the enemy was consolidating its operations into strategically-placed campsites, abandoning the smaller ones once they'd been stripped of anything useful. The sites were chosen to dominate and control all activity in a particular region. The great striders then began systematically destroying communications facilities, power plants, major transmission lines, bridges, and anything else that might link or aid our security services.

I became separated from Mayer and the others during the battle, and so as evening approached, I had to decide what to do next. The way south still seemed open to me, although for how long, I had no idea. Our bicycles were gone, probably grabbed by refugees, many of whom were still milling about in the late afternoon sun. I decided to head to San Francisco. I was curious as to what was happening in that great city by the Bay. Since I had no transportation, I walked.

Parts of San Rafael were burning fiercely, but as I headed south through the lower reaches of town, I gradually passed out of the damaged area. Most of the stores had been ransacked by looters, but I did manage to find some bottled water at a service station, along with a few chocolate bars and crackers and stale sandwiches. I wolfed down the food and drank a bottle of water. I rigged a makeshift pack from rags to carry additional provisions, and loaded the sack with as much as I could tote. I was parched enough that the water was quickly consumed.

The refugees diminished rapidly as I moved south. Apparently, everyone thought that San Francisco was a danger area, and had headed west towards the coast. I encountered one or two strays here and there, and a little brown dog who was so skittish that he wouldn't come anywhere near me; I threw him a cookie, which he gobbled down immediately before running off in the other direction. I have no idea what became of him—or of so many others that I encountered on my journey.

I walked for hours as the sun drifted ever lower in the sky. I was almost on my last legs by sunset. Every time I stopped, though, my fears would get the better of me, and soon I would get up and resume my plodding course southwards. At last I was able to spy the Golden Gate Bridge shining in the distance, although I couldn't tell how far away it was.

Suddenly and without warning I was violently ill, vomiting most of my dinner onto the grass by the road; one of the sandwiches must have gone bad. I suppose this was around four; I'm not really sure—it was late afternoon. I lay down in a garden to rest. I seem to recall talking to myself during that last interval, something about Becky and the Martians. I was very thirsty, having drunk all of my water.

I was angry with my wife all of a sudden. I don't really know why. Perhaps it was my worrying about what'd happened to her in Sonoma, combined with my desire to see her safe again. I hated the fact that I had to cope with this godawful burden on top of everything else. It was totally unfair to her, of course, but that's the way I felt—and I'm trying to relate what happened to me with as much honesty as possible.

I don't remember exactly what came next. I was just so damned tired. At some point I became aware of a figure standing in front of me: someone in a soot-smudged, short-sleeved shirt with white collar, his pinched face staring down at me in concern. Framing him was the splendor of a mackerel sky, rows and rows of orange and pink clouds streaking the horizon, illuminated by the brilliant sunset.

I sat up and groaned.

"Water?" I managed to gasp.

He shook his head "no."

"You've been asking me that ever since I found you," the minister said.

As soon as he spoke I realized that "he" was actually a "she." The closely-cropped hair and the narrow, gaunt body had initially thrown me off.

For a moment we were silent, taking stock of each other. I'm sure that she found me a strange sight indeed, with my filthy pants and shirt, and my face and shoulders blackened by the ever-present smoke. The minister had a weak chin, short, black hair, and large, pale brown eyes staring vacantly at me. She spoke again, her gaze turning to the sky.

"What does it all mean?" she asked.

"Who are you?"

"The Reverend Lesley," she said—I didn't know then whether "Lesley" was a first or last name—"St. Gandalf's was my church."

I just stared. What could I say? God had nothing to offer me.

She extended her thin white hand and then spoke almost a complaint. I had no sense that her words were addressed to me:

"Why did it happen? What have I done? This morning I conducted the service as usual, asking God to save our town and preserve our church. This afternoon the Martians came, saw, and conquered; and then—and then—it was Sodom and Gomorrah again! All my work undone. All my work thrown back at me. What did I do to deserve this? What kind of devils are these Martians?"

"Where are we?" I asked, trying to clear my throat. I was so parched that it was hard for me to speak.

"Corte Madera, I think," she said. "Or maybe Mill Valley, I'm not really sure."

She sat down beside me, gripping her knees very tightly, and then turned to look at me again. For a moment she just stared silently at my face.

"The agent of God came walking through the city streets, its hand of death pointed right at St. Gandalf's," she said, "and suddenly—fire, brimstone, and destruction!"

She waved her hands again.

"All my work—my Sunday school, my preaching, my building of a congregation—it's gone. Why is God punishing *me*? Everything that I had that was good is dead; everything that was truly fine is finished. Oh, that beautiful place of worship— it's demolished! My life has been swept away from me! Why? Why? *Why?*"

She began ranting then.

"'The smoke of her burning goeth up for ever and ever'!" she said, standing up and gesturing at the horizon, her face contorted in disgust.

I was finally beginning to understand. Her tragedy—she was obviously a refugee from the destruction of San Rafael— had driven her to the brink of insanity. She was suffering from massive psychological shock and trauma. Her world, her hold on reality, had been so firmly displaced by events that it was irretrievable.

"How far are we from Mill Valley?" I said matter-of-factly, trying to restore the conversation to some semblance of normalcy.

"But what are we to do?" she said, completely ignoring my question. "Who are these creatures of Satan everywhere around us? Has the Earth been given over to them?"

"*Ma'am*. Are we very far from Mill Valley?"

"Only this morning I officiated at an early celebration of the…."

"Yes, Reverend," I said quietly, "but you have to look after yourself now. You can always rebuild your church, but you must conserve your strength. While there's life, there's hope. God hath spared you for a reason."

"Hope?" She looked over at me with her large brown eyes. They reminded me of a cocker spaniel's.

"Yes," I said. "*Hope! Hope that we'll survive this invasion! Hope that we'll begin life anew. Hope that we'll live rather than die!*"

I told her that our military would soon rally and the Martians would be defeated. Those of us who survived would have to pick up our shovels and begin reconstructing our lives. She listened to me very intently, but as I rambled on, her attention gradually faded, and she looked again at the distant, declining sun, which had now reached the horizon. (I often had the same problem with my history and philosophy students!)

"It's the beginning of the end," she finally said, interrupting my most learnèd discourse and thoroughly irritating me in the process. *How dare she!* "The great and terrible day of the Lord, when all men shall be called to account, when men shall call upon the mountains and the rocks to fall upon them and hide them, yes, hide them from the face of Him that sitteth upon the throne on high, when the great Judge shall levy out the fines and punishments for all our sins! 'Yea, though we walk through the valley of the shadow of death'…."

I ceased reasoning with this woman. There wasn't any point. I struggled to my feet, put my hands on her shoulders, and shook her hard to get her attention.

"Come on, wake up, Lesley!" I said. "I know you're scared!

So are the rest of us. Quit your whining. What good's religion if it fails the weight of tragedy? Think of all the earthquakes and floods, wars and volcanoes. Think of the lives that have been lost. Do you believe God's given San Rafael a pass? He's not an insurance agent, you know."

For a time she just sat there blankly, her face an unreadable mask.

"They're invulnerable," she said. "They're pitiless. They care nothing for man. They're either the agents of God or the tools of the Devil. But which? It doth make a difference."

"Look, Reverend," I said, "you haven't seen nearly as much fighting as I have. I've watched them demolish our military. But I also saw one of the alien machines destroyed this afternoon, and it was *your* church, Lesley, that destroyed it. Isn't *that* the act of a just God?"

"Destroyed?" she said. "Yes, of course, it was, wasn't it? But how can one of God's agents be destroyed *by* God?"

"Who the hell knows?" I was losing patience. "Nonetheless, I saw it happen, and so did you. I have no doubt that our forces will prevail. We just had the misfortune to wind up in the middle of things, and to see much of what we cared about damaged. But we survived, both of us, and that has to mean something. *It has to mean something, Lesley!* We've both been given a second chance."

"Yes, a second chance," she said. "I hadn't thought of it that way, but you're right, of course. A second chance to make things right again. But how do we rebuild? How do we start over?

"What's that light up there?" she asked abruptly, pointing at the eastern sky.

I looked where it was darkest on the horizon. I could see a thin white line etching its way towards us.

"Must be one of our missiles," I said. "It's our boys at work!"

But even as we watched, the tip of the candle suddenly flared brightly and then vanished into the ebon background.

"What happened?"

"I'm not sure," I said, "but that flicker tells me that our men are still trying to push back the storm. Something *will* work, Reverend, of that I have no doubt. But we've got to move. The Martians will be coming this way before much longer."

She sprang to her feet and gestured towards the distant north.

"Listen!" she said.

From beyond the low hills came the dull resonance, the understated booming, of dim, distant guns, followed by a remote, even weird crying sound, the alien wail of the Martians. Then everything went still again.

It was dark now. A lone bird began singing from a nearly tree. What it was doing here at this time of the year I had no idea: probably a refugee like us. High above us in the sky a crescent moon hung faintly pale against the encroaching dark. Smoke from San Rafael still permeated our clothing.

"We should find some shelter for the night," I said. "A place that's safe and warm."

But as things actually happened, we chose wrongly—and part of that wrongness was undoubtedly choosing each other.

CHAPTER FOURTEEN
BROTHER STEPHEN

Am I not a man and a brother?
—Josiah Wedgwood

STEPHEN SMITH, 26 DECEMBER, MARS YEAR I
SAN BERNARDINO COUNTY, CALIFORNIA, PLANET EARTH

My younger brother Stephen was living in Loma Linda, a suburb of Los Angeles, when the Martians first landed. He'd completed his medical studies the year before, and was now serving as an intern at a university there, working long, grueling shifts. Consequently, he heard very little about the Martians until he went off duty early Christmas morning.

For whatever reason, and we have no idea why, most of the original complement of Martian spaceships fell either in the San Francisco Bay Area or the Los Angeles Metropolitan Region. The first of them to impact the Southland smacked into an old inn and resort near La Quinta, southwest of Palm Springs, on noon of Christmas Day; and the rest soon followed, day after day, striking mostly the inland communities of Southern California. Perhaps the Martians had some idea of driving the population together in the great urban centers, although as things worked out, the aliens actually moved too slowly to capture many of the refugees. We really don't know why.

That night a capsule fell on the Inland Empire, and suddenly my brother's plight became more serious. The news reports were now showing the danger posed by the Martian fighting-machines. Everywhere the alien ships were unfolding themselves, with the usual deadly consequences. With an enemy vessel located less than a dozen miles away in San Bernardino, Steve knew that he had to evacuate right away.

Of course, the power stayed on longer in the Southland, which enabled the folks there to follow the news for one or two days more, depending on where they lived. Also, there were a number of military bases located in Southern California, and the response by the authorities was somewhat quicker, given the fact that the news regarding the events up north had already been disseminated to the media.

On St. Stephen's Day (ironically enough) an evacuation of the area was ordered by Major General John Edgar Smuts. The population was told to retreat west to the coast, northeast to the San Joaquin Valley, or south to San Diego, whichever was easiest. Stephen could already see a column of smoke rising from northeastern San Bernardino. The fire caused by the landing had ignited the brush when the Santa Ana winds blew in around noon, and so the authorities were facing two major problems. Southern California had had very little rain that season. Sometime later that day the San Bernardino ship finally unfolded, and the first casualties occurred on a university campus there.

My brother felt no anxiety about us, because I'd talked with him briefly after the first ship had landed in Novato, and he figured we'd long since evacuated. The news from the Bay Area became spotty, though, after communications and power lines were cut. Steve wasn't married, had had no time, really, to pursue a social life. He lived in a walk-up apartment off the end of Mountain View. But he suffered from the same incessant curiosity that I did, and so he immediately headed to the area where the Martians had established their pit in San Bernardino.

He knew from news reports that the San Bernardino capsule had landed near Park Avenue and College Parkway. Interstate 215 had been blocked by the police at its junction with Highway

210, but he used the city streets to sneak within a mile of the landing site, and then ran his motorbike up a hill behind the campus, not far from the San Andreas Fault, where he had a bird's-eye view of the proceedings. Only the bulk of the library building blocked a portion of his vision. He told me afterwards that he'd just wanted to see the aliens for himself before they were all killed. He also tried calling me again on his cell phone, but of course by then the towers were down all over the Bay Area, and remained so until long after the crisis had passed.

At first Steve could only see a line of black smoke. As I mentioned already, the Santa Ana winds were blowing about 30-40 MPH, generally to the west or northwest, pushing the brush fire away from the campus towards the housing communities and businesses that lined I-215, and crossing the tracks of the main rail line that ran on the other side of the freeway up to Cajon Pass. This posed a major problem for the authorities, because it effectively blocked one of the few exit points out of Southern California. They were trying to stop the fire from spreading any further west. The military convoys that had been sent from Camp Pendleton and Fort Irwin had to fight through dense smoke even to establish a perimeter around the Martian pit. The number of very large campus buildings made their task even more difficult.

Steve watched while several of the structures were occupied by the troops, who established machine-gun emplacements on top of the library building (which directly overlooked the pit), and also on the roof of an adjoining faculty office structure.

As soon as the Martian "egg" began to crack, our boys unleashed everything they had, forcing the aliens to bottle up again immediately. Already several of their vessels had been destroyed around the country through aggressive artillery and missile attacks at the first sign of activity in the pits. Nothing else happened in San Bernardino for another hour, until late afternoon.

Then the Martians unslipped their ship very quickly, thrusting through the opening a protective canopy that would become the carapace of a fighting-machine. Our concentrated fire proved ineffective, and Steve was soon witnessing the destructive power of the alien sting-rays, as they zapped our emplacements into oblivion. Edwards Air Force Base had sent a squad of fighters to strafe the Martians, but this too had minimal effect. The aliens had already adjusted their strategy to account for the best we had to offer.

Finally, Smuts ordered his remaining forces to retreat. This was cunning of him, because he had used the initial occupation period to lace the surrounding grounds with very large land mines and other explosives, and to wire several of the larger buildings with munitions designed to implode them.

As the soldiers pulled back, the Martians emerged from their pit in force, quickly erecting several of the great striders, and knocking out any opposition they encountered. Then they began aggressively moving forward against our army, destroying everything they encountered. But as they stepped onto the open stretches of the campus lawn, several mines blew up, over-turning one of the fighting-machines. This stopped them for awhile, because they had to set their fallen comrade to rights; they also used the time to mount a third strider.

Smuts had left some guerrilla forces in place to taunt the Martians with hand-held missiles and bazookas and similar kinds of "stingers," and this prompted the alien machines to move forward perhaps more quickly than they'd intended, without first assessing the situation. Smuts had placed his men within the concrete buildings fronting the quad on the south side of where the Administrative Center had once stood. Of course, the tripods attacked these facilities aggressively, moving ever closer to pick off the little irritants that were "stinging" them incessantly. When the striders reached the faculty office building, the remaining soldiers withdrew and blew the struc-ture, collapsing it onto a fighting-machine. The tons of concrete completely buried one of the Martians, destroying it.

Thereafter the striders remained at a respectful distance while they systematically demolished all of the other buildings on campus. Smuts's men had put up a good fight, but it wasn't enough. The Martians had prevailed once again.

Steve left the scene not long thereafter, and headed straight home. He packed his few belongings into a carryall, and attached it the back of his motorcycle. Since Interstate 10 was blocked near Palm Springs and I-215 was cut off in San Bernardino, he decided to head west.

First, though, he checked with his hospital to see if his services were required, but they were already evacuating their patients to the coast. At this point Steve had had very little sleep during the previous two days, and was beginning to feel extreme fatigue. Also about this time the power went out in the Inland Empire, and although it came on again briefly later, it was gone for good by nightfall.

Everywhere the roads were packed by people trying to escape the Martian invaders. Steve took the back roads to the Moreno Valley. The Santa Anas were still blowing steadily from the high desert down to the ocean, acting like a natural heater to bake everything between the inland areas and the coastline.

Steve stopped for dinner at a café just the other side of Riverside. The power was still on there.

"There's fighting near Indio," one of the patrons said.

Everyone was discussing the war.

"What'll it be?" the waitress asked my brother.

"Aren't you going to evacuate?" he asked.

"Nah," she said, "they'll put this right in a day or two."

"Coffee," he said, "lots of coffee. What's your special?"

"Pork chops, but they're kinda greasy. Try the New Yorker instead."

"New Yorker it is, medium rare, baked, and salad with vinegar and oil on the side. Aren't you afraid?"

"Come on, who'd want anything in Moreno Valley?"

"You've got a point," he said.

The place seemed busy enough, and nobody appeared worried about the day's developments.

In fact, as the hour progressed, more and more customers

kept crowding through the door, until the restaurant ran out of booths.

"Mind if we sit here?" said a woman with her ten-year-old daughter in tow, as she slipped into the booth opposite him. She was short and dark-haired and slightly overweight. Her child was a thinner version of herself, armed with braces and eyeglasses.

"Go ahead." Steve waved his fork while munching steadily on his lettuce.

"The freeway's just terrible," she said. "It's taken me two hours to get here from Redlands."

"Bumper to bumper, eh?" he said.

She shook her head in frustration. "I'm Cassie, by the way." She held out her hand.

"Steve," he said.

"And I'm Erie," the girl said very emphatically. "That's short for Erin."

His two companions ordered their dinners. Their first choice was already gone: the café was running short of food.

"We're heading to Laguna," Cassie said. "My sister lives there."

"A bit out of your way, isn't it?"

"We'll try cutting across on the Ortega Highway, if it's open," she said. "What about you?"

"They're evacuating people from the coast any way they can, using ships from the Naval Base in San Diego, as well as freighters, pleasure craft, and sailboats. So I guess I'll head there."

His New Yorker plopped down in front of him. It actually looked fairly good.

"Ketchup or steak sauce?" the waitress asked.

"No thanks," he said, waving her off. "I'm just trying to get to San Pedro or Newport Beach, and then we'll see what's possible."

"You look tired," the woman said.

"Yeah, too many late nights, too much of everything."

The waitress brought halibut for Cassie and a hamburger for her daughter.

They ate in silence for a few moments.

"I've...," they both started to say at the same time—and then laughed.

"I've got plenty of room in my SUV," Cassie suddenly said. "We could use some help."

"Already got a motorbike," he said, and then paid an inordinate amount of attention to his food.

"I mean, I'm not trying to...." She swallowed heavily and sipped her iced tea. "It's just that.... Oh, shit, I always do this. Look, Steve, you seem like a nice enough guy. I'm just worried, that's all. I don't know what's going to happen."

"None of us do," he said.

He finished his meal, and then watched silently while his companions ate theirs.

"Dessert, anyone?" their waitress asked.

"Not for me," he said.

"Not for me, either." Cassie patted her stomach and groaned.

"I want some pie." Her daughter, like so many children, favored sweets.

"We'll take it with us." Her mother reached for the bill.

"OK." Steve looked directly into her eyes.

"OK?" Her face was a puzzle.

"Yeah, people have to help each other out these days."

She obviously hadn't expected his reply.

"Uh, what do you do, Steve?"

"I'm a doctor, an internist actually, specializing in cardiology."

She nodded her head. It was good enough for her.

"I'm a dental hygienist."

"And *I* go to school," Erin said. "But Mom says we're on vacation now."

"Yes, we're all on vacation." Steve smiled at the thought. "A very *long* vacation."

He paid the bill for all of them, putting it on his MasterCard, which was still good as long as the power was working. Outside, it was almost dark. He loaded his bike into the rear of the SUV, making room by shifting around their clothes and baggage.

"Good, you've got plenty of food and water back here."

"I tried to think of everything," she said. "I don't know if I planned right, but…."

"You did the best you could," he said. "That's all you can do. You drive, Cassie: it's your car and I'm just dog-tired."

It took them more than an hour to inch their way the ten miles down to Perris, and another hour to get to Lake Elsinore, and he slept the whole way, snoring gently in the back seat while Cassie drove on.

"Steve!" The cry jolted him wide awake.

They'd followed State Route 74, the so-called Ortega Highway, around the northern end of the lake, and there, where it turned away from the lake to start up the mountains, was a barricade that hadn't been present before.

A group of armed men had parked several large trucks right across the highway, blocking all access.

"Pull over to the side," Steve said, "and I'll talk to them."

He wandered up the highway from the perimeter road fronting Lake Elsinore.

"Hey, guys!" he said. "What's up?"

Route 74 was vacant behind them.

"We're the tax collectors," one man said, stepping in front of the truck line. He carried a hunting rifle slung under his right arm.

"Tax collectors, huh? What kind of tax are we talking about?"

"Three hundred dollars per car, cash on the line."

"Yeah, we don't take plastic!" one of his companions said.

They all laughed.

"Isn't that a bit illegal?" Steve asked.

"Well, maybe it is and maybe it ain't, but you don't pay us the money, sonny, you ain't goin' nowhere up that there mountain."

"Haven't got it," Steve said, and began walking away.

"Hey!" one of the men said. "We also take trade."

My brother stopped and turned around. "What kind of trade?"

"Well, that little filly you got over there. She'll do just fine for an hour or two."

"I'll think about it," Steve said, turning and continuing to amble back to the SUV.

"You do that," the first man said, "and remember when you come crawling back here tomorrow. Right now the price's three hundred bucks; tomorrow it'll be higher, I friggin' guarantee you."

Just as Steve reached the SUV, a Highway Patrol car came slewing around the corner, and ran up the short stretch of Highway 74 to the barricade.

"You men there, what are you doing?" echoed the voice from the official vehicle's loudspeaker.

The "tax collectors" dodged behind their trucks, and abruptly and without warning opened fire. Multiple shots hit the police car, killing the officer inside, stray bullets whizzing by Steve's head. He jumped into the SUV, slammed the door, and yelled "Floor it!"

They continued down the perimeter road along the lake. A few miles away, another traffic jam slowed them down.

"We've got to find shelter for the night," Steve said.

"Where?" Cassie asked.

He pointed to an unlit house set back from the street.

"Try there."

When he pounded on the front door, no one answered, so they drove around the place, and hid the SUV from the sight of the road. Then they prepared to camp.

"I've just got the two sleeping bags," Cassie said.

"Keep 'em for yourselves. I have a pillow and a blanket in my pack. That's enough."

"We could break into the place," she said.

He shook his head. "That wouldn't be right."

And that was Monday night.

They awoke the next morning to the sound of repeated gunfire off to the north.

"The 'tax collectors'," Steve said, groaning as he tried to sit up. He was stiff from sleeping on the ground.

"You think they finally caught up with them?" Cassie asked.

"Had to. The authorities wouldn't allow something like that to continue."

They started loading their things back into the SUV.

"Crap!" Steve said, pointing to a hole in the side of the vehicle.

He started going through everything, closely examining the contents, and then shook his head.

"What's the matter?" Cassie wanted to know.

He grunted and frowned: "Bike's ruined."

He hauled it out and showed her the damage to the engine.

"Can't do anything about it," he said, tossing the cycle to one side.

Then he indicated a nearby faucet.

"Best fill up every container you've got," he said.

Afterwards they drove into the little town of Lake Elsinore, and found a small, family-run restaurant that was still open.

"Don't know how long the eggs will last," the proprietress said, "but you're welcome to them while we've got 'em. Coffee, honey?"

"Please," Steve said, and they had a quiet breakfast together.

"Any papers?" he asked.

"The *Valley Chronicle* published a one-sheeter this morning, but most of the news is on TV." She used her remote to turn up the sound.

"Fighting is reported throughout the San Bernardino area, in Palm Springs, and near Palmdale and Victorville," the Channel 14 newscaster said. "We've got reliable reports that the Martians are on the move again, and that the military is deploying its forces to meet the threat. People are being encouraged to evacuate to the coast, where a massive operation is underway to transport the population to safer areas, particularly San Diego and Mexico.

"The southern freeways remain open, but are heavily crowded with bumper-to-bumper traffic; the same is true of the

Pacific Coast Highway. Average speed on these roads is less than ten miles per hour. Several of our newscopters have been shot down, and the rest of the fleet has been confiscated by the Air Force, so we can't give you our usual live coverage. Power has been lost in most of the outlying communities of the L.A. Basin. The Mayor continues to urge calm, and the Governor has issued a statement from his hotel in Austria, telling everyone to be brave and 'kick some Martian butt'. That's a direct quote."

"Calm and brave, right," Steve said, "just like him. Say, any service stations still open?" he asked the owner.

"Try Ben's Den over on Water Street," she said. "If anyone's got gas, he does. Tell him JoAnn sent you."

After finishing their meal, they topped off their tank, and then headed back to the Ortega Highway, which was finally open, but completely filled with traffic.

"You really want to do this?" Steve asked.

He was driving now.

"My sister's in Laguna," she said.

"But is she even there?"

Cassie tried calling on her cell phone.

"Nothing," she said.

"Here're our choices: we can go north to Orange County, where the roads will be terribly impacted; we can take I-15 south, with the same result; or we can chance the Ortega Highway over the hump. It's about thirty miles through the Elsinore Mountains to San Juan Capistrano, but once we start, there's no way out: we either come or we go. If we run into some guys like the ones we met last night, we'll be completely at their mercy."

She sighed. "I don't know what to do," she said. "Let's try it, Steve. I don't know why, but I trust you."

"I trust you too," Erie's voice said from the back seat.

"OK, then," he said, and turned onto the highway, forcing his way into the line of vehicles.

The Ortega Highway swings back and forth across the flank of the mountains just north of Elsinore Peak, a 3,500-foot expanse of dry scrub and bushes and trees. Spread along the top of the plateau is the Cleveland National Forest, which includes live-oaks and pine trees as well as scrub and chaparral. As the automobile crawled up the side of the mountain, they had a splendid view of the entire Moreno and Temescal Valleys.

Suddenly they could hear the rumble of heavy firing somewhere in the east.

"Look," Erie yelled, "over there!"

She pointed out the window.

Far off in the distance they could make out the spindly skeletons of three of the Martian fighting-machines, slowly but inevitably working their way down the Moreno Valley.

"They must have destroyed March Air Reserve Base," Steve said, pointing to the huge clouds of smoke reaching into the heavens above 2,500-foot-high Steele Peak, which blocked their direct view of the old military facility.

Their SUV continued to inch its way up the flank of the mountain at a stately five miles per hour.

"They're coming!" Erie suddenly screamed.

"They're still a long way off," Steve said. "It's OK, really."

But they could see that the striders were moving visibly closer, even as they watched. Cassie and her daughter both had their heads hanging out of the windows on the right-hand side of the car.

"What's *that*?" Cassie asked.

Steve glanced over. The Martian machines were coming down the slope from Perris, spraying some kind of black cloud towards the town of Lake Elsinore.

"What are they doing, Steve?"

"I have absolutely no idea," he said, "but it doesn't look good. This isn't their usual weapon."

"Please go faster," Erie said.

"I'm going as fast as I can, Little One," he said.

"Mommy, I'm scared."

"Me too, Erin," her mother said, "but we need to be brave now. Steve will get us through."

But that journey, my brother later told me, was the longest of his life, and he prayed to God all through that interminable trip, not for his own salvation, but to spare the lives of Cassie and her daughter. It took them two hours to reach the top, while the Temescal Valley and Lake Elsinore and surrounding communities all became completely enshrouded in the oily fog. He had no idea what was going on down there, but he knew it couldn't be good.

He felt an exultation of spirit when they reached the plateau of the Elsinore Mountains. It was around noon, so they broke out some simple fare for lunch, passing it around in the car, even as they continued to inch forward towards Orange County.

No one said anything, not even Erie. It wasn't necessary. Just their companionship was enough.

If I get no more than this, Steve remembered thinking to himself, *I'll be well satisfied*. He looked at his fellow travelers and smiled.

"I think we made it," he said. "I really do."

Cassie smiled back at him.

"I know I have," she said.

CHAPTER FIFTEEN
MY DARLING BECKY

There is in every true woman's heart a spark of heavenly fire, which lies dormant in the broad daylight of prosperity; but which kindles up, and beams and blazes in the dark hour of adversity.

—Washington Irving

ALEX SMITH, 26 DECEMBER, MARS YEAR I
SONOMA COUNTY, CALIFORNIA, PLANET EARTH

The more time I had to think about it, the more I feared for the life and safety of my dear wife, Rebecca. I'd left with her Aunt Anita and Anita's beau, Dave Kwon, in Sonoma, on the day after Christmas. It now seemed forever to me, but only a few days had actually passed.

I'd thought that she'd be safe there, but one of the Martian machines from Richmond had veered north to Vallejo at the top of San Pablo Bay, and was preparing to move northwest into Napa and Sonoma and ultimately to Santa Rosa, destroying the railroads there as well as the communication centers. Sonoma was on a straight line from Vallejo to Santa Rosa and was bound to be affected. Thankfully, I didn't know about any of this at the time.

About three in the morning the police cars went blaring up and down the city streets, telling the people of Sonoma to evacuate, that the Martians were coming, and that they had fifteen minutes to leave. Becky got Anita and Dave into their old pickup, and crammed into the front seat as a third, with the dog tied in back in the open bed. My wife drove.

They headed up State Route 12, passing through Boyes Hot Springs and Glen Ellen. The police had routed the fugitives onto both lanes of the highway; in a few places they were able to crowd the cars three across by using the shoulders. They averaged about fifteen miles an hour.

As they were leaving, they could hear a series of huge blasts, punctuated with gunfire and the zapping sounds made by the alien weapons; and could see occasional flashes of green light in the direction of Sonoma. Anita was whimpering, she was so scared, and so was the little schnauzer in back, whose name was Fritzie; he was a sweet little thing, very bright and affectionate.

They'd just passed Glen Ellen when they were forced to stop. They tried to see what was happening up front, but the lights of the Highway Patrol vehicles obscured everything, together with clouds of gray smoke.

Then they heard something that absolutely terrified them: a deep boom-boom-boom noise. The ground began to vibrate, and they suddenly realized that one of the Martian striders was almost upon them. Anita screamed for help; Becky reached over and grabbed her aunt, telling her to be absolutely quiet. Then she turned off the lights.

Boom-boom-boom it went, pounding ever closer. Suddenly the car in front of them was smashed out of existence, as an enormous pad came out of the sky to crunch the vehicle into a flat metal flan, like something done by an auto wrecker. They could see the shaft of the leg extending up into the heavens, God knows how high; and then it lifted again, carrying pieces of the SUV and its inhabitants with it—and boom-boom-boom, continued on towards Santa Rosa.

"We can't go forward," my wife said.

"We can't go back either," Dave said. "We're stuck!"

And it was true: the wrecks that now littered the road made it impossible to travel any further on Highway 12.

"You know, there's a cutoff that runs from Glen Ellen to Oakville," Dave said. "We could walk the mile or so back to Glen Ellen, and then head into the woods."

"I don't know how far I can manage on foot," Aunt Anita said.

Her knees were bad, Becky knew, and her weight would make it difficult for her to walk any great distance.

"We'll do the best we can," my wife said.

They packed up whatever they could carry, got Fritzie out of the truck bed, and then started trudging their way down the edge of the highway in the dark. They proceeded very slowly, both because of occasional motorcyclists, private and official, that were scooting by, and because of other pedestrians, some of whom were moving in the opposite direction.

When they reached Glen Ellen, it was obvious that Anita wouldn't be able to continue much further, and that they all had to rest in any case. By this time it was starting to get light.

Glen Ellen is actually located a little to the west of Highway 12. Several secondary roads connect there, one leading off to the east, and several to the west. They stopped and found a motel where the proprietor took pity on them, giving them bagels and orange juice.

"You really need to get out of here," the man said. "The Martians are all over Sonoma, I hear, and they've passed this way several times already, heading towards Santa Rosa."

"Where can we go?" Becky asked.

"Don't know," the man said. "Maybe west would be best, but I couldn't swear to it."

"No," Anita said. "I absolutely can't go any further."

So they stayed in Glen Ellen for the rest of that day, and saw no more Martians, ironically enough, although they heard periodically from different law enforcement officers that the aliens were still roaming around somewhere. They were all so tired by then that they didn't really care that much. The power had failed, so there was no hard news of any kind; indeed, nothing was working except the tap water. Occasionally a police car would check on them.

Finally the authorities got a convoy of trucks through, and evacuated all the people they could find to Rohnert Park in the west. Fritzie sat up on Anita's lap, looking thoroughly disgruntled by the proceedings.

I heard all of this many weeks later from the proprietor of the motel, Berke Fernández; but he knew nothing of what'd become of Becky and her aunt thereafter. He chose to remain with his property throughout the crisis, and somehow survived everything that followed.

CHAPTER SIXTEEN
THE BLACK DEATH

I counted two and seventy stenches,
All well defined, and several stinks.
> —Samuel Taylor Coleridge

ALEX SMITH, 27 DECEMBER, MARS YEAR I
MARIN COUNTY, CALIFORNIA, PLANET EARTH

About the time that the minister and I had our first *tête-à-tête*, the Martians were moving again. As far as I can tell from the conflicting accounts that were published later, most of the enemy remained busy with the great construction projects in their respective pits until about nine in the evening, generating huge volumes of dark green smoke. I think they must have been assembling their weapons of mass destruction.

The aliens must have been dissatisfied with the progress of the war thus far. They'd lost several machines to our attacks, and while they'd greatly and quickly overpowered our forces in each case, they couldn't really afford a war of attrition. The supply lines to the home world were just too long and uncertain.

That night they began advancing again, slowly and cautiously, making their way south towards San Francisco in the west and to San José in the east. The two machines that had been assembled in Mountain View remained standing there, silent and alert, apparently serving as anchors for their companions' great sweep southward.

The striders didn't usually advance as a single grouped body, but often in a formation that resembled a loose, looping triangle, each separated from its fellows by a mile or two. Sometimes the point of one triangle was joined to another. The apex of each triangle could then wander left or right as needed for mop-up operations. They communicated with each other through siren-like howls, running up and down the scale from one note to another, if that's what it was. No one has ever deciphered this language. I eventually concluded that the whoops and hollers were more like signals than anything else.

Of course, we'd heard the long wailing during the Battle of San Rafael, before the Martians retreated to Richmond. They didn't stay there for long, though, crossing San Pablo Bay again later that night. The National Guardsmen, consisting mostly of unseasoned volunteers, were now holding our front lines; most of our regular forces had been decimated during those first few days.

A typical engagement usually ran something like this: the Guardsmen would fire one wild, premature, and wholly ineffectual volley, just enough to identify where they were, and then the Martians would either destroy them with their sting-rays, or bypass them altogether to attack our HQ and C&C facilities. Afterwards, they'd often return to the front lines to finish the job. In this way our forces were quite literally picked apart, unit by unit, and destroyed as an effective "fighting machine."

One group of tanks rallied at Hayward and ambushed a Martian strider moving south towards them, laying down very accurate fire, as deliberately as if they had been performing an exercise on a range somewhere.

The Martian machine advanced a few paces, staggered, and went down with a great whump of dust. Everyone cheered. The toppled alien, however, set up a prolonged ululation, an unholy racket indeed, and immediately a second glittering giant answered him, appearing over the trees just to the north. One leg of the damaged strider had been smashed by our shells. The second and third volleys flew wide of the Martian on the ground, and simultaneously its companion brought its ray-gun to bear on our tanks. The vehicles blew up, ammunition and all, and only one or two of our boys escaped.

The downed machine was eventually repaired and put back into service.

We could hear a continuous booming to the north and east on the other side of the Bay.

A few minutes past ten that night, the minister and I were still hiding in the shrubs along the road; I think we were somewhere in Mill Valley. Then three great machines loomed out of the darkness to the north. We could just make them out by the pale light of the moon, glittering as they twisted and turned in their wobbling style of walk.

A dozen rockets suddenly shot from the hills behind them, but eleven were immediately knocked from the sky by the green rays, and the twelfth impacted a tree short of its target. The Martians sometimes seemed to have difficulty locating our men, who must have broken into small guerrilla groups to attack the striders from cover. Four more of the fighting-machines soon joined the group, sweeping up and down the countryside to our left, looking for the soldiers who'd dared attack them.

"We need to find cover," I said.

The minister cried faintly in her throat and began dashing down the road, but I knew it was no good running from a Martian, so I turned aside and crawled through some nettles and underbrush into the broad drainage ditch that ran by the side of the street. She looked back, saw what I was doing, and returned to join me.

Two of the great tripods halted near us, perhaps having seen our movement; the nearer of the machines was facing Tamalpais Valley, while the other strider was outlined indistinctly against the sky. I couldn't be sure of its exact location.

The unworldly howling had ceased; the machines then took positions equally spaced from each other, working in absolute silence. They actually formed a half-circle, I later learned, with about twelve miles between the horns at its furthest extent.

We still had soldiers out there somewhere, targeting at least part of the crescent formation—at San Rafael and Novato and San Anselmo and Fairfax and Woodacre, and even at Point Reyes on the coast. Behind hills and woods, in ravines and gullies, across the flat meadows, wherever a group of trees or houses provided sufficient cover, our men patiently waited for the enemy's next move. I don't know if General Harroll was directing the activity, or if some other officer was in charge. Everyone knew, though, that this represented our final throw of the dice. The Martians just had to advance a little further into our line of fire, and instantly those motionless black forms, those guns and tanks glittering so darkly in the night, would explode into thunderous fury, would light up the sky with their weapons, and then water the soil with their valiant blood.

How much did the aliens actually understand? No one has ever answered that question to my satisfaction. Did the Martians appreciate the bravery of our boys? Or did they interpret our occasional spurts of activity, the sudden stinging of our shells, as the onslaught of a hive of bees, something to be brushed aside? Did they dream of killing us? What did they want? I had no idea, and neither did anyone else.

I've asked myself these questions a hundred times or more, and still I have no answer that makes much sense, although I know more now than I did then. As I watched those vast, impersonal sentinels standing so very close to us that night, I realized how utterly alien they were, and how strange we must seem to them. Was some understanding between the two species even possible?

Then came a sound like the distant concussion of a gun, followed by a long whoosh, and then another, and yet another. The Martian near us raised a tube on high and discharged it with a heavy boom that made the ground heave. The one further north answered it. There wasn't any flash or smoke, just this ominous series of dull detonations, followed by the whooshing sound I'd heard previously.

This was obviously something new! I was so curious that I

completely forgot my fear and climbed onto an adjoining wall. I stood there staring southeast towards Almonte. Just then I heard another loud report, and could feel rather than see a large projectile hurtling overhead down the valley towards the Bay. I expected to observe some flash of its detonation where it landed, but instead all I could see was the dark sky above, dimly lit by the moon, and a kind of mist spreading wide and low below me near the coast. The silence returned.

"What's happening?" the minister hissed, crouching beside me.

"I have no idea," I said.

A bat flickered by and vanished from sight. A distant shouting began—and then abruptly ceased. I looked up again at the Martian machine, and saw that it was now moving southeast along the creek bed, with a swift, rolling motion generated by the working of its three legs.

Every moment I expected some hidden emplacement of ours to attack the striders, but the evening remained calm and silent. This was very strange indeed. The figure of the Martian grew smaller as it receded, and presently the mist and night swallowed it up completely. We climbed higher along the wall as it paralleled the road, trying to see something, anything, that might tell us what was going on. Towards Almonte I could perceive a darkened hollow with a hill poking out of it; and then, on the other side of the stream, another. I couldn't make any sense of it. What the hell was happening here?

I looked to the north, and there I saw a third of the black clouds hugging the ground.

Everything had become very still. Far away to the southeast, I heard the Martians hooting to one another, and then the air quivered again with the distant thud of their guns. But our own weapons made no reply.

"We need to get to higher ground," I said, suddenly seized with apprehension.

I don't know why I was so worried, but there was something very wrong about what I'd observed. So we headed immediately up the road leading out of Mill Valley to a hilly area between the two gullies. I just didn't like the look of that black vapor.

Later I learned much more about the Black Death, as it came to be called, but everything then was still a mystery to us. It was just my gut instinct that drove us up that hill and saved our sorry lives.

The poisonous gas was dispensed in several ways. It could be shot some distance in canisters that would crack open on impact, thereby dispersing their noxious load, or by directly spraying the vapor over the areas that the aliens wanted cleansed of life. The fog killed everything that breathed it.

It was heavy, this gas, heavier than the densest smoke. It would sink through the air and pour over the ground in a manner that was almost liquid, abandoning the hills and streaming into the valleys and ditches and waterways. Wherever it encountered water a chemical reaction occurred, neutralizing the stuff and covering the stream or pond or ocean with a powdery dark scum that sank slowly to the bottom. The vapor didn't diffuse in air as a gas might, but hung together in oily banks, flowing sluggishly down the slope of the land and driving reluctantly before the wind, very slowly combining with the moisture of the atmosphere, and sinking to earth in the form of an inert black dust. Our scientists have never been able to recreate the stuff in their labs.

Anyone who reached high ground could easily escape its effects, if they understood what was happening. In San Francisco, for example, a number of people on the upper floors of high-rise hotels survived the initial onslaught of the Martians, and eventually lived to tell about their experiences.

As a rule, though, the Martians didn't wait for the vapor to disperse naturally, but cleared the air by wading into the stuff and neutralizing it with some kind of gaseous counteragent.

Late that night we heard some of our own guns again, firing in the distance at a Martian machine. We also saw another Martian ship land, I'm not sure where, somewhere to the south of us. It was a brilliant emerald meteor high in the sky, a beautiful sight really, if it hadn't been so ominous.

The Martians had methodically cleared the countryside of most of the pesky "bugs" that were irritating them, much as we might smoke out a bees' nest. From Novato to San Francisco millions of human beings died during that long, dark night, quickly and horribly and completely. Each discharge of an alien weapon resulted in the wholesale slaughter of tens of thousands of innocent men, women, and children.

We didn't realize this, of course, for some days, but were lucky enough to save ourselves accidentally.

The great striders had almost ceased using their sting-rays, either because they had a limited supply of the energy needed to produce them, or because they wanted to preserve rather than destroy our countryside and cities. After that terrible night everyone knew that no earthly army could stand against them.

Thus, most resistance against the invaders had ceased by dawn of the next day. The military command withdrew its forces—there weren't all that many soldiers remaining—to safer locations, leaving just a few bands of sappers and guerrillas. The local governments abandoned their efforts to maintain order, and evacuated their personnel to other locales, along with anyone else who could be persuaded to go. The cities in the San Francisco Bay Area were abandoned to the enemy. The Martians lost no time in occupying San Francisco proper, establishing their major base there.

Reverend Lesley, for once, had nothing to say. I think that even she was appalled by the wholesale slaughter of human life—although I'm not certain to this day whether the Martians actually intended to wipe us out completely, or were merely trying to control the surviving members of our population for their own purposes, whatever those might be.

Perhaps the future would provide answers to these questions. Perhaps the Martians themselves would someday enlighten us.

Hell, I was just glad to be alive.

CHAPTER SEVENTEEN
EXODUS, STAGE RIGHT

Babylon is fallen, is fallen, that great city.
—Holy Bible, *Revelation 14:8*

ALEX SMITH, 28 DECEMBER, MARS YEAR I
SAN FRANCISCO, CALIFORNIA, PLANET EARTH

Although electricity in the Bay Area had failed several days before, people were still living there, but as that third morning after Christmas dawned crisp and bright, all the survivors were ordered out of the City of San Francisco and surrounding communities. It was now obvious that the Martians would soon occupy the place, and that anyone left behind would not survive very long.

Indeed, there were more people remaining than the authorities had ever imagined, tens of thousands of them, and evacuating the multitudes was no easy task. Some were loaded on ships at the Embarcadero, some sent south on trains, some put on BART or buses or trucks or bikes or skateboards or anything else that was mobile.

By mid-morning, though, the Police Department began to lose coherency as an organization, falling apart as individual officers fled with their families for safer climes. Official government was just about finished in the city.

The freeways out of town were all jammed, although some effort was being made by the Highway Patrol to clear away any vehicles blocking traffic. One of the major problems confronting the evacuation was the fact that two Martian fighting-machines were planted at Mountain View, just west of San José. These'd landed fairly early in the picture, but hadn't moved any further than the area immediately surrounding the impact sites. They'd obviously been positioned to anchor the southern hub of the alien advance.

As transportation efforts eased, the remaining refugees began fighting among themselves for room in private automobiles, vans, delivery trucks, or whatever was available, often paying exorbitant prices for the privilege. Those who couldn't pay tried taking matters in their own hands, which resulted in several violent shoot-outs with many casualties. Helicopters were used to airlift hospital patients to waiting ships off-shore.

As the day advanced and the bus, BART, and train drivers refused to return to San Francisco, the people began fleeing in an ever-thickening multitude to the south—by foot, by bicycle, even by grocery store cart. At noon a Martian strider was seen on the Marin side of the Golden Gate Bridge, which was being defended on the San Francisco end by some hasty emplacements erected at the Presidio, the long-decommissioned Army base. It was important to keep the Bridge clear as long as possible, because the ports of both San Francisco and Oakland are located within the Bay, with the only exit into the Pacific Ocean being through the Golden Gate. People were still being evacuated through the strait by ship.

There was a brief firefight at Fort Baker on the tip of the Marin Peninsula, but it ended with the usual result. This was followed by an exaltation of the Black Death, but its effect was minimal, since the intervening ocean neutralized its potency before it could reach land on the other side. The Martian striders would have to enter the city proper to seize control. Nothing happened immediately, however.

A freight train consisting of empty boxcars and flatcars had been run all the way up to the Ferry Building on the Embarcadero. Refugees piled into the gondolas any way they could, and still there were more people wanting to leave. Why they'd waited so long is a mystery to me. The train started backing its line of cars south along the waterfront, eventually plowing through the shrieking hordes that tried to block it, crushing a number of refugees, but eventually getting out of the city with some difficulty, and saving perhaps a thousand souls.

The Martians moved into the city around dinner time, spraying the area near the waterfront and the Presidio with the Black Death, killing anyone who couldn't get to high ground.

The few survivors fled into the higher parts of the city—the ziggurats of Babylon, you might say—where they waited and watched as the Martians spread out, establishing bases at strategic points. Of course, I knew nothing of this until later, but I had my own hell to experience first!

CHAPTER EIGHTEEN
ONE FOR ALL, ALL FOR ONE

One for all, all for one we gage.
—William Shakespeare

STEPHEN SMITH, 27-29 DECEMBER, MARS YEAR I
ORANGE COUNTY, CALIFORNIA, PLANET EARTH

Far to the south my brother Stephen, his friend Cassie, and her daughter Erie, had just managed to escape the Martian advance down the Moreno and Temescal Valleys to the area around Lake Elsinore. They fled up the side of the Elsinore Mountains on the Ortega Highway. This winding road, also called State Highway 74, traverses the San Mateo Canyon Wilderness Area between Los Pinos Peak and Elsinore Peak, eventually following the long canyon of the San Juan River down to San Juan Capistrano in Orange County. It's a beautiful drive through the Cleveland National Forest, although the "forest" proper just consists of scrub pines and shrubs and brush. As with all Southern California mountain regions, this area is normally parched, with very little rain or other moisture except in mid-winter.

Far below them in the valley, Steve had witnessed the first unleashing of the Black Death in the Southland. As their SUV topped the crest, however, the trio felt safe again for the first time in several days.

"I think we made it," Steve said.

But they still had thirty miles to go on this two-lane road, and the traffic moved very slowly indeed, averaging no more than five miles per hour.

Cassie again tried calling her sister, Elizabeth Fisher, in Laguna Beach, but with no luck.

"Can't get a signal," she said.

"We need to find the quickest way possible out of Southern California," Steve said. "Liz will have to fend for herself."

Then the double line of cars in front of them stopped altogether (both lanes were being used for westward travel). Horns began sounding. Finally Steve got out of the vehicle to see what was happening, but the nature of the road was such that there was no way he could determine what the conditions were up front.

"What do we do now?" Cassie asked.

"We wait," my brother said.

He turned off the motor to conserve fuel.

The Santa Ana winds were blowing about thirty miles per hour, creating very dry and warm conditions throughout Southern California. The temperatures in the valleys were running about eighty-five degrees, hot but not unusually so for December; up on the plateau it was perhaps ten degrees cooler, but since they were sitting in the open sun, it seemed warmer than that.

"Open all the windows," Steve said.

"I need to pee," Erie said.

"I'll take her," Cassie said.

She led the child off into the bushes away from the road, where she couldn't be seen.

In the distance Steve could hear the put-put-put of a motorcycle slowly driving up the shoulder of the road to the west. It stopped frequently. Everyone was getting out of their cars and standing around. It was too warm to remain inside.

"Know anything?" one man asked.

But no one did. Communications were completely cut.

Eventually the cycle showed up. It was a lone Highway Patrolman.

"What's up?" Steve asked.

"The road's blocked by an overturned truck down in the canyon," the cop said. "There's no way to clear the accident. You'll have to walk out. Lake Elsinore's quite a bit closer."

"The Martians are down there," Steve said. "What about Orange County?"

"The buggers haven't reached there yet, at least as of two hours ago, but I don't how long that'll hold. There're massive evacuation efforts by ship and train taking place along the coast, moving people south to the border. If you can get there before the Martians do, you and your family will have a fighting chance of getting out."

Then he drove on to warn the others. He was back again in an hour.

"Elsinore?" Steve asked.

The man shook his head. His face was grim.

"You don't want to go there!" was all he said.

"What's happening, Steve?" Cassie asked.

He explained the situation.

"We have to get out," he said. "If we wait until the Martians reach San Juan Capistrano and the beach areas, then we're cut off for good."

"But it's at least twenty-five miles."

"I know," he said. "Once we get past the wreck, though, maybe someone will give us a lift the rest of the way."

Then he gathered up the water and the lighter food packages. Cassie had brought several backpacks, and these he allocated to the two adults.

"We're going on a little hike," he told Erie.

"Oh, goodie!" she said.

She was at the age where everything was still an adventure.

They started down the road about mid-afternoon.

The highway was crowded with refugees. Most of the fugitives were trudging along at a slow but steady pace, hiking west into the smiling orb of the sun, sipping their bottles of water and groaning over their aching feet. They encountered occasional forested sections along the way that provided them with enough shade to allow a brief rest in a cooler environment. One of the ranchers there was handing out water and ice, the former pumped straight and cold from his well.

They stuck close to the highway. Although there were other dirt roads heading off to either side, Steve knew from previous experience that this was the only way through the Wilderness for at least fifteen miles in either direction. It was the Ortega Highway—or nothing.

That evening they stayed near a large house where the owner was fixing barbecued beans and franks on an open barbecue pit fire for anyone who wanted them.

"Got enough here to feed an army for a year," he said. "Ain't doin' me much good, that's for dang sure."

Steve thought it was one of the best meals that he'd ever had.

They were allowed to sleep in one of the ranch's barns. The hay was rough and poking, but softer than the bare ground would have been.

"God, I'm tired," Cassie said, stretching her arms in the loft. She chuckled: "Everyone seems to think I'm your wife."

"Maybe you are," he said, smiling at the thought. "I don't care what people think, Cassie. I just want to get you and Erie to safety, any way I can."

But she was already asleep, and so was the little girl.

My brother found sleep hard to find, though, even with the lassitude he could feel seeping into his bones. The trauma of the past few days was suddenly catching up with him. He wondered how many men had died yesterday and today, and how many more would follow tomorrow. He would have pondered more upon these things, except that he too fell into a deep slumber.

Sometime in the middle of the night he woke briefly to find his two companions cuddled up next to him. Maybe it was the warmth of their bodies that had stirred him. They already felt like a family. He found, surprisingly, that he didn't mind the thought. Then he slept again.

The rancher, a man named Ricardo Valdeste ("Call me

'Rich'"), offered them fried eggs the next morning, the third day after Christmas.

"Got a whole coop full of the damn things," he said. "If I don't use 'em, they just go to waste."

"Aren't you evacuating?" Steve asked.

"Hell, I've spent nigh on to forty years up here on this damned mountain," Valdeste said. "I've seen fires and I've seen rain. I've seen sunny days I never thought would end. I'm not leaving it now. If the Martians come, they come. If I die, I die. I'm seventy-five years young. Hey, I've lived a good life. Ain't goin' be around that much longer anyways."

"We won't forget your kindness," Steve said, shaking the man's hand. "If we survive, we'll be back to check on you."

"I do 'preciate it, son," Rich said. "Now you and your pretty wife and daughter better skedaddle on down this mountain. You don't want to lose 'em."

"No, sir, I don't," Steve said, and meant it too.

Valdeste had shown them a lane on a detailed forestry map that would save them several miles of walking.

"You have to go up and down a bit more," he said, pointing at the inset, "but you'll pick up a couple of hours. You take this with you. I don't need it."

Then the rancher wished them well, and the fugitives headed off into the wilderness.

The path was no more than a trail, really, but it wound its way through a wooded area that was actually quite pleasant, and certainly cooler than the hot asphalt had been. It was almost like walking in a park, save for the hilly sections. Steve carried Erie up the steepest of the slopes. They rested frequently. They saw no one.

About noon they stopped to eat some jerky and fruit and cookies, washing them down with bottled water. Erie went off briefly to do her thing—"not too far, mind," her mother cautioned—and the adults were alone for the first time since they'd met, just two days earlier.

"When this is all over," Cassie said quietly, "I'd really like to see you again, if that's OK."

"It's OK," he said, smiling.

He reached out and took her hand, and she gripped it hard. Then they both jumped to their feet at the sudden scream of Cassie's daughter.

Erie was just down the trail, her hands holding up her pants. Confronting her from twenty feet away was the tawny face of a cougar, its incisors bared. Steve didn't even think; he rushed right by the girl straight at the cat, waving his arms and shouting at the top of his voice. Scared by the unexpected confrontation with this large, noisy monster, the big mountain lion abruptly turned tail and ran away. Steve grabbed the girl and Cassie joined him, putting her arms around both of them.

"You're all right," he said, over and over again, holding the girl close.

When everyone had found their breaths, they gathered up their things, and headed down the trail.

They reached San Juan Canyon and the blacktop road before dinner time, falling in with the long line of refugees slowly trudging their way towards the coast.

"How far is the wreck?" he asked one of the men.

"About a mile on, I think."

The San Juan River, although dry part of the year, had carved a considerable channel through the rock, and the towering walls of the canyon closed in on them, providing some shade amid the strange formations on either side.

"They're almost like sculptures," Cassie said, looking up at the carved and colorful rock faces.

They reached the site of the accident an hour later. A big rig had jackknifed right across both lanes of the road, jamming into one wall of the canyon and hanging out over the river bed on the other side, draped onto the guardrails.

"They won't clear this one up easily," Steve said.

There were several police cars clustered on the west side of the wreck, and at least one open-topped truck.

"There must be over two hundred people here," Cassie said.

The cops were giving out numbers to those waiting for transportation. When Steve asked how long it would be, one of the police just shrugged.

"Maybe tonight, maybe tomorrow," he said. "We've gotten fewer and fewer trucks and buses as the day's gone on, so I don't think we'll see very many more tonight. You might want to find a place to settle down with your family."

"What about Orange County?" Steve asked.

"You mean the Martians? They aren't there yet, but I doubt they'll wait too long. We're still taking people off in ships. If you can find your way there in time, there'll be a boat for you somewhere."

My brother went back to Cassie and told her what the police had said.

"We're going to have to stop here tonight," he said. "They do have some hot food and cold water down there. It's not much, but it's better than what we have."

"I'd give anything for a shower," she said, sighing and brushing a lock of hair off her sweaty forehead. "All right, let's go."

The meal consisted of lukewarm hamburgers and limp fries and almost cold pop. It was filling, if nothing else. Then they found a place underneath one of the rock overhangs, and snuggled down together with a blanket, Steve's arm draped around Cassie on one side and Erie on the other, and managed to sleep a bit through the night. Their "bed" was uncomfortable, but at least they had each other.

The next day, the winds let up a bit, and the temperature was more bearable. There was even a hint of mist in the air.

They managed to board a yellow school bus the next morning. They sat in one row close together, their packs stuffed down around their feet. It took them an hour to wind down the rest of the canyon to the residential area on the east side of San Juan Capistrano.

The junction of Highway 74 with Interstate 5 was heavily congested, with the freeway being almost totally blocked by traffic. Still, the police kept the underpasses sufficiently clear that some travel was possible, and the bus finally deposited the three fugitives at Mission San Juan Capistrano, which was being used as a transfer site for the evacuees. There they were forced to register as refugees.

Steve gave them his full name (Stephen Jackson Smith), and then Cassie had to sign for herself (Cassandra Elizabeth Austen) and her daughter (Erin Eliza Weckesser).

"You don't use your husband's name?" the official asked.

"No, I've never gotten around to changing it," she said very sweetly, "and my daughter was by my first husband."

"What's the situation down south?" Steve asked.

"I-5 and the railroad are blocked at Oceanside," the man said. "You'll have to go out either through San Clemente or San Onofre State Beaches."

"How soon?"

"By nightfall. We have to move quickly now before the Martians show up. You're in Group 225. When you hear your number called, report to the bus out front.

"Next!" the man said, motioning them on.

They were passing out snacks, packaged peanuts, pretzels, water, and cookies at a stand in front of the Mission, so the trio sat down together there and rested for awhile.

"Steve...," Cassie said.

He just shook his head.

"Wait till we're safe," he said.

CHAPTER NINETEEN
THE *BRANDYWINE* DECANTED

Behold, now, another providence of God.
A ship comes into the harbor.
—William Bradford

Stephen Smith, 29 December, Mars Year I
Orange County, California, Planet Earth

The old Mission at San Juan Capistrano was serving as temporary headquarters for the evacuation of refugees from the Orange County and Inland areas. Steve and his two charges, Cassie Austen and her daughter Erie, arrived there in early afternoon, and were assigned numbers in the queue. A few hours later they boarded a bus and were driven to San Clemente, where the fugitives were slowly being loaded onto boats for evacuation.

Many of the refugees were hungry, tired, ill, depressed, and yearning to breathe free. The aid workers were distributing food packets and bottled water, but not much of anything else. There was no place to sit or wait: they either had to stand or plop on the ground. Despite the dire circumstances, the crowds were remarkably quiet and orderly. Even the children seemed subdued; perhaps they realized the seriousness of their plight. Steve said that he noticed several individuals who started crying for no apparent reason, and then stopped; and others who expressed anger or outrage at the ease with which the Martians had subdued mankind. Overall, though, people mostly tried to help other people.

Of the alien machines there was no sign. Steve was told that the enemy had occupied all of the inland valleys of Southern California, but thus far had only reached the coastline at Oceanside, thereby putting San Diego in jeopardy. Most of Los Angeles proper was still free, and still had electrical power and water; and Orange County remained unoccupied.

The authorities found it difficult to retain control in the big urban areas. Property rights were ignored and looting was commonplace. Men tried to defend their stores, their homes, their livelihoods with any weapons at their disposal, but it was a futile gesture against the rampaging mobs. Real knowledge of the invaders was sorely lacking. Folks had heard wild tales about the striders, sting-rays, and the Black Death, but much of it was based on false information. My brother listened to the lone, battery-operated radio that was available on the beach, which said that the city fathers of Los Angeles had gathered at Santa Monica, and were preparing to evacuate north up State Highway 1, if necessary.

The Martians were rumored to be invading Tarzana, Fontana, Beaumont, Corona, or any of a dozen other places throughout the L.A. Basin, but it was all a bunch of hooey. The military and the Mayor of Los Angeles knew where the Martians were actually located; their slow advance towards the coast was being carefully plotted on maps.

The Navy had dispatched several warships from San Diego to San Pedro, the main port facility of Los Angeles. The evacuation operation was being coordinated out of the U.S. Naval Reservation in San Diego. Ships of all kinds had been seized with the cooperation of their owners, and were ferrying boatloads of fugitives from the Los Angeles area to San Diego, Hawaii, Tijuana, and Ensenada. Some of the bigger vessels could only operate near the docks of San Pedro, but many others used small motor craft to land on the numerous beaches of Southern California, and ferry the refugees out to the waiting ships offshore. Some of these vessels had made ten or a dozen trips to and from San Diego in the preceding two days.

Steve saw dozens, even hundreds of small ships lying off the state beaches at Doheny, San Onofre, and San Clemente. These were arranged in a sickle-shaped mass near an off-shore fogbank. Closer in he could see a multitude of small fishing boats, yachts, motorboats, and even sailboats; and further out were anchored the larger commercial vessels. Nearer the beach was a dense swarm of rowboats and smaller motor craft ferrying people to and from the larger ships anchored in deep water.

A couple of miles from shore he also spotted a large warship. He noted down the particulars, and was later able to identify it as the Ticonderoga Class Guided Missile Cruiser, the *U.S.S. Brandywine*, its identification number (82) clearly visible across its gray steel prow. It was the only such vessel in sight, but far away to both the left and the right over the smooth sea—and that day there was a dead calm, fortunately—he could spy a trail of dark smoke that marked several other ships in the Pacific Fleet, ready to give their all to protect the vital lifeline they had established.

About mid-afternoon my brother and his two companions heard their numbers called. They boarded a motorboat (Erie got her feet wet!) and plowed through the surf without difficulty. For years afterwards, folks remarked on the calmness of the waves during that fateful day. They headed towards a large pleasure yacht anchored a few hundred yards offshore. As they approached the vessel from its rear, they could see its name proudly displayed on its stern—*The Unsinkable Mollie K.*

"A good omen," Cassie said.

They were welcomed on board the beautifully maintained craft, the ship's hands helping them up the ladder.

There were already fifteen or twenty fugitives lining the rails, but the captain continued to hold his position close to the coast for over an hour, picking up as many passengers as he dared, until the decks were almost dangerously overcrowded. He probably would have remained even longer if it hadn't been for the sound of guns erupting immediately to the south. The

Martians had apparently reached the Camp Pendleton Marine Corps Base just beyond San Clemente, where our boys were putting up a fierce resistance.

The large cruiser offshore abruptly hoisted anchor. A jet of dark smoke shot from its funnel as it moved forward to provide cover for the evacuees. Any ships that were full promptly set sail for the open sea, but many of the other captains courageously ordered their vessels to move *towards* the coastline, giving the remaining refugees their last best chance of escaping the coming battle.

The noise rapidly grew louder. My brother could now hear the *zzzttt-zzzttt* of the Martian sting-rays in addition to the roar of our artillery and tank guns, together with the popping of the gas canisters as they were flung by the aliens at our men at Camp Pendleton. To the north, three other naval warships rose one after the other out of the sea, outlined beneath their clouds of black smoke, as they drove forward to assist the effort.

The yacht suddenly pulled anchor and began moving west towards the distant fog bank. The California coast was growing a little hazy when a Martian suddenly appeared, small and faint on the southern horizon, advancing north by northwest along the surf-line from the direction of San Diego. The captain started swearing at the top of his lungs at the slowness of his ship's passage, but there were so many vessels hugging the coast at this point that it was impossible to proceed quickly without risking a disastrous collision. Every eye on board was riveted by that distant metal shape standing higher than the trees, as it strode confidently up the beach with its leisurely parody of a human gait.

This was the second Martian machine that my brother had ever seen, after the distant strider that he'd spied near Lake Elsinore. He stood there transfixed at the sight, watching this huge erector set as it suddenly began to wade into the sea. Far to the south, skirting some stunted trees, came another strider, and then another, plowing through a shiny mudflat that seemed to hang halfway between sea and sky. They were all stalking north from Oceanside, apparently having defeated the Marines at Camp Pendleton. *The Unsinkable Mollie K.* receded with terrifying slowness from this ominous advance.

Glancing around, my brother saw each of the refugee ships sailing away from the approaching Martian machine, one vessel passing behind another, another coming around broadside, bellowing and honking at each other, individual motorboats rushing hither and thither and yon. One was too slow, and was swatted into kindling by the swing of a Martian tentacle. Another pair collided in their haste, dumping their passengers into the ocean.

Then the swift yaw of the yacht flung Steve headlong onto the railing and backwards onto the deck, almost casting him overboard.

"Steve!" Cassie said, rushing with Erie to his aid. They held onto each other and the rail as tight as they could.

Cheers echoed across the water. The yacht lurched and rolled once and then twice and then once again.

Passing to starboard not a hundred yards away was a vast steel hulk. The blade of its prow tore through the water, tossing huge waves of foam to either side. The yacht was sucked down to the point where the starboard deck almost touched the waterline.

The salt spray blinded Steve for a moment. When his eyes cleared again, he saw that the warship had a large, humped, gray superstructure over its center of gravity to house the vessel's guided missile system. The *Brandywine* was sailing to the rescue!

The oncoming Martian machines were now standing far out from shore, their bodies almost completely submerged, with just their carapaces showing. Seen from this perspective, they appeared far less formidable than the warship steaming towards them. Strangely, the aliens seemed to regard this new antagonist with some puzzlement. This was typical of their general reaction.

When confronted with something that they'd never encountered before, they became cautious almost to the point of paranoia. It was astonishing, really. They wouldn't do anything to respond to a threat until they'd actually seen a particular weapon in action. If you could have found something that would have blown them away the first time it was used, they wouldn't have stood a chance. Unfortunately, that never happened.

They may also have thought that this was another component of their own invasion fleet. The *Brandywine* held off firing immediately, even though it was armed with a wide array of guided missiles. I think this was a deliberate tactic on the part of the captain, who'd been told that more distant attacks on the Martian fighting-machines had always failed; or it may simply have been to protect the vulnerable fleet of rescue vessels interposed between the forces. In any event, the warship drove at top speed directly towards the three tripods standing out from shore.

The ship was moving at such a pace that in a minute it had traversed half the space between the yacht and the striders. Suddenly the foremost Martian machine discharged a canister of the Black Death at the oncoming cruiser, but it glanced off its side, generating an inky, oily jet that rolled seaward; its poison was immediately neutralized by interaction with the seawater.

Astoundingly, the Martians retreated! Their gaunt figures rose out of the water as they moved towards the shore. One of them suddenly raised a tentacle and shot a sting-ray at the cruiser. It must have driven through the steel hull of the ship like a white-hot iron rod thrust through paper, but it failed to incapacitate the vessel.

In response the *Brandywine* fired a Tomahawk missile, and the Martian reeled backwards from its impact. In another moment it had toppled over completely into the sea, exploding into a great mass of water and green-tinted steam. The warship then launched several additional missiles, one splashing into the water close by a freighter, one ricocheting towards several other civilian vessels before finally sinking a transport, and the others missing the enemy altogether.

The warship continued to head straight for the second Martian strider, and was within a hundred yards of the alien machine when the latter's sting-ray came to bear. With a blinding flash the ship's foredeck, missile dome, and smoke-stack leaped upward in a paroxysm of fire; but the ship was so close to the alien weapon that its flaming wreckage crashed right into the great fighting-machine, crumpling it like a piece of cardboard. Steve and Cassie and Erie were shouting at the top of their lungs, along with all of the other passengers.

"Two!" yelled the captain, holding up a pair of fingers.

Everyone was cheering our victory.

The smoke obscured the scene for many minutes. All this time the yacht had continued heading out to sea, further away from the fight; and when the smoke finally cleared, nothing of the *Brandywine* could be seen. The third Martian machine had also vanished, presumably retreating back to shore. The warships steaming down from the north were now quite close to the action.

The yacht continued on its journey seaward, and the cruisers and destroyers receded slowly towards the coast, which was now hidden by a marbled bank of vapor, smoke, and black gas, eddying and combining in the strangest ways. The fleet of refugee ships scattered to the southwest. Then the warships continued south, abruptly passing into the thickening haze of evening. The coastline grew faint, until at last it was indistinguishable amid the low banks of clouds that were gathering over the sinking sun.

Steve held Cassie and Erie close to him.

"Look, Uncle Steve," the little girl said, pointing up at the sky.

Something leaped out of the gray dusk, rushing very swiftly into the luminous space above the western horizon, something flat and broad and very large, something that swept around in a vast curve, grew smaller, sank slowly, and then vanished again into the mystery of the night. And as it pirouetted above them it rained down darkness upon the land, and all was shrouded in mystery and death and the final end of mankind's short-lived civilization.

It wasn't until much later that we identified the thing as the first example of the Martian flying-machines.

But *The Unsinkable Mollie K.* steamed on towards the western horizon, ferrying its precious cargo of humanity to safety.

My brother survived the war, thank God—and so did his wife Cassie and his daughter Erie.

PART TWO
THE EARTH IN THRALL

Were Earth itself in ruin laid
The wreck would find him undismayed.

—Horace

Men will lie on their backs,
Talking about the fall of man,
And never make an effort to get up.

—Henry David Thoreau

CHAPTER TWENTY
UNDER FOOT, UNDER WOOD

Better make a weak man your enemy than your friend.
—Josh Billings

ALEX SMITH, 28 DECEMBER, MARS YEAR I
MARIN COUNTY, CALIFORNIA, PLANET EARTH

Had the Martians just wanted to destroy our cities, they could easily have done so on the evening of the Twenty-Eighth, when they began their move into the San Francisco Peninsula and the outlying areas of the Los Angeles Metropolitan Region. Refugees by the hundreds of thousands flooded the roads up and down the California coast and in the inland valleys. Some traveled by car, some by bicycles or motorcycles, and some on foot, but all fled the advance of the alien machines. Where the freeways became clogged, motorists just abandoned their vehicles and walked away. The worst traffic jams ever recorded in California history, maybe in the history of the United States or of the world, had suddenly become a stark reality.

It was the beginning of the end of all we held dear.

It was the beginning of the rout of our civilization.

It was the eclipse of man's rule on Earth.

Beyond the brown hills that rise north and east of San Francisco, the glittering Martians went to and fro, calmly and methodically spreading their poisonous gas over each patch of countryside and town, spraying it again whenever it served their purpose, and taking possession of the conquered land. I don't think they wanted to exterminate us as much as demoralize any organized resistance—or so I would judge from later events. They systematically destroyed our weapons, cut every phone line and power relay and cell or transmission tower, and wrecked some of the major freeway intersections. They were purposely and deliberately and methodically hamstringing mankind. They seemed in no particular hurry to extend their field of operations, and didn't even reach beyond the central core of San Francisco until the next morning. Many individuals had remained in their homes during the Martians' initial incursion the previous night, and no doubt many perished there, suffocated by the Black Death.

San Francisco Bay remained a jumble of interlocked shipping. Some captains were tempted by the enormous sums offered them by wealthy fugitives; less prosperous refugees who found their way to these vessels were often tossed overboard and drowned, unless they could pay the going price. About six on the evening of the Twenty-Eighth the aliens unleashed a cloud of black fog between and around the arches of the San Francisco-Oakland Bay Bridge, but it quickly dissipated itself in the salt water.

The Bay itself became a jigsaw puzzle of confusion and chaos, with collisions between vessels almost epidemic—and for awhile the single exit point beneath the Golden Gate Bridge was so jammed with boats and barges that they threatened to block the passage completely. Fortunately, enough level heads prevailed that the wrecks were cleared away and the passage reopened. No one was allowed to board the ships from either the Presidio or the Bridge itself.

Early on, the Martians ignored the refugees, but that night they decided to seal the strait for good, thereby removing a major evacuation route. About seven, a strider appeared on Angel Island and started wading out towards Alcatraz Island, crushing the boats as it went, until nothing but wreckage remained. I don't know why Alcatraz was deemed important, except that a strider poised there had an unencumbered view of the Golden

Gate and the piers on the waterfront all the way down to the Embarcadero. A number of these structures were destroyed over the next day, although the Bridge itself remained largely intact, a testimony to its sound construction. The traffic lanes on the Bridge were blocked with wrecks and abandoned vehicles, so much so that the Martians apparently didn't consider it a threat—fortunately for me.

At dawn on the third day after Christmas I realized that the wall we'd been climbing during the night actually fronted on an old house, one of a long line of such structures at the upper reaches of the town of Mill Valley. We decided to take refuge there until the Black Death had passed.

I broke a window to enter a house over Reverend Lesley's objections—"We will be judged by the Living God for all our sins," she said—and found it well provisioned. We stayed there all that night—that *Dies Iræ* ("day of wrath") of panic and pandemonium—safe in a little island of daylight cut off by the Black Death from the rest of the world, while the Martians began their occupation of San Francisco. We could do nothing but wait and hope.

My mind kept returning to Becky. I figured she was safe in Sonoma, was possibly even mourning me as dead or injured. But what if she *wasn't*? What if the Martians had suddenly moved north from Novato? This seemed unlikely to me, but the enemy had proved so unpredictable thus far that anything was possible—and I now had enough time on my hands to consider the very worst.

My musings became almost an obsession. I could think of nothing else for hours but what might be happening to her, turning over each new twist and turn until I was crazy with worry. My only consolation was the belief that the Martians were now moving *en masse* towards San Francisco—and thus away from Becky. I would not have been comforted knowing the reality of the situation.

However, I soon grew very tired of my ministerial companion's constant complaints, of her continuing despair, and so I kept my distance, staying in a children's bedroom filled with toys, dolls, and computers. I even tried connecting to the Internet, but everything was still down. None of the accouterments of modern civilization would do anything more than beep at me, and I was already getting plenty of that from Lesley. My cell phone was also dead. I felt completely cut off from the rest of the world.

When the minister barged in again to complain about the food, I told her where she could shove it. Such unexpectedly uncouth language seemed to take her aback. She walked away, leaving me in blessèd silence.

We were temporarily hemmed in by the Black Death. I saw signs of life in the adjoining structure late that night—a face showing at a window and some lights that flickered (perhaps candles); and later I heard the slam of a door. I don't know who they were or what became of them, just that they were gone by morning, when we investigated the place. The Black Death drifted slowly down towards the sea, creeping away from us on little rats' feet. I could easily measure its withdrawal from the attic window when the light returned on the Twenty-Ninth.

A Martian machine strode across the adjoining field about nine that morning, neutralizing the remaining gas with a stream of some chemical that hissed against the walls of our house, smashing all the glass that it touched, and singeing Lesley's hand as she fled from the living room. It had the peculiar odor of chlorine or bromine or something like that ("borine," I thought, chuckling at my own witticism, which would have been lost on the minister).

Late that morning I slowly crept downstairs across the sodden carpet to peer outside. The country to the southeast was completely dark, as though a black snowstorm had passed over it. Looking down the valley towards the Bay, I was astonished to see a kind of reddish tinge intermingling with the soot on the scorched slopes of the brown-green hills above Mill Valley.

Then I realized we were free again. I decided to depart at once, but Lesley wouldn't hear of it.

"We're safe here," she kept repeating, "safe, safe, *safe!*"

Good riddance, I thought to myself, and decided to leave without her. I found some food and bottled water, even a first-aid kit in a bathroom cabinet, and a couple of clean shirts in one of the bedrooms. The weather was getting funky again, as it had a tendency to do at this time of the year, with mists and rains and rather cool nights.

When the minister realized that I was leaving her alone, she suddenly roused herself and demanded that we travel together. Shitty shit, shit! I didn't have the gumption to refuse her. I actually felt sorry for the woman. I think it was leftover guilt from leaving my wife alone. Well, in retrospect I shouldn't have tried!

Everything appeared quiet outside, so we started walking southeast around noon on the blackened road towards Almonte.

Dead bodies lay strewn by the way, contorted and twisted in their pain and wretchedness, dogs and cats and birds as well as men, plus the usual assortment of wrecked automobiles and trucks, all layered with a leavening of the inert black dust. That pall of powder, that thick coat of cinders, made me think of the destruction of the ancient cities of Pompeii and Herculaneum, and how they'd been immersed by a volcanic eruption that had left them buried for thousands of years.

We reached the village of Almonte without further difficulty. We were constantly besieged by the strange, even bizarre landscape around us, now almost surreal in its appearance; and we were relieved to find that one large patch of green on the side of a hill had somehow escaped the suffocating drift of the dust. It was covered with a peculiar kind of bush with long, narrow leaves. Lesley made the Sign of the Cross at it and mumbled something about "need" or "Swede" that I couldn't quite make out.

I also noticed a reddish tinge to the soil, and when I bent down to examine this phenomenon more closely, I saw that the ground was covered with the minute ruby sprouts of a myriad of new plants.

"Look at this!" I said, but Lesley would have nothing to do

with my philosophical observations, having no curiosity about such things whatsoever.

A mile or so to the east we came back to the 101 Freeway, and there we saw some men and women hurrying off in the distance towards the town of Tamalpais Valley. I didn't even try to hail them, although these were the first living folks we'd encountered in the outside world in several days.

By this time we were both hungry and thirsty, so I raided a 7-11 Store near the highway. Lesley insisted on leaving a twenty-dollar bill on the counter, which I thought unnecessary. Nothing was cold, of course, but the packaged goods were still sound, and the pop and bottled water didn't age. I supplemented my pack with as much as I could reasonably carry.

We decided then and there to follow the freeway south to San Francisco, starting the next day. It was only about five miles or so to the Golden Gate Bridge.

In the meantime, we needed to start looking for another safe house for the night. There were plenty of prospects in the immediate vicinity. First of all, though, I wanted to reconnoiter the local area, to see if any of the Martians yet lingered.

On the other side of the inlet the theological seminary was burning, much to Lesley's consternation.

"God wouldn't have allowed such a thing," she said. "He just wouldn't."

"Maybe they were heretics," I said.

She admitted that they belonged to some other denomination, but the idea still seemed to disturb her.

"A great many have died," I said, "and thousands of buildings have been destroyed. What difference does one more make?"

She looked at me with utter contempt.

"You're a tool of the Devil," she said. "No one who believed in God would ever say such things. That's a sacred place."

"I'm a tool of no one, and I paint what I see. Look around you, Reverend. What do *you* see?"

Lesley uttered a cry halfway between a croak and a lament.

Down by the water's edge, a grove of trees was still smoldering.

"I do regret the loss of the trees, though," I said.

Then I continued down the road to Tamalpais Valley.

This town had been unaffected either by the sting-ray or the Black Death, and I saw a few people still wandering around, though no one had much news. Like us, they were taking advantage of the lull to shift their quarters to someplace safer. I think that many of the houses here were still occupied by their original inhabitants, too scared even for flight. And who knows, maybe staying put was as good an option as anything else. I know from stories published after the war that some people survived the entire invasion without ever having left their homes.

We could see evidence of the hurried evacuation all along the road. I remember particularly the three smashed motorcycles lying together in a surrealistic heap, pounded into the road by the wheels of the cars and trucks that had subsequently passed over them. We crossed the Overwood Creek Bridge about mid-afternoon; I noticed some reddish clumps of vegetation floating down the stream, some of them bigger than basketballs. I had no idea what they were, and there really wasn't time for close scrutiny. I did wonder, though, if they were connected to the shoots that I'd seen earlier that day up the hill.

At Popcastle we again encountered a shroud of black dust that was the remnant of the neutralized poison gas, and heaps of dead bodies everywhere; but spied nothing of the Martians until we were almost at Marin City.

In the distance I could see three individuals running down a side street towards the Bay, but otherwise the place seemed deserted. Up in the hills the remnants of Fort Baker were still smoldering, but we saw no further signs of the Black Death.

As we approached Marin City, a group of people suddenly ran straight at us, and the upper section of a great Martian fighting-machine loomed over the nearby houses not more than a hundred yards away. I was scared half to death. Had the strider just glanced down at us then, I would have died for sure—but once again I was spared, for what reason I have no idea. We didn't dare go on. We hid for a few moments in a back-yard storage shed. There the minister curled herself into a ball, weeping silently and refusing to stir.

I was determined to reach Sausalito, though, and so an hour or two later I set out again by myself. I crept around some shrubs and stepped into a passageway beside a big house, emerging into the open on the road towards the Bay. The minister—I just couldn't shake the bloody woman no matter what I did—suddenly came scurrying after me. I tried to outrun her.

That was the stupidest damned thing that I ever did in my life. I should have known that the aliens were still there. Lesley had just caught up with me when we saw the fighting-machine we'd seen before, striding over a field not far from Tamalpais Valley. Four or five little black figures scurried before it like mice, and it soon became evident that the machine was actually herding them. In three strides it was among the fugitives, but instead of using its sting-ray to blast them out of existence, it systematically picked them up one by one, tossing them into the great metal carrier on its back, like some vineyard worker harvesting clusters of grapes.

It was then, for the very first time, that I realized that the Martians might have some purpose in mind for us other than death. The two of us just stood there in the open, utterly appalled at the sight, and then turned and fled through the gate behind us into a walled garden, falling into, rather than deliberately finding, a ditch. We lay there, scarcely daring to whisper to each other, until the sun went down.

Lesley just whimpered constantly, like a puppy crying for its dam.

There were worse things than being alone.

CHAPTER TWENTY-ONE
BLOW THE MAN DOWN!

Oh, blow the man down, bullies, blow the man down!
To me way-aye, blow the man down.
Oh, blow the man down, bullies, blow him right down!
Give me some time to blow the man down!
                    —Anonymous shanty

ALEX SMITH, 29 DECEMBER, MARS YEAR I
MARIN COUNTY, CALIFORNIA, PLANET EARTH

I suppose it was around four before we found enough courage to start again, sneaking out among the bushes and over the lawn, watching the near-darkness for any sign of the enemy. We saw evidence of the aliens all around us. In one place we blundered upon a scorched and blackened area, now ashen, littered with a number of dead bodies. They'd been horribly burned about their heads and trunks, but their legs and shoes remained mostly intact.

Leland Heights had escaped destruction, but the place seemed silent and deserted. At first we saw no one there, living or dead, although it was really too dark for us to probe the side streets. Then my companion suddenly began complaining out loud of her hunger and thirst (for one so slim, she protested overmuch, I think). I suggested that we break into one of the houses. This time Lesley failed to protest our "transgression of God's immutable laws."

The first place we tried was a small cottage. I found nothing there but moldy cheese and bread, but plenty of good water to drink; someone had already stripped the place of canned goods. I located a small hand ax out in the tool shed in the back yard.

But the noise we'd generated had attracted the attention of a third party.

As we started to cross the road again, we were suddenly confronted by the indistinct shadows of eight or ten men.

"Freeze!" came the command—and we did!

Lesley started to protest, and was told to shut up. She did.

They took us to a large house several streets away, and led us into a lighted room inside. The doors and windows had all been carefully shrouded to prevent any of the candles from being detected by the aliens.

For the first time we could see who'd captured us—and they could do the same. Most of the men (and one woman) wore soiled uniforms of one sort or another, and all carried weapons.

"Identify yourselves!" their leader said.

I gave them an abbreviated version of our story.

"I'm Captain Stromwick," the commander said. "We're the Army in this area."

"Which unit?" I asked.

"Various units," the officer said. "We're all survivors of engagements with the enemy. We're the leftovers, you might say. And you've just been drafted, folks."

"I don't have any military training," I said. "I'm a college professor."

"And I'm a minister," Lesley said.

"You're now both Privates in the United States Army," Stromwick said. "For the duration, you might say. You'll report to Sergeant Mayer."

It was the Guardsman whom I'd first encountered near Novato! Somehow he'd survived.

"Smith," he said, "is it really you!" He emerged from the shadow of a doorway.

We embraced briefly. It'd had only been a few days, but it

seemed like a lifetime.

"How'd you escape?" we both asked simultaneously.

"I just ducked and ran," Mayer finally said. "I ran and ran until I could run no more, and then I hid in a shed until they went away."

I told him a bit more of my story, and how I'd encountered Lesley.

"A woman, huh?" he said.

"Sort of," was the only response I could make.

"I'm the representative on Earth of God's holy word," the minister said.

"Sure you are," I said, "and I'm the Ayatollah Khomeini."

"Blasphemer!"

"Enough!" the officer said. "You're all members of Uncle Sam's Club now. And we're still fighting this war."

"How!?" I just couldn't help my remark. "How, sir? I've seen the enemy machines. They've smashed any opposition they've encountered. They're harvesting our people now, for what purpose I haven't the faintest idea. They don't make the same mistake twice, Captain. What do you think *you* can do that men in tanks *couldn't* do?"

"Quit feeling sorry for myself, for one thing," he said. Then he motioned with his hands. "Come on, gather 'round, all of you.

"Look, men, these machines are operated by living creatures. I've seen them close up. I headed a team that examined a downed strider. The way it fell, its carapace had cracked open on impact, apparently after hitting a concrete wall. The cab was filled with a foul-smelling fluid. The creature inside looked like a cross between an octopus and a slug. It was breathing—barely—when we found it, but died shortly thereafter. God, what a stench!

"We've been using the wrong tactics. The control modules in the machines are faced with a kind of glass—stronger than any earthly equivalent that I've seen—but breakable nonetheless. An RPG, or even an ordinary grenade, is powerful enough to penetrate the stuff. I know this because I tried several tests with the remnants we had. The problem is getting the explosives to the right place at the right time. We never had a chance to use our knowledge before the final attack up north wiped out our command-and-control center.

"However, I see several possibilities. If we could topple one of the striders, we could use our grenades to penetrate the cab. Or we could find a location where we'd have a clear shot at the thing with our RPGs, giving us some real chance of hitting the thing's porthole."

"But the machines usually travel in groups of three," I said. "How do you separate one from the others? Without that separation, sir, it wouldn't matter if we brought down a strider—the others would quickly rally to the aid of its comrade."

"We'll have to use a decoy," he said, nodding his head. "One of us will have to create a diversion."

We all looked at each other. Everyone there knew exactly what *that* meant.

Just then one of the other companies of this makeshift command returned.

"Report!" Stromwick ordered.

"They've cleared out for now, sir, at least on the north side of town," the noncom said. "We left a sentry there as ordered."

"Very well," the captain said. "Fix yourself a cold meal, and be quick and quiet about it. Then get some sleep." He looked at our not-so-eager faces. "Mayer!"

"Yes, sir."

"Take two men and relieve the guards outside. When the south patrol returns, I want to see Sergeant Raymar right away."

"Yes, sir." He left immediately.

"The rest of you are dismissed, except for Smith."

Then the officer turned to me: "How well do you know this area?"

"I've driven the freeway many times, and I've taken a few jaunts through the countryside over the years. But, to answer your question: not very well, actually."

"You've had no military service?"

"None at all, sir."

"Good," the officer said. "Then you'll create our diversion for us."

"Me?" I was aghast. "But...."

"You're not much good for anything else. Neither is Lesley. And I don't have time to train you. So you're going to have to help us in other ways. I can set the trap. Somebody has to bait it if we're going to pull this off. Like I said, Smith, a diversion."

"But I could get killed!"

"Yes, you could. So could we all. So what? We're all expendable."

I could see that I wasn't going to get along very well with Captain Stromwick, but I held my tongue. Arguing with him wouldn't help my situation if I wanted to survive.

"Get some rest," the officer finally said. "We need to reconnoiter in the morning."

Lesley was in the kitchen of the house, complaining again about the cold and the bad food. Gad, I was tired of her unrelenting whining.

"Shut up!" I said, pawing through the cache of canned goods.

I found a container of chicken noodle soup that tasted good even unheated. I washed it down with some tepid diet cola—like drinking battery acid. Then I grabbed a sleeping bag in one of the other rooms, and curled up in a corner.

I was shaken awake shortly after dawn. I went outside to take a crap and then ate again. The endless cycle, endlessly repeated—eat and shit, shit and eat. Seemed kind of futile when you thought about it much.

About an hour later the Captain ordered a dozen of us to form up, and slowly led the way under a hazy sun. It was looking to rain, I thought, noting the dark clouds forming to the west.

"Pay attention, Smith!" Stromwick hissed.

We kept our eyes open after that for any of the Martian machines, but saw nothing. They appeared to have left the area completely.

"What if they're gone?" I asked.

"They'll be back," the Captain said. He pointed to the freeway, less than a mile distant. "They follow the main roads, just like we do."

By this time we'd crept right to the edge of the village, and were facing a series of rolling hills and a few open fields, intermingled with houses and businesses.

"Be careful, men," Stromwick said.

He led the way again through a weed patch that was sprouting new growth from the recent winter mist. Some of it, I noted, sported a distinctly reddish hue—I didn't recognize the plants that were growing. They seemed, well, odd somehow, like they didn't belong here. I wondered if they were inadvertent imports from the marine traffic that frequented the Bay.

But I had no time to think about such things, when the officer suddenly hissed, "Cover!"

We all hit the dirt right away—even Lesley. Now I could hear it—the thump, thump, thump of a Martian strider coming towards us from a great distance to the north. Soon there was another, and then another, all following in order, one down the middle of the freeway, crushing the cars that littered the road, and the other two flanking it about a quarter mile to either side. Suddenly I was very much afraid that we'd be spotted in our weedy environment, and I wanted to run—oh, so very fast— as far away as possible. Ironically, though, I was too scared to move.

Thump, thump, thump.

The ground itself was shaking with the weight of the things. I was surprised, really, that they seemed to maintain such a stable attitude with all that mass perched on high.

Thump, thump, thump!

Closer and closer they came. They had reached almost to our position when I dared a slight glance upwards. I could see what Captain Stromwick meant: each strider was topped with a swivel-head similar to that of a praying mantis. There was a clear panel evident right in the front of the cab, where the controller could see what was happening in front of it. It would have to turn its entire head, however, to get a feeling for the surrounding environment. This seemed to me a basic design flaw, but perhaps it was intended to keep the vulnerable part of the machine as small as possible. Surely there must have been other sensors available within the compartment, perhaps the Martian equivalent to our radar.

But they didn't spot us, and they continued on their trek to the Babylon by the Bay to the south, leaving us in temporary peace.

I saw then how it could be done! Diversion, hell!

* * * * * * *

I sketched the thing on the back side of a mortgage bill.

"Look, sir," I said, showing the Captain, "there's a bridge about a mile up the freeway that crosses a four-lane road plus a railroad track."

"Yeah, I 'member that," Mayer said.

"The aliens think in just one dimension."

"What do you mean?" Stromwick asked.

"Well, if something works for them, however poorly, they don't try anything else unless they're forced to. Look at their response to the clashes we've had with them. We destroy one of their machines, and they alter their plans accordingly. The same thing never works as well a second time: they adjust their tactics, and they seem to communicate with all of their forces simultaneously.

"But…if we can somehow keep moving faster than they can, we might be able to destroy some of their assets before they can react.

"Now, they're using the freeway much like we did: as a main transportation route to and from their initial pit sites down to San Francisco, where they must be building their central base. With their mass and height, the machines have flattened much of the roadway back down to its original surface, creating a relatively unencumbered passageway.

"This bridge I mentioned is the longest freestanding span on Highway 101 for about five miles. If we could somehow collapse the damned thing while one of the striders is crossing it, its two companions would immediate come to its aid, and be vulnerable to attack while bending down to help their stricken friend. We might get three for one."

I held up the sheet for everyone to see my drawing.

"That might work," the officer said, nodding his head. "How much ordnance have we got?" he asked Mayer.

"Some plastic explosives, sir," the noncom said, "some shells left over from that last artillery piece that was destroyed, a couple of tank shells and rockets, and quite a few grenades and RPGs."

"We'll save the latter for the follow-up attack," Stromwick said. "Can we blow the bridge?"

"Maybe, sir. I'll have to see what I can put together."

"Report back to me after you've taken an inventory. Meanwhile, the rest of you get some R&R. Maltz, you take your men out on the first patrol."

"Yes, sir."

"And Smith!"

"Yes, sir."

"Good thinking."

"Thank you, sir."

* * * * * * *

Later that afternoon we headed to the rendezvous point out near 101, each of us organized in groups of five or six. Even the explosives were distributed in different packs. We reached the bridge well before dark, and Maltz and Glasgow, our most experienced demolition men, began putting together the bombs. I don't pretend to know what they did. They kept us civvies pretty well back from the action. I think they were afraid that people like Lesley and I might accidentally trip something—or screw it up, more to the point.

Finally, everything was ready as the sun was starting to set. We found cover on either side of the overpass amid the wreckage. And still we saw no aliens. Had we missed the main event? Were the machines already gathered together in the Baghdad by the Bay?

We had to have light to conduct the attack, so Stromwick pulled us out before darkness descended. We spent the night huddled in a nearby business office. Outside a light rain began to fall, drip, drip, dripping on the asphalt parking lot. At least we were dry and relatively warm inside.

We heard two sets of fighting-machines rumble down the freeway in the middle of the night, but we could do nothing to stop them. We got what sleep we could, and just waited for dawn.

The next morning—it was the last day of the year, I think (I was starting to lose track of time)—we were roused before first light, and given our rations by the noncoms during roll call.

"Bethancourt!" Mayer hissed, but Bethancourt didn't respond. He must have snuck away during the night.

"Shit!" somebody said.

I wasn't sure if he was the smart one or not. There were still too many hazards present to be wandering around by yourself out in the dark.

Then we formed up into four different companies, each man with his own duties. I was given a pistol and some ammo, which is all I knew how to use.

They placed me and Lesley in a bunker off to one side of the overpass. The minister was rattling off prayers under her breath, and was quite literally shaking with fear.

Then we waited again, for at least two hours. I was almost to the point where I had to pee when I heard the familiar distant thumping of the Martian feet.

No one had to tell us to get ready. We all knew what we had to do.

Maltz blew the bridge when the central alien strider was

halfway across. Everything worked to perfection. The machine fell fifty feet into the hole, its legs being severely mangled by the explosion and chunks of flying concrete. What we hadn't anticipated was the collateral effect of the blast on its two companions, which were blown right over on their sides. Before they could recover, we'd lobbed several grenades at their cabs and blasted their coverings, killing the drivers inside almost instantaneously.

We were standing around the destroyed fighters, screaming our bloody heads off in insane triumph and even shooting our guns into the sky, when we heard the wailing sound off in the distance.

"Ooh-lah!" it shrieked, much like a bunch of cats howling in the middle of the night, only worse, far worse.

"Take cover!" the Captain said, and we ran like hell, all of us, our military discipline sloughing away with each step.

I had no idea that the damned alien machines could move so fast. I'd never actually seen them "run." But suddenly they were upon us, blazing away—and our attempts to fight back were crushed so easily that we might as well have been ants defending our pitiful little sand hills. Stromwick was killed at the onset, although he did manage to fire one RPG round at a strider. He damaged a tripod's leg before being crushed beneath its splayed pad. The rest of the squad was either killed or harvested.

I was blown into a ditch, which ironically saved my life. Lesley found a hole somewhere else, which saved hers.

I thought then that we were the only two survivors of the attack, although I realized later that, as in so many other things, I really didn't have the whole story.

* * * * * * *

I guess I must have lain there for perhaps two hours. I waited until my hearing started to return and the machines finally abandoned the site, having salvaged what they could of their wrecked comrades (I don't think they got very much).

I was so banged up that I could hardly walk, but I dragged myself the mile and a half back to our HQ, since I knew I could find rations there. I choked down what I could from one of the cans (to this day, I have no idea what I ate then), and then slept the rest of the day and through much of the night.

Towards dawn, a noise startled me awake. I grabbed my pistol and snuck to the back of the house, where someone or some*thing* was trying to get in. I almost shot Reverend Lesley when she pulled the door open, but there was just enough light to discern her features.

"Lesley!" I said. "You survived!"

I was almost happy to see her, as despicable as she was.

"Smith!" she said, and flung her arms around me in a misguided exhibition of passion that she instantly regretted. "Uh, s-s-sorry!" she hissed, drawing herself back again.

"Did you see anybody else?" I asked.

"No one," she said. "I think they're all dead."

"We should really find out for sure."

"I don't want to go back there again."

But I pressed the issue, so sometime around noon we carefully and very slowly made our way back to the site of the engagement with the aliens. I counted at least fifteen bodies or body parts. Many of them had been dismembered.

"Where are the rest?"

"They may have been harvested if they were still alive," I said. "Or perhaps they're buried under the rubble, or scattered—or maybe a few of them escaped, just like us."

"They were *not* good people," the minister said.

"They were braver than either of us," I said, and she dropped her eyes to the ground. She didn't say much after that.

We went back to the house.

"What are we going to do?" she asked.

"I want to see what's happening in San Francisco."

"Why?"

"That's where the Martians have been gathering."

"But...."

"It's also where the resistance will be, if there's anything left of it," I said.

"Oh," and after that she gave up. She didn't want to be left alone.

We left the next day, carrying what we could, heading towards Sausalito. We had to proceed very slowly, both because occasional groups of striders would come marching through at irregular intervals, and because I was so stiff from being banged around that I had a hard time sustaining any long march.

We stopped overnight in a junkyard, where we found refuge in the main office.

We were sound asleep when they attacked—a band of at least ten humans armed with small weapons. They took our food and arms and spare clothes—anything that might be useful.

"You're even worse than the Martians," I said.

"God will punish you!" Lesley said.

"We've got kids," one of them said. "What would *you* do?"

"Obey God's laws," the minister said.

"Yeah, right!"

So we had to find a new place of refuge, and a new store of supplies.

Not far from Sausalito we located a large white house within an arbor, not at all obvious from the road, and in the kitchen found some loaves of bread that were still passable if one trimmed the mold off the edges, some soup, and a canned ham. The fridge also housed several six-packs of warm beer and iced tea, a spoiled casserole of baked beans (God, what a stench!), and some brown lettuce in the produce tray. We weren't sure how much of this was still edible, but we were a lot less fussy about such things by then.

The cupboard also contained some cheap bottles of wine, a couple dozen cans of fruit and salmon and such, unopened jars of peanut butter and mayonnaise, two boxes of crackers, a jar of pickles, a sack of flour, and several packages of cookies, among other odds and ends, including three or four ant trails. Oh, well, they were as entitled to their feast as we were.

That night we sat in the darkness around the kitchen table—we didn't dare light a candle—and munched on bread and ham and cheese, all of which still tasted pretty good, washing it down with two bottles of warm ale. It was certainly better than nothing, although the minister made her usual face. Reverend Lesley had now decided, oddly enough, that we should move south immediately, but I thought we ought to rebuild our strength first (we were both dog-tired), and wait until morning.

Then it happened, just like that!

We heard a whistling sound coming at us out of the sky. A blinding flash of green light made everything in the kitchen stand out in vivid shadows of emerald and black. The enormous explosion shoved us to the floor with a crash of breaking glass and falling masonry. The entire house rattled and settled, and a shower of ceiling plaster rained down on our bare heads. My first thought was that the San Andreas Fault had finally snapped its leash and precipitated the damned earthquake that everyone's been predicting for years.

I was knocked against the oven and stunned senseless. I lay there unconscious for a long time, the minister later told me. When I came to, I was swimming in darkness again. She was dabbing water all over my throbbing head, begging me to wake up.

For a long time I couldn't remember who I was or what had happened to me. Things came back to me very, very slowly. The bruise on my temple throbbed unceasingly.

"Are you feeling better?" Lesley whispered.

I couldn't answer. Then I sat up, and the whole room swam. I vomited suddenly to one side.

"Oh, shit," was all I could say.

I felt terribly sick and disoriented.

"Don't move," she said. "The floor's covered with glass. You can't get up without making some noise, and I think *they're* outside."

"Who?" I said rather stupidly.

The obvious answer just didn't occur to me in my weakened

state.

"The *Martians*!"

I couldn't argue with her, couldn't argue with anyone, really, since I was feeling so bad. We both sat there perfectly still, each nursing our respective hurts (Lesley had been cut on the forehead). I could hardly hear her breathing. Everything was silent, except once when something very near to us, maybe a piece of plaster, slid to the floor with a rattling sound. Outside I could sense an intermittent, metallic rustle.

"Hear that?" the minister asked, when the noise repeated itself.

"Yes," I said, still groggy.

"It's the Martians!"

I listened more intently.

"Doesn't sound like the sting-ray."

"It's them!"

I somehow thought that one of the great fighting-machines had stumbled against our house, like the one that had demolished Lesley's church in San Rafael. I still wasn't thinking straight.

All that night we scarcely moved from our positions. When the minister had to pee, she used an empty pan. At dawn a pale light finally began filtering into the kitchen, not from the window, which remained totally black, but through a triangular hole that had been created between a crossbeam and a pile of broken bricks in the wall behind us. The interior of our prison cell was then revealed to us in all its glory.

The window had been forced inward by a mass of plants and soil and rocks, which had flowed over the table at which we'd been sitting. Outside, dirt was banked high against the house. Up above we could just see the dangling edge of a severed drainpipe. The floor was littered with smashed and bent pots and pans and broken glass. The other end of the kitchen appeared totally blocked, and we deduced from this that the rest of the house had probably collapsed from the impact. But the impact of what?

Contrasting with this ruin was the brightly colored refrigerator, the pastel green cupboards, and the wallpaper, which was designed to imitate alternating blue and white tiles. A couple of yellow recipe sheets were tacked to the walls, looking like large insects that had been mounted there by some insane entomologist. The combination of this color scheme was utterly bilious to me.

As the light improved, we could see a gap in the wall, and through it a Martian fighting-machine standing sentinel over the still-glowing spaceship in the pit. It was then that I realized what'd happened. The sight so terrified us that we crawled as carefully as we could out of the twilight of the ruined kitchen into the safer recesses of the storeroom right behind it.

"The ship!" I whispered to myself. "It hit the house and buried us under the ruins!"

For a time the minister was silent.

"Lord God have mercy upon us!" she finally said.

Then I heard her whimpering again, or maybe she was praying. She was getting on my nerves once more.

We lay very still for many hours. I could scarcely breathe, I was so scared; and I sat with my eyes fixed on the faint light of the kitchen door, just daring the Martians to enter. I could barely make out Lesley's face, a dim, dark, oval shape, with her white collar and cuffs. Outside there began a rough metal hammering, then a violent hooting sound ("*Ooh-Hooh*"), and after a brief interval, a hissing like the escape of steam. These noises continued intermittently through the night, but seemed to increase in volume as time went on.

Soon our time was punctuated by the measured thudding of the Martian engines, together with an underlying vibration that made everything around us constantly shake and quiver. Once darkness fell, the ghostly kitchen was shrouded in black, and we felt safe enough to emerge from our cocoon for the first time in many hours. We'd crouched in the storeroom all day, silent and shivering and utterly worn out.

I was wide awake again—hungry and thirsty and with a pressing need to empty my bladder. The ache in my belly became so urgent that it forced me to immediate action. Then I told the minister that I was going for water, and felt my way back into the kitchen. She made no answer, but as soon as I began drinking, the faint noise that I made stirred her as well, and I heard her crawling towards me.

We felt around for food and drink, and wolfed it down, mold and all. Once Lesley tried to take something from my hand, and I think I growled at her and slapped her fist away. We'd been reduced to scrounging like animals. For a time I *was* an animal, just another beast striving to survive for another hour or another day and another morsel of food. I also didn't hesitate to empty my bowels in front of her into whatever vacant canister or bottle was available.

I hated the feeling of being trapped.

I hated the thought of dying.

And, most of all, oh yes, most of all, *I hated Reverend Lesley!*

CHAPTER TWENTY-TWO
THE RUINED HOUSE

Habitant of castle gray, creeping thing in sober way.
—William Ellery Channing

Alex Smith, 3 Bi-January, Mars Year i
Marin County, California, Planet Earth

After eating our fill we crept back into the storage area, and I dozed again. When I awoke I was alone. The thudding continued without cease, giving me a persistent, throbbing headache to go with the head injury that I'd received. I whispered Lesley's name several times, and at last felt my way to the door of the kitchen. It was now daylight, and I saw her lying with her face pressed against the hole that looked out onto the Martian pit. Her shoulders were hunched over, and her head was hidden from me.

I could hear loud, rhythmic noises outside, like those generated by a garage; and the ruined kitchen continued to rock with an incessant thud-thud-thudding sound that reminded me of the bass reverberations of hip-hop music—what I call "rap-shit." Through the gap in the wall I could just see the top of a tree touched with gold and the warm blue of a tranquil evening sky. I could even hear a bird or two chirping away over the clatter. I advanced carefully amidst the broken glass littering the floor, struggling to keep silent.

I touched Lesley's leg, and she jumped so violently that a

piece of plaster went sliding down the outside of the house and fell into the pit with a loud rattling noise. I gripped her arm, fearing that she might cry out, and for a long time we crouched there motionless. Then I turned to see how much of our wall remained. The falling masonry had opened a vertical slit in the debris; by raising myself cautiously over a beam I was able to peer through the gap onto what a few nights ago had been a quiet suburban California street.

The ship had plopped onto the home next door, utterly obliterating the building. It now lay buried in a hole that was already larger than the pit I'd seen at Novato. The earth surrounding it had splashed upward under the impact of the landing—"splashed" is the only word that describes it—creating mounds of dirt that hid the adjoining houses from sight.

Our own structure had collapsed onto its front section, destroying most of the ground floor; but the kitchen and storeroom and the entrance to the basement had somehow escaped, although buried under tons of soil. It was closed off except in the direction of the ship. We were perched on the edge of the huge circular excavation that the aliens were creating. The heavy equipment generating the beating noise was hidden from us. A pale green vapor rose like a veil across our peephole, giving off a faint metallic odor.

The spaceship had already unfolded itself: on the far rim stood one of the great striders, its hatch ajar, looming stiff and stark against the evening sky. At first I hardly noticed it, because of the extraordinary device I saw at the center of the pit.

It was one of those things that have since been labeled "handling-machines," the study of which has given us some basic knowledge of Martian science. It had the appearance of a spider with six jointed, articulate legs, plus an arrangement of metal attachments and tentacles protruding from its body. These arms were often retracted, but this particular machine was using three of its "hands" to fish out a number of rods, plates, and bars that had lined the interior of the ship, apparently serving to strengthen its structure during its transit to Earth.

The bars were being deposited on the surface next to the pit.

Its motion was so swift and perfect that at first I didn't even regard it as a machine, in spite of its glitter. The fighting-machines were marvelous things, to be sure, but nothing compared to this. Folks who've never seen these devices scarcely have any idea of the "living" quality they evinced.

You may recall the photos published in *People* in one of the first accounts of the war. Malletoni made a very hasty study of the striders, with appropriate illustrations of the surviving wrecks. The article presented them as rigid tripods, lacking flexibility or subtlety, suggesting that Earth had been attacked by a horde of stiff-necked robots. Of course, nothing was further from the truth. The issue sold out immediately. The documentaries on CNN and the *National Geographic* Channel were similarly "dry" and uninformative, giving a barebones description of the Martian devices, but little more. They universally failed to convey the vitality of the alien machinery.

At first, as I said, the handling-device didn't impress me much as a *machine*. It appeared almost like a large crab with a glittering carapace. A Martian sat inside and directed the thing with its own tentacles, the equivalent of the creature's central brain. But then I realized just how much the mechanism resembled the *other* Martian devices, and even the aliens themselves, with its gray-brown, shiny, almost leathery covering—and the true nature of the "handler" suddenly dawned on me. The artifact combined both organic materials and metal alloys, blending them together in an intricate combination of power and efficiency and beauty. None of our engineers has ever been able to duplicate one of these machines, or even to get one of the relics left by the aliens working again.

I wanted objectively to record the events that I witnessed here. Suddenly I was aware of a rancid odor emanating from the pit, like a pail of shellfish that's been left out in the sun too long. It was sickening.

I then examined the Martians themselves more closely. Already I'd formed a general impression of these creatures. The initial nausea I'd experienced no longer bothered me, although the pervasive stench was unsettling at times. Since I was fully hidden, I could easily observe the comings and goings in the pit.

The aliens' bodies consisted of a huge, humped, round head about four feet in diameter, with a silly, oversized, almost cartoonish grin plastered over the front. They had no nose as such—the Martians didn't seem to have any sense of smell, and I wasn't really sure at that point how they breathed. I saw a pair of very large, dark-hued eyes, almost black in color, and beneath them a kind of fleshy beak, similar to that of an octopus or squid. The creatures were finally dissected by Herr Doktor Franz-Ferdinand von Jarmann in the months following the war; he stated that they combined elements of shellfish, insects, and crustaceans, all mixed together in ways that should have been biologically impossible.

At the back of the "body"—I don't know how else to describe it—was a small "drum" that served as an ear, although it must have been almost useless in our dense atmosphere. Grouped around the mouth was a set of short feelers, almost like wormy whiskers. At the base of the creature's body were sixteen slender, whip-like tentacles, arranged in two bunches of eight each. Four were longer than the others. These Martian "hands," as Jarmann termed them, seemed both flexible and versatile. The aliens seemed to be trying to raise their bodies using these "hands," but this was difficult with the increased weight generated by our gravity. On Mars they could have moved around with ease, but on Earth it's a wonder they could even breathe.

The creatures' internal anatomy, as Doktor Jarmann's lengthy investigations have since shown, was fairly simple, being dominated by a large brain. They also had rather a bulky lung into which the mouth opened, a large heart, and unusually thin blood vessels. The pulmonary distress caused by our denser atmosphere and gravitational force was all too evident in the constant convulsive movements of the creatures' outer skin.

The Martians had no digestive tract as such. They were mostly heads—just heads. Stomach, intestines, and colon were nonexistent. They "ate" by drinking the living fluid of warm-blooded creatures directly into their veins, piped there by means of a small tube that they extended from their mouths. I suppose you could call them vampires of a sort. I later witnessed one of the feedings myself.

This type of diet might seem gross to us, but our own eating habits would probably appear just as disgusting to an intelligent rabbit, if such existed.

The advantages of this kind of physiology are clear. Our bodies have to turn solid food into useful nutrients. The Martians bypass such necessities by being biological parasites. They may regard us as little more than sources of potential nourishment.

Although there's some evidence (see "A Diet of Worms?" by Lance K. Perth, *The Journal of Exobiology*) that they also fed on the blood of other mammals during their brief sojourn on earth, the aliens seemed to prefer man as their primary source of nourishment. This can partially be explained by the remains of the victims they brought with them as provisions from Mars. These creatures, to judge by the shriveled bodies recovered from the alien ships, were bipeds with flimsy skeletons and a feeble musculature, standing about six feet high, and having round, erect heads, with large eyes protruding from flinty sockets. A number were included in each ship, but all were killed before the aliens landed on Earth. Perhaps this was just as well, for merely attempting to stand upright on our planet would have broken every bone in their fragile bodies. There's some question, however, whether the aliens actually found human blood "tasty," or whether it even provided sufficient nutrients to sustain their lives for any great length of time—or even if this was their preferred choice.

Professor Jarmann has noted three other areas where the Martian physiology likely differed from our own. They apparently didn't sleep, any more than our own hearts sleep. The aliens would have experienced little or no sense of fatigue as we know it. On Earth their movements required enormous expenditures of energy, far greater than they would have needed on their homeworld; and yet to the very end they kept pressing forward, never ceasing their efforts. During a twenty-four-hour period they performed twenty-four hours of work, just like a nest of ants or wasps.

The Martians had also dispensed with sex. A young alien was actually born on Earth; it was found attached to its parent, partially budded off, just as certain sea creatures on our world propagate asexually. In man, indeed, in all of the higher terrestrial animals, asexual reproduction has long since been abandoned; on Mars, however, evolution apparently veered in another direction.

This development had previously been postulated by several well-known sci-fi writers. *The Coming of the Eggheads*, by Bunny Barlevin, postulates that giant, pea-brained chickens will one day rise from their coops to conquer mankind, spreading their seeds of sappiness throughout modern civilization. Menlo P. Menville's *Big Brains of San Berdoo* suggests that we have nothing to fear but our organs themselves; the revolting revulsion that we'll feel when our real personas begin to emerge from their collective chrysalides is beyond mankind's complete comprehension; several critics felt, however, that it was *his* novel that was beyond *anyone's* comprehension. *Robot Get Your Gun*, published in hardcover by Underhill Books, notes that the perfection of mechanical devices must ultimately supersede organic limbs, and that organs such as hair, nose, teeth, ears, and chin will become nonessential parts of the human anatomy in the future. Only the brain, author Lambie Wilhelm suggests, will remain necessary, with just one other part of the body making a strong case for survival—the hand, the "teacher and agent of the brain." While the rest of the body dwindles, she imagines, the hand will grow ever larger through constant, unceasing activity.

We can certainly laugh at such "imaginotions," and yet the Martians obviously suppressed their animal side to increase their intelligence. A gradual development of brain and hands (the latter becoming tentacles) at the expense of the rest of their bodies altered their physiology permanently; their brains grew ever larger (in effect, they became talking heads, much like politicians), without any of the emotional baggage that burdens most human beings (lawyers being the lone exception).

Doktor Jarmann has also established, in his stirring essay, "De Exo-Physiologia Parvula Martianorum" (published in *Zeitschrift der Pikkoloflöte-Musik*) that the bacteria and viruses that have caused so much havoc on our planet probably don't exist on Mars, or (more likely) were eradicated by Martian science millennia ago. The aliens apparently never experience disease, dying eventually of old age, although the outside limit of that age is unknown. Dr. Terrot Callander has suggested that the Martians never stop growing throughout their lifetimes, and that the invasion fleet may have consisted only of juveniles bred for that purpose. Graeny Michaels takes issue with that notion, however, believing that the aliens were fully aware of what they were doing, most of the time.

Finally, there's the curious question of the red weed.

Vegetation on Mars, like the soil from which it is nurtured, displays a vivid, blood-red tinge to its leaves, stems, and blossoms. None of the rovers that we've sent to the Red Planet have noticed these plants, so it's likely that they've long since retreated from the harsh conditions of the surface, particularly at the equator, and now exist only in specially cultivated patches underground, or possibly in very small scattered tufts somewhere near the Martian poles, where water ice is known to exist. At any rate, the seeds that the aliens brought with them to Earth only gave rise to red-hued growths.

The plant known popularly as the red weed, however, was the only one to gain widespread footing in terrestrial soil. The red creeper, a different species altogether, appeared mostly in wooded areas, with very few people actually observing it. The red-faced groper only grew in very small patches in swampy areas, although it seemed to flourish in the Sacramento climate, and was particularly attracted to human females. The crimson tide was a kind of kelp that infested the California coast for awhile. The ruddy root grew mostly underground; hence, it was mostly never found, except in fine restaurants. The pink pincushion was a type of nettle with a sheen of prickly metal. The carmine copperhead has only recently been identified as peculiar to the Mojave Desert. Undoubtedly, more such plants will be discovered as time goes on, although none of them seems to have adapted very well to the conditions on our world.

For a time the red weed flourished astonishingly well wherever there was water or even the hint of dampness. It'd spread up the sides of our pit by the third or fourth day of our imprisonment, and its cactus-like branches soon formed a rosy fringe to the edges of our triangular window on the world. Afterwards, I found it scattered all throughout the country, especially around fresh-water springs and rivers and ditches—and at the edges of the ocean.

Why did the Martians seed the Earth? This is one of the great unsolved mysteries of the aliens, because they made no obvious effort to consume the weed. Perhaps the plants produced nutrients the Martians required, or maybe the crimson growth was intended as food for other alien animals that would have been brought to our world at some later date. Some writers, especially Dulcimer de Nardo, have suggested that the Martians found the reddish hue esthetically pleasing. No one really knows for sure.

Their eyes had a visual range not unlike our own, except that, according to Doctor Lando Pfischmonger, the colors dark blue and violet would have seemed black to them. Biologists have postulated that they communicated with each other through their hooting sounds and gross gesticulations (indeed, this was first asserted in the above-mentioned *People* article, "I Survived the Martians," by Marco Polo Malletoni). However, no human who survived the war saw as much of the Martians as I did. I observed them from close range over a long period of time. I've seen four, five, even six of the creatures sluggishly performing the most elaborately complicated operations together without making either a sound or obvious gesture to each other. Their peculiar hoot-hoot noise invariably preceded their feeding and accompanied certain other actions, but it had no specific tone; this was, I believe, not actually a signal, but just noise that accompanied certain set activities. Maybe in the distant past, the Martians communicated verbally, but I doubt that's been true for a very long time.

I have a certain knowledge of basic psychology, and I'm absolutely convinced from my observations that the Martians communicated telepathically with each other (however, Dr. Roweena Warner believes that telepathic communication between Earth and the home world would have required more energy than the Martians could have possibly generated—there's really no way of proving or disproving this notion). I never believed in telepathy before, but it's the only explanation that seems to fit the facts.

The Martians wore no clothing. Their concept of ornament was necessarily different from ours. They seemed less sensitive to changes of temperature than we are. They were sluggish in our atmosphere, but that never stopped them from attaining their goals. Their extensive use of artificial limbs and implements made them individually more powerful than any single human being, enabling them to live and move on a planet where the force of gravity would have otherwise rendered them completely ineffectual.

That's not to say, of course, the Martians were all-knowing or invincible. Their largest machines were the giant tripods, and this three-in-one pattern can been seen in many of their constructions. They made very little use of pivots. Their machines employed a complicated system of sliding parts moving over very small but beautifully curved friction bearings, the longer levers being activated by a sort of sham musculature of disks housed in elastic sheaths; these disks were activated by an electrical current. Thus, they were able to achieve a fluid, almost animal-like motion in their mechanical creations. They also used biological components to help control and manipulate their machines, but since few of these survived the war intact, we have very little idea of how they actually worked.

Such quasi-muscles helped power the crab-like handling-machine which I'd observed unpacking the spaceship. That's why the machine seemed almost more alive than the Martian directing it. By comparison, the aliens themselves appeared ineffectual, lying there panting in the glaring sunlight, stirring their feeble tentacles right and left, sopping up warmth, and thrashing about limply after their long journey across space. One of them was bathing itself in a pool of water to one side of the pit, and presently I saw it change places with another. I wondered then if the creatures were originally aquatic in nature.

While I was observing these sluggish movements, the minister tugged my arm, trying to pull me back so she could take her turn. The slit only permitted one of us to peer outside at a time, so I had to relinquish my entertainment while she exercised that privilege for a few hours.

When I resumed my post, the busy little handling-machine had already assembled several pieces of the apparatus it had taken from the ship, molding them into a shape like its own. To the left the digger came into view, emitting jets of green vapor and working its way 'round and 'round the pit, excavating and banking the dirt in a methodical series of actions designed to enlarge the Martians' living quarters. This is what'd caused the regular beating noise and the rhythmic shocks that had kept our ruinous refuge aquiver all through the night. It piped and whistled to itself almost cheerfully as it worked and worked and worked, endlessly making its rounds. So far as I could tell, the thing operated completely on its own.

I observed the invaders first-hand during those long days of captivity, finding them utterly fascinating. Their motives, their intentions, their basic thoughts all still seem a marvel to me.

If only I'd found some way to communicate with the enemy.

If only I'd found some way to communicate with the minister.

CHAPTER TWENTY-THREE
ENDLESS DAYS

The enemy faints not, nor faileth,
And as things have been, they remain.
—Arthur Hugh Clough

ALEX SMITH, 3 BI-JANUARY, MARS YEAR I
MARIN COUNTY, CALIFORNIA, PLANET EARTH

The arrival of a second fighting-machine drove us back into the storeroom, for we feared that two Martian striders might spot us more easily. Within a few days, however, we realized that a creature operating in the bright sunshine couldn't possibly penetrate our dark hole, and we became increasingly bold.

Still, any hint of movement outside drove us immediately back into the storage nook. As bad as things were, the attraction of our local entertainment center was for us irresistible. I remember how, in spite of our ongoing peril, we still competed every morning for the privilege of watching the aliens. We'd race across the kitchen at first light, trying not to make any noise, while silently pushing back and forth at each other, within just a few feet of instant death if we were exposed.

Of course, we were totally incompatible. Our danger and isolation only emphasized this fact. I hated Lesley's helplessness and cowardice and rigid stupidity. Her endless protests drove me at times almost to the point of screaming. She was like a spoiled child: if something didn't go her way, she'd weep silently for hours, lamenting her fate and crying out under her breath to *her* God to save *her* sorry soul.

She also ate too much, despite her slender frame. I told her that our only chance of survival was to remain hidden until the Martians left, however long that took, and that we needed to conserve our stores. She paid me no mind. She ate and drank whatever she wanted whenever she wished, without any consideration for me. She slept very little. She nagged me constantly. I think she must have been more than a bit crazy.

As time passed, I became increasingly irritated with her attitude, until I finally had to use threats to keep her in line. That stopped her whining for a few days. But she was one of those folks who was only concerned with herself and her own place in the universe, a place justified in her thinking by her personal relationship with God. You just can't reason with someone like that.

We fought our mini-conflict in a dark, dim contest of whispers, snatched food, and grasping hands—while just outside our prison, the pitiless sunlight of that terrible winter illuminated the strange, ongoing drama of the Martians puttering about in their pit.

When I looked again through the hole, I saw that the aliens had been reinforced by three striders. These had brought with them some odd devices arrayed in an orderly fashion around the ship. The second handling-machine was now complete, and was servicing one of the new constructions. The latter had a body like a large gasoline can, above which oscillated a pear-shaped basin from which a stream of white powder was flowing into a container below.

This was the "ore-processor," as I called it. With two of its "hands" the handling-machine was digging out lumps of clay and flinging them into the receptacle at the top of the new device, while another arm periodically opened a door and removed rusty, blackened pieces of residue from inside the machine. A third device transported the powder from the basin along a channel towards some mechanism hidden from me by a mound of blue dust. This unseen third machine generated a little thread of green smoke that rose vertically into the air.

The handling-machine, with almost a musical clinking, extended a tentacle like an articulated telescope, something that up till now had just been a blunt knob on its body, until the far end was hidden behind the mound of clay. Then it lifted a bar of white aluminum into sight, new and untarnished and brightly shining, and deposited it beside a growing stack of other ingots by the side of the pit. Between sunrise and sunset this dexterous little creature (for it seemed almost alive) ground out and baked more than a hundred such bars from the crude ore, and the mound of residue rose steadily until it slopped over the rim of the pit.

The contrast between the swift, complex movements of these machines and the inert, panting clumsiness of their masters never ceased to amaze me, and for days I had to tell myself repeatedly that the *latter* were the living, breathing, *directing* half of these symbiotic creatures.

The minister was on duty when the first humans were brought in. I was sitting just below her on the kitchen floor, listening for any tidbits, when she suddenly leapt backwards, almost losing her balance (which would have been a disaster). She slid down the rubbish heap next to me, gesticulating and moaning incomprehensibly. For a moment I almost panicked. She just kept jabbing her finger at the peephole. Curiosity finally got the better of me, and I gingerly stepped across her body and crawled forward to our makeshift observation post.

At first I couldn't see any reason for Lesley's frantic behavior. Twilight had fallen by then, and I could just make out a few stars twinkling faintly above—but the pit itself was partially illuminated by the flickering green fire that always gleamed while the aluminum bars were being forged. The mingling of emerald light with the shifting, rusty black shadows was strangely seductive. Over and through the pit flew hordes of bats, oblivious to the sight and sound of the Martians, picking out bugs attracted by the light. I once saw one of the furry critters snatched out of the air; but after trying to suck the life out of the ugly little beast, the Martian flung it away in evident disgust. Bat juice apparently didn't taste very good to the aliens (actually, it didn't sound good to me either!).

I couldn't see the Martians, because the mound of blue-green residue had risen to a point where it blocked my sight; there was a fighting-machine standing on one rim, its legs partially retracted. Then, amidst the clamor of the machinery I suddenly heard the almost inaudible murmur of human voices, and I nearly shouted out a response before my sense got the better of me.

I watched the strider intently, satisfying myself that the hood did indeed contain a Martian. The green glow reflected the oily gleam of its skin and the brightness of its dark eyes. I could also see some kind of fluid sloshing around in the cab, maybe to provide a resting place for the creature or some kind of nourishment. Then I heard someone scream. A long tentacle reached over the shoulder of the machine to the little cage that it bore on its back. It lifted something high overhead, a black, vague outline struggling and writhing against the backdrop of the starlit sky.

Then I realized—all of a sudden—that it was a man!

He was visible for just a second: a stout, ruddy, middle-aged individual, still well dressed. A few days earlier he might have been someone important. His eyes were bulging in fear. The green-gold light gleamed sickly on his forehead. Then he was pulled behind the mound, and after a moment of profound silence, a terrible shrieking began, followed by a sustained, even cheerful hooting noise from the Martians (*"Oh-leh!"*).

I slid down the rubbish pile, struggled to my feet, and bolted into the storeroom. The minister was crouching silently on the floor there with her arms over her head; she looked at me in horror.

That night we stayed in the anteroom, unable to sleep, trying to balance our fear with the terrible fascination of the Martians. I felt we ought to do something, and tried to think of a way of escaping our predicament, but with no luck. The only way out was through the pit—period!—and we couldn't risk trying to sneak past the ever-vigilant aliens.

The next day, however, I reconsidered our situation. Reverend Lesley had never been very rational, and was even less so now, being reduced to occasional whimpers at the implication of what we'd seen. For all intents and purposes she'd regressed to the level of a beast.

Our one chance depended on the Martians eventually abandoning the pit when they'd finished with whatever it was they were doing. I knew that this had happened at some of their secondary camps, because I'd seen the evidence myself in Novato. If they remained awhile, they might ease their guard eventually, thus affording us some possibility of actually getting away.

I also thought about trying to dig ourselves out through the rubble in the other direction, but this seemed to me so difficult with the poor tools that we had at our disposal that I immediately dismissed the notion. For one thing, I'd have to do all the digging myself, since I couldn't rely on the minister for support; for another, it appeared from what I could tell that both floors of the structure had collapsed onto the foundation. Removing the debris would require considerable time and effort, and might well generate a great deal of noise in the process.

It was on the third day, if my memory is correct, that I saw the boy killed. This was the only time that I actually observed the Martians feeding. One of them held the teen down while another extended its, well, for want of a better word, "proboscis," and then they took turns, three or four of them, draining away the victim's vital fluids. His body gradually turned white as I watched. They sucked him completely dry, every drop, and then stripped away the remaining flesh, feeding it into another one of their machines, evidently to be used for some kind of fuel. (Jarmann believes that the aliens were able to reprocess human flesh into manipulable hydrocarbons for use as lubricants and such.) The skeletal remains were dumped on the growing trash heap of Martian civilization.

After that, I avoided the peephole for the better part of a day. I went into the storeroom, removed its door, and managed to pry up a couple of floorboards without making a racket. I spent several hours working with my makeshift shovel as quietly as possible; but when the hole was only a couple of feet deep, the loose earth collapsed around it rather noisily. I dared not continue. Then I lay down on the floor for a long time. After that I abandoned any idea of digging my way out.

I also entertained very little hope of being freed by other humans. But on the fourth or fifth evening I once more heard the sound of heavy guns pounding in the distance. Some of our boys had survived!—or perhaps reinforcements had been sent from elsewhere in the state.

It was very late and the moon was shining brightly. The Martians had taken away the excavating-machine and ore-processor, and, save for a strider that still stood sentinel at the far side of the pit, and a handling-machine that was buried out of sight immediately beneath my vantage point, the place now seemed deserted. The pit was dark except for a pale glow emanating from the handler and the sickly light of the moon; the silence was interrupted only by the occasional clicking of the handling-machine as it measured the marigolds.

That night had a serenity to it that belied our peril, and I felt a sense of peace for the first time in many days, I don't know why. Then I heard a dog howling in the distance, and that familiar sound made me sit up and take notice. Immediately thereafter I distinctly perceived a booming noise like the sound of great guns in play. I counted six reports, and after a long interval, six more.

And that was all.

CHAPTER TWENTY-FOUR
THE LIFE AND DEATH
OF A MINISTER

Say not "Good night"; but in some
brighter clime bid me "Good morning."
　　　　　　　　—Anna Letitia Barbauld

ALEX SMITH, 8 BI-JANUARY, MARS YEAR I
MARIN COUNTY, CALIFORNIA, PLANET EARTH

On the sixth day (I think) of our imprisonment, I stepped back from our window on the outside world and suddenly found myself alone. Lesley had retreated to the storeroom. I went to find her, creeping quietly into the rear of our little establishment. Then I heard the sound of drinking. I reached into the darkness, and my fingers wrapped around a bottle of burgundy, which I tried to yank from the woman.

"What the hell are you doing?" I hissed. "You're putting us both in danger!"

She grabbed ahold of the bottom of the container, and tried to pull it out of my hands. Then the bottle fell between us and broke on the floor. We stood there whispering threats to each other in low tones. In the end I told her that I was implementing a rationing program. I divided the remaining foodstuffs into portions that would last us ten more days. That afternoon she made a feeble effort to crawl by me while I was dozing, but I woke up immediately and stopped her. All day and all night we sat there face to face. I was tired. I was cranky. And all she could do was quietly weep and complain incessantly of her hunger. It was just a night and day, but it seemed to me—it seems even now—interminable.

For two days we argued off and on about inconsequential things. There were times when I struck her, I'm ashamed to say, times when I cajoled her, and once when I even tried to bribe her with the last bottle of booze. I knew the faucet in the kitchen could still provide me with a trickle of bad-tasting water. But she just wouldn't listen to reason.

"God is judging me," she said. "He hath singled me out for punishment!"

Oh God, I just wished she would shut her mouth forever!

She became careless of her movements and any noise she made while moving around in our prison. I began to realize that my sole companion in this damnable darkness was insane.

My own mind may also have wandered a bit during this period. I had strange, even wild dreams whenever I dropped off. Maybe the struggle with Lesley was one of the things that ultimately kept me sane—and alive.

On the eighth day she began to speak aloud instead of whispering, and nothing that I tried would stop her.

"Is it just, God?" she said, over and over again. "Is it *just?* On me and mine be the punishment laid. We have sinned, we have fallen short. There was poverty, sorrow; the poor were trodden in the dust, and I held my peace. I preached acceptable folly—my God, what folly!—when I should have stood up, though I died for them, and called upon them to repent—*repent!* Oppressors of the poor and needy! The wine press of God!"

Once more she would speak again of her hunger, praying, begging, weeping, even badgering me to give her more food. She then perceived that she had a hold over me—and now she threatened to bring the Martians down upon us unless I agreed to release the supplies. I defied her.

She continued to warble in her loud, obnoxious, whiny voice through most of the eighth and ninth days, making threats and entreaties intermingled with a torrent of half-sane and frothy repentances for her sham service of God. I actually started to pity her. Then she slept awhile. When she woke, she began again, so loudly, in fact, that I had to make her stop at any cost.

"Shut up!" I said.

She went down on her knees.

"I've been still too long," she said in a loud voice that must have reached all the way to the lower circles of Hell, "and now I must bear witness. Woe unto this unfaithful city! Woe! Woe! *Woe!* To the inhabitants of the Earth by reason of the other voices of the trumpet—"

"Shut up!" I repeated, rising to my feet, terrified lest the aliens should hear. "For God's sake, woman—"

"Nay!" shouted the minister at the top of her voice, standing and extending her arms to the left and right. "Speak! The word of the Lord is upon me!"

In three strides she was at the kitchen door.

"I must go to bear witness against the aliens! I must depart! It has already been too long delayed."

I put out my hand and grabbed the first thing that came to me, a large carving knife still dangling from its original hook. In a flash I was after her, overtaking her halfway across the kitchen. I raised the blade on high—and then struck her with the butt! She slumped immediately to the floor. I stood over her body, panting. At last she was silent! *Finally!*

Then I heard a noise just outside, a scraping of the plaster, and the hole in the wall suddenly went dark. I looked up and saw the lower half of the handling-machine moving slowly across the opening. I was scared shitless.

One of the tentacles came curling like a serpent through the debris, swishing back and forth as it sought its prey. Then another limb appeared, feeling its way over the fallen beams. I just stood there watching the alien "arms" reaching towards me. Outside I could actually see the Martian driver visible through its glass plate: the ugly, bulging face, the dark, bestial eyes peering intently into the darkness from the liquid bath in which it was embedded. The metal snakes kept feeling their way forward through the opening in the wall. I froze completely.

Then at last I came to my senses. With a huge effort I stumbled over the outstretched body of the minister, and stepped quietly towards the storeroom door. The first tentacle now stretched out about the length of a man, twisting and turning this way and that with its strange, jerky movements. For awhile I continued to watch the thing, fascinated in spite of myself by that slow, fitful advance. Then I forced myself back into the safety of the alcove. I was trembling so much by this point that I could barely stand. I opened the door of the partially blocked cellar, and stared back into the faintly lit kitchen, listening intently. Had the Martian seen anything? What was it doing?

Something was moving out there, something was very quietly but purposefully exploring our little world. Every now and then I could hear it tap against the wall, or start questing again with a faint metallic sound, like the jangling of keys on a ring. Then a heavy body—I knew whose it was—was dragged across the floor of the kitchen towards the opening. I crept to the door and peered out. The driver in the handler was examining the minister's head. *Jesus H. Christ!* I gave no thought to Lesley's welfare, but only hoped that the creature wouldn't infer my presence from the blow I'd given her.

I crept back into the cellar, shut the door, and covered myself as much as I could with boards and fallen debris. Every now and then I paused, absolutely rigid, to listen again.

Then the faint jingling returned. Santa and all his reindeers, I thought!—and nearly burst out laughing in spite of myself. The thing was slowly feeling its way around the ruined kitchen. Then it moved into the storage nook. *Shit!* Maybe—oh, God, maybe!—it was too short to reach me.

At that point I actually prayed for my life. I hadn't prayed for anything since I was a kid. The tentacle scraped faintly at the cellar door. Quote the raven, "nevermore"! Ah, distinctly I remember, it was in the dark December….

But of course, it was January now.

Things were quiet for a bit, and that was almost worse than the scratching sounds. Suddenly I heard it fumbling at *my* chamber door! *The Martians understood doors!*

It worried at the knob for a moment, a very *long* moment.

The door swung open!

In the gray light I could barely see the damned thing, like some rogue elephant's trunk waving towards me, touching the walls and examining the ceiling and feeling the broken stairs. It was blindman's buff all over again. The tentacle looked like a black worm swaying its little head to and fro, sniffing and snuffling me out. *Shitters quitters!*

It touched the end of my shoe. I nearly screamed out loud. I bit the heel of my hand to keep quiet. The blood was salty in my mouth (do the aliens taste salt?). For a time the thing remained motionless. I even wondered if it might have withdrawn. Then it grabbed onto something big with an abrupt click and scratch—for a moment I thought it was *me*—*God, I thought it was me!*—and took whatever it was with it. Apparently it'd grabbed a piece of wood or something to examine. Who the bloody hell knows?—or cares, even.

I slightly shifted my position—my back was cramping—and then listened again, oh, gentlefolks, did I ever listen, I strained myself listening, I *heard* myself listening. And all the while I whispered sweet passionate prayers to Jesus for my safety. It was the Reverend's ultimate revenge: *I had become Lesley!*

Once again I heard the same deliberate tinkling sound creeping towards me. Slowly but steadily it drew ever nearer, scratching against the walls and tapping on the remaining debris. I knew I was dead for sure this time. I suddenly felt a great release. I didn't care any more. I would give myself up willingly.

And then—and then the thing just rapped smartly on my door and shoved it shut with a giant bang. I must have jumped halfway to the ceiling. I heard it gradually retreat back through the outside rooms, rattling cans and smashing bottles. I heard nothing else but silence, a silence that passed into an infinity of suspense.

Had it *actually* withdrawn? It'd fooled me so many times in the past hour or two that I wasn't really sure. I finally decided that it was gone.

I lay there all through the tenth day. I remained sequestered in the close, close darkness of the basement, buried among the leftover pieces of man's existence, not daring even to crawl out for the drink that I so desperately craved. I couldn't find the strength to leave my security blanket. I couldn't even move.

Oh, dear God in heaven.

Lesley, please forgive me!

CHAPTER TWENTY-FIVE
THE SWEETNESS OF THE AIR

The God who gave us life, gave us liberty at the same time.
—Thomas Jefferson

ALEX SMITH, 13 BI-JANUARY, MARS YEAR I
MARIN COUNTY, CALIFORNIA, PLANET EARTH

By the eleventh day I was getting so weak that I finally found the gumption to abandon my refuge. The kitchen and the store-room were empty. The Martians had apparently confiscated every scrap of food, perhaps to sustain their human captives. For the first time I despaired: I'd had nothing to eat or drink for several days, and I didn't know where to go or what to do.

My mouth and throat had swelled up and my strength was ebbing very rapidly. I sat alone in the darkness of the storage nook while I sank further into my funk. I would have killed for a piece of bread. I thought I might have lost my hearing as well, because the noises from the pit had ceased. But I didn't feel strong enough to crawl to the peephole to check on what was happening outside.

On Day Twelve, however, I knew I had to do something or die. I wasn't going to last much longer. So I took a chance, crept out into the kitchen, and attacked the leaking faucet that stood on the sink. I got a couple of handfuls of green, rusty water. It tasted like shit—but it was the nectar of the gods! Despite the noises I made slurping the foul liquid, nothing with tentacles poked its way through the hole.

I kept thinking about the minister and her awful death. I felt guilty over my treatment of the woman, who had obviously gone completely gaga. I wondered how much I'd contributed to her dementia.

The next day I drank some more water and then dozed. My dreams were filled with food and of vague plans of escape. I conjured a series of nightmares about the death of the minister, and one of Becky; but, asleep or awake, the hunger in my belly kept me drinking constantly. The light outside had changed to a dull rouge, like the color of blood.

On Day Fourteen I snuck into the kitchen again, and I was astonished to find that fronds of the red weed were now poking through the hole in the wall, turning the half-light of the place into a crimson-hued obscurity.

It was early on the following day that I heard the dog scratching outside. When I investigated, I saw its nose peering through the red weeds. At my sudden appearance the terrified creature began barking quite furiously.

I thought that if I could induce the mutt to come a little closer ("Here, doggy, doggy!"), I might just be able to kill and eat him, or at least to shut the bugger up, lest his actions attract the Martians.

I crept forward very slowly, softly whispering "Good dog! Good dog!"—but it suddenly withdrew its head and disappeared.

The pit remained absolutely still thereafter. Then I heard the flutter of a bird's wings and a hoarse, harsh cawing.

For a long while I lay next to the peephole, not daring to touch the red plants that now obscured it. Once or twice I heard a faint pitter-patter—perhaps the feet of the dog again—running on the sand below me, and there were more bird sounds. Finally, emboldened by the silence, I found the courage to look out.

Except in one corner, where a multitude of crows hopped and fought over the remains of the men the Martians had consumed, there wasn't a living thing to be seen anywhere.

I could hardly believe my eyes. The machines were gone. Save for the mound of grayish-blue powder in one corner and some leftover bars of aluminum in another, the place was just an empty circle in the sand.

Slowly I thrust myself outside, and finally stood staggering in the open air for the first time in two weeks. I could see clearly in every direction. The aliens were gone! The pit dropped off right at my feet, but I found a slope that would take me to the top of the ruins. I trembled in anticipation of my escape.

Even so, I hesitated for about ten minutes; and then, with my heart pounding in my chest, I scrambled to the top of the mound under which I'd been buried so long.

I carefully looked in every direction.

No Martians!

When I'd last viewed this area, it'd been a neatly paved street of comfortable houses interspersed with well-trimmed shade trees. Now I stood on a mound of smashed bricks, plaster, clay, lumber, and gravel, over which had grown a mass of red, cactus-shaped plants, almost knee-high, without a shoot of green anywhere to dispute their hegemony. The surviving trees of Earth were sere and dead; in the distance, however, I could see a network of red thread intertwined around some still living branches. How long the latter would survive was unknown.

The neighboring homes had all been wrecked, although none had burned; some of their walls still stood intact, sometimes as high as the second story, with smashed windows and shattered doors. The red weed had spread riotously through their roofless rooms. Before me was the great pit, where the crows now fought over the scraps of man. I could also see and hear other birds hopping among the ruins. Far away I spied a gaunt cat slinking along a wall, but no traces of any *living* man whatsoever.

The day seemed, by contrast with my dark confinement, dazzlingly bright, the sky a brilliant blue. The alien invasion had at least rid us of smog and other pollutants!

A gentle breeze moved the red weed in a pavane that parodied popular dance: every inch of unoccupied ground waved at me, gently swaying back and forth, back and forth. I was mesmerized by its stately pantomime of planet-cide. The perfume of its little purple pustules penetrated my befuddled brain.

And oh! Oh! The very sweetness of the air!

CHAPTER TWENTY-SIX
FIFTEEN GLORIOUS DAYS,
FIFTEEN FUN-FILLED NIGHTS

I am weary of days and hours,
Blown buds of barren flowers.
—Algernon Charles Swinburne

ALEX SMITH, 17 BI-JANUARY, MARS YEAR I
MARIN COUNTY, CALIFORNIA, PLANET EARTH

For the longest time I just stood there, heedless of my own safety. A Martian could have walked by at any time and harvested me. While imprisoned I'd only been aware of my immediate surroundings. I hadn't had any notion of what'd been happening in the world outside. I'd expected to see some ruins, of course—but I suddenly found myself occupying a place that was literally "not of this Earth!" This wasn't the world I'd abandoned two weeks earlier.

It was the first time that I felt that we were no longer masters of our world, just mere animals among many others, all now crushed under the Martian heel. Our lot, it seemed to me, was to lurk and to watch, to run and to hide, whenever our masters walked among us. The rule of man had passed.

But soon this feeling also passed, and I became aware of a terrible hunger gnawing at my insides. In the distance I could see a house that was relatively undamaged. I went creeping towards it knee-deep (sometimes neck-deep) in the red weed, hardly able to stand upright at times, seeking that little piece of paradise. There was a fence around the place, but when I tried to climb over it, I was just too weak. I finally found a gate where I could tumble into the yard. I broke a window. Inside I discovered a few odds and ends stashed away undiscovered in a bottom pantry (everything else had already been looted), mostly canned goods and some pop. I grabbed a can of salsa and popped the top.

It was hot!

It was *really* hot! I was crying as I shoved spoonful after spoonful into my gullet.

But hellfire and damnation, it tasted like manna from heaven!

I don't think I've ever had anything better.

And the warm soda?—hey, I chugged half of it in one swallow to wash away the burning sensation of the Mexican food.

I found a few cans of fruit, vegetables, soup, and beans, all of it still good.

But I also found I couldn't eat very much of anything. My stomach had shriveled during my captivity, and I feared over-taxing it with something that it couldn't digest.

I fell asleep propped up against the cabinet right there on the kitchen floor.

When I awoke, it was dark, and suddenly I *really* had to poop! I ran outside without even checking for aliens, and did my American duty all over the red weed, yes, sir, I did!

Then I went back and ate some more. And slept some more. And pooped some more! And ate some more again!

I spent several days there rebuilding my strength, and throughout that sojourn, so unlike my recent confinement in Hell, I gradually regained my strength and natural good spirits.

I had no idea at this point what day it was. I'd lost track of time during my captivity. I think I spent fifteen days there, but I'm not really sure. The last few episodes tended to blur together in my memory. I was trying to forget *everything* about Reverend Lesley.

On the third day of my release, I put together a makeshift pack, adding the lightest cans I could find for my trip. I exchanged my clothes with some that I'd found in one of the bedrooms—they didn't fit well, but then neither did my own duds anymore. I still wanted to see the big city—and what had happened to it. I hadn't been cured, dear friends, of my deadly itch of curiosity, oh no!

A block or two down the road I splashed through a brown sheet of shallow water covering a place where a park used to be. I was surprised at this variation from the dry California land-scape, but I soon discovered that the red weed tended to create standing pools of water wherever it grew. Liquid, almost *any* liquid, made the weed grow at an extraordinary rate, until it became huge in size. The resulting mass would quickly choke any waterway or drainage area, thereby creating mini-swamp-lands which allowed it to flourish even more. The weed was transforming the landscape in more ways than one.

In the end, though, the red weed succumbed to disease almost as quickly as it'd spread initially. Some kind of canker, the botanists said, something that devastated its vascular system, choked the weed back on itself. The red growth rotted like a thing already dead, its fronds becoming bleached, then shriveling and turning brittle. In the final stage they'd break at the least little touch. The water that had stimulated its early growth then carried its vestiges out to sea. Or so we believed then. But as always with the Martians, we never investigated far enough, we never probed beneath the surface, we never asked or answered the real questions.

And the chief of these was "why?"

On my journey I had to drink some of the muddy water. When I exhausted my cans, I also tried gnawing on the roots of the red weed; they were pulpish and watery in nature, and tasted like a cross between turnips and jícamas that have gone a little past their prime, leaving a slightly bitter flavor in one's mouth. Still, they stayed down and provided nourishment, and once I got past the slightly unusual taste, I didn't hesitate to use them to supplement my diet.

The swampy areas were sufficiently shallow for me to wade across them without difficulty, although the weed itself tended to impede my progress. There were wet patches everywhere, even on some of the roads, and I had to be careful that I didn't slip. I was still very weak from my long ordeal. I managed to find the state highway again by noticing occasional houses and the lines of power pools and lights, and so made my way down towards Sausalito.

Here the scenery changed once more, from the strange and unfamiliar to the standard urban wreckage I'd seen everywhere else that the aliens had visited: patches that exhibited the devastation of a tornado, interspersed with houses whose blinds were neatly drawn and doors primly closed, as if their inhabitants were still sleeping within (maybe they were). Ironically, *this* landscape seemed almost stranger to me now than the places that had been terraformed—or, more correctly, Marsaformed! The weed was less abundant here, for reasons I didn't understand, and the tall trees along the lane were completely free of the alien creeper. I hunted assiduously for food in these places, but they'd already been ransacked thoroughly of anything worthwhile. I rested for the remainder of the day in a real bed, being too fatigued to press on.

All this time I saw no living humans and no sign whatever of the Martians. I did encounter a couple of hungry-looking dogs, but both bolted on sight. It doesn't take long for the veneer of civilization to vanish, even among our beloved pets. Later that day I saw two human skeletons—not bodies, but skeletons picked quite clean—and in the woods nearby I found the crushed and scattered remains of several cats and rabbits and even the skull of a sheep or goat. But although I gnawed the bones in my mouth, there was no nourishment left in them. I was growing hungry again: the Martian vegetation didn't provide much nourishment to the human soul.

In the hours before sunset I struggled along the road towards Fort Baker, where I saw further signs of the sting-rays at work. In a nearby house I found—oh glorious day!—a sack of sprouting potatoes that helped assuage my hunger. I ate them raw with a little salt. From Fort Baker one could look down upon the Golden Gate Bridge. What I spied were blackened trees, darkened ruins, and the remnants of a flooded ditch, red-tinged with the weed. I heard nothing but silence. How swiftly the world had fallen beneath the sway of the invaders!

For a time I wondered whether mankind itself had been wiped from the Earth. I stood there alone, potentially the last man left alive.

I stayed in Fort Baker overnight. The next morning I slowly trudged across the great bridge that spanned the Golden Gate, avoiding the wrecked and tangled cars, trucks, and vans. The only men I encountered were long dead. I stopped at mid-span, and gazed back into San Francisco Bay, filled now with the wreckage of great and small ships, blotted with dark oil stains and patches of the crimson kelp.

The air was crystal clear. I thought I saw a strider perched on Treasure Island, but it might have been the wavering of the light. Then I turned widdershins and gazed out to sea, drowning my eyes in the great ocean expanse laid there before me, wanting to lose myself in the endless waves of blue. I almost ended it there. I even stood on the railing, holding onto a guy wire as I swayed in the breeze.

Then I sighed and stepped back down onto the roadway. I looked back into the harbor. The central span of the Oakland Bridge was gone. I saw no smoke, no smog, no nothing. Man had been vanquished in little less than a month. But suddenly I laughed out loud, almost hysterically, because I realized that, in spite of everything, the Golden Gate Bridge was still standing! *I* was still standing. Surely that meant something. It had to. I would see what I could see, and hang the bloody consequences!

So I entered upon the great city of San Francisco, Babylon-by-the-Bay. And the first thing that I saw there was the skeleton of a man, his arms separated several yards from the rest of his body.

"And a very fine morning to you too," I said.

I didn't care now who heard me—or what.

As I plodded on into the city, I became more and more convinced that the extermination of mankind had already been accomplished in this part of the world, save for a few stragglers such as myself—and we wouldn't be far behind. The Martians, I thought, had moved elsewhere, had left this country desolate, were now seeking their prey in some more distant community. Perhaps they were destroying Berlin or Paris or Washington, D.C., or maybe they'd moved east over the mountains into Nevada.

I again laughed out loud at the thought of the aliens encountering the gamblers of Reno or Las Vegas, of being confronted at the city gates by a crowd of feckless, useless individuals calling themselves men and women.

"Double or nothing?" one of them might say.

"Double or nothing?" I screamed to the wind.

"Double or nothing!" one of the Martians might have said.

Who the hell knows?

Who the hell cares?

CHAPTER TWENTY-SEVEN
THE KING OF S(N)OB HILL

Whoso diggeth a pit shall fall therein;
And he that rolleth a stone, it will return upon him.
—Holy Bible, *Proverbs 26:27*

Alex Smith, 20 Bi-January, Mars Year I
San Francisco, California, Planet Earth

I found refuge that night in a hotel on Nob Hill, sleeping in a clean, made-up bed for the first time in weeks. I'd ransacked a couple of rooms for food, until I found some cans of pineapple, a rack of drinks, and those endless packages of salted nuts. Gad, if I never see another roasted peanut or almond again in all my life, it'll be too damned soon. And there was enough booze in those little storage cabinets that they so tastefully provided the guests that I could have swept my sorrows away for weeks. I sipped at a few of the mini-bottles before giving it up. Ultimately, they just made me sick.

I was careful not to use the flashlights I'd uncovered or the candles, fearing that some Martian might come knocking for dinner during the night.

Something drove me to prowl the huge place, floor by floor and window by window, peering out every so often for some sign of the invaders, but I managed finally to stop my wandering and settle down for the night. The hotel was so big that it ironically made me feel less secure. Thus, despite my fatigue, I slept very little, tossing and turning with wretched, repeated dreams of Lesley and Becky and the monsters chasing me around in circles. But as I lay in bed early the next morning, I found myself thinking clearly once again, something that I hadn't been able to do since my last argument with the minister.

I had to get on with things—whatever those might be.

The death of Reverend Lesley and the fate of my wife still preoccupied me whenever I had a spare moment. I also needed to know the current whereabouts of the Martians if I was going to survive.

Regarding the good Reverend, well, what can one say? It was she or I. If I had to make the same choices all over again, I'm quite sure that I'd do exactly the same thing. Lesley was unable to cope with the alteration of her world. She was one of those individuals who based her image of herself on her accouterments: in this case, her position and her church. Take those away, and the structure of her personality suddenly collapsed. God had unforgivably dealt her a losing hand. The Martians just didn't fit into her worldview. Neither did I.

And Becky?—well, she was either alive or dead. I had no way of knowing what'd happened to her. I probably shouldn't have left her with her aunt, but I did, and now I was paying the price: guilt, guilt, *guilty* as charged, Your Honor! There was absolutely nothing I could do about the situation now. I still remained an observer at the very heart of the matter. For some reason, for some strange and awful reason, I was the one person in the world who was in the right place at the right time to record the invasion of the Martians.

So I needed to know where the aliens had gone, or even if they were still around. I needed to find out because, well, because I *needed* to, that's all. I wanted to know. Even today, I *still* want to know. *Why, why, why?* I try to frame questions that are simple enough to answer but complicated enough to hold my interest. And always I come back to the basic question of "why?"

I got up and staggered into the bathroom, making use of the facilities. Better that than a ditch! The water was mostly off this far up from the street. I just got a trickle from the faucet. The haggard image glaring back at me from the mirror was the face of a stranger: salt-and-pepper beard (it itched abominably), lined forehead, gaunt face, matted hair shooting every which way, and old, even ancient eyes.

"Here's lookin' at you, kid," I sighed.

I managed to locate some clean clothing in one of the dresser drawers. Like the previous set, they didn't fit me exactly, but I didn't think the aliens would mind. Then I went down to the ruins of the hotel restaurant to scrounge a breakfast. Surely there must be something left down there.

I was opening cupboard doors and storage cabinets and bins, looking for anything that hadn't spoiled, when I heard a noise just behind me.

"Hands up!" came the command.

Slowly I complied.

"Now turn around."

I very carefully obeyed. Standing in front of me was a forty-something woman with short, dark hair, a Giants baseball cap, and a really big gun pointed right at my heart.

"What are you doing?"

"Probably the same as you," I said. "I was looking for something to eat, if you really want to know."

"I don't, especially. If I give you some food, will you go away?"

"Well, here I am, practically the only man left on Earth, so far as I can tell; we haven't even been introduced yet, and already you want me to leave. How about putting that gun down?"

"I don't think so," she said.

"At least tell me your name. I'm Alex Smith, by the way."

"Umm, Nomsah. Nomsah Vassilidis."

"Now that's an odd one. I know, because I study names. That's just not something you hear everyday."

I looked at her more closely in the dim light.

"Haven't I seen you somewhere before?"

"I've heard that line too," she said. "No. I think you can have a couple of mini-boxes of cereal and maybe a can of peaches, and then you'll be on your way, sir, or you'll be very, very dead, sir. I'm good at predicting things, and this is one future I can assure you *will* actually happen. I'm not interested in playing games.

"I'm certain you're a fine, upstanding gentleman in real life. I'm certain you have nothing but good in mind for me. But I can't take that chance, and neither can you, really. So, Alex Smith, whoever the hell you are, take the damned food I'm offering you, and get out of here before I shoot you dead in bed. Because I will, sir, in just about two goddamned minutes, sir."

What choice did I have? At least I got something to eat.

The morning was bright and clear again, and the eastern sky glowed pink, tinged with fine little golden clouds. The vista reminded me of one of those TV programs about "Beautiful California"—you know, the ones where everything is bright and rosy and "we don't talk about poverty here, oh no."

Somewhere near Chinatown I saw the ruins of the panic that must have poured through the city when the evacuations began. A minivan had slewed halfway up the curb by the side of the road, inscribed with the young, seductive, come-hither image of "Madame Stavroula, Grand Mystic and Traveling Tarot Card Reader," who for just a hundred bucks would tell you your future and your fortune, with a money-back guarantee. She looked like a gypsy in her waist-long hair and multi-colored shawl and quasi-medieval outfit, but the effect was partially ruined by the granny glasses and thick pancake make-up. I wondered who'd refunded *her* deposit.

Nearby I saw some blood-stained bone fragments next to a vaguely spurting fire hydrant, no doubt all that remained of the dear Madame, at least on *this* sphere. My movements had become slow and even lazy, as if I had all the time in the world. I thought again of going north to Sonoma to find my wife, although I knew that I probably had little chance of surviving such a trip. I realized suddenly that I was very lonely.

I found cover under a bunch of oleanders in a park near the

North Beach area. Patches of red illuminated the paths, but I saw relatively little of the weed there, which seemed, well, odd. Then the sun emerged from behind a cloud, flooding everything with newfound light and vitality. I encountered a swarm of miniature yellow frogs frolicking in a swampy pond amidst the eucalyptus trees, and I drew a lesson from their example.

I would live.

I would survive to tell my story.

These creatures had no more inkling of the aliens than ants did of man.

Suddenly I knew I was being watched. Turning around, I saw a dark figure crouching behind a clump of roses. I stepped towards him, and he pulled out a rifle. I held out my hands where he could see them. He just stood there silent and motionless, waiting for me to approach.

I noticed that he was dressed in camouflage clothing such as a soldier might wear, and I wondered if he was one of the "weekend warriors" who'd gone out to meet the Martian onslaught a month ago. He looked as though he'd been dragged through several ditches and weed patches. His clothes were dirty and tattered, his face streaked with mud, his nose dripping, his dark hair completely unkempt. His entire body was gaunt from stress and hunger. There was a red slash across the lower part of his face that gave him an ugly smirk; it looked as though it might be infected.

"Halt!" he said in his hoarse voice. "Halt, I say. Who are you and where are you from?"

"Novato," I said. "I was at the first pit that the Martians made."

"What's your name, soldier?"

I was tempted to say, "Call me Ishmael," but instead just mumbled something about "Smith."

He paid no attention to anything I said.

"There's no food here. This is *my* place. From this hill down to the Bay and back again and up to the edge of the park, it's *my* place, all mine. I'm the commander of the company here, and there're only enough supplies for us. What do you want?"

I considered my answer carefully. This man was skating right on the edge.

"I was trapped in the ruins of a house for two weeks. I don't know anything about what's happened in the interim, except that everyone seems to have disappeared."

He looked at me uncertainly. His finger twitched on the rifle.

"Could you possibly lower that gun?" I said.

"I'll be damned!" he said. "It's *you!* It's the man from Novato! I thought you'd been killed."

Then I recognized him.

"You're the National Guardsman from my garden."

"Yeah, I'm Mayer. We're the lucky ones! Imagine seeing you again after all this time! I thought you'd been blasted for sure. Bugger-food, you know." He put down his rifle and held out his hand, and I shook it most gratefully. "I crawled into a drain," he said. "But they didn't kill everyone, not after that first bout. And later, well, later they all went away, and I headed off towards San Quentin, taking a shortcut across the fields." Then he stopped. "You've gone part gray! Imagine that! And your beard, you didn't have a beard before, that's why I didn't recognize you. You look like an old fart now." Suddenly he realized what he'd said. "Sorry," he said, "sorry, I didn't mean to insult you."

I shook my head.

"We've all been through a lot," I said.

There was a squawk in the trees. Mayer jumped up, grabbed his weapon, and stood sentinel until the sound repeated itself.

"Just a damn crow." He gestured with his gun, visibly relaxing. "Lot of 'em about these days. You know, this park's a bit too open for me. Let's get under cover where we can talk some more."

"Have you seen any of the Martians?"

"Nah, they've all gone to the other side of the city somewheres," he said. "They've got a camp over there. At night, the sky lights up with their doin's. It's just like a big city itself, and in the glare you can barely see them movin', shadows outlined among the shadows. In daylight you can't see much of anything, unless you get too close, and you don't want to do that! But here, well, here I haven't seen them for"—he counted on his fingers—"five days, I guess. Then I spotted a couple of the big machines carrying something really large, dunno what it was. And night before last"—he stopped and waved again at the distant horizon—"it was just more lights, you know, but they had something up in the sky, this kind of jet, I guess, but bigger than anything I've seen before. Now that our fighters are gone, I think they're building their own warplanes. Maybe they want to rule the rest of the world, huh?"

At his direction, I dropped to my hands and knees to crawl under the rose bushes, cringing every time one of the thorns grabbed my clothing.

"So they're flying now?"

"Oh yeah," he said, "they fly! You know, it was so large, the thing was so damn friggin' big, that it blotted out the whole sky. Geez, I saw the stars covered over one by one as the machine drifted by. It scared the holy shit out of me, tell you the truth, even more than the sting-ray did, and that was bad enough. Had to change my pants, if you know what I mean."

I allowed as how I did. I settled my bottom into a little dirt hollow and made myself comfortable.

"Then it's all over," I said quietly. "If they can do that, they can do anything. We don't stand a chance."

He nodded in agreement.

"Yeah, that's what I think too. But maybe they'll leave us alone for awhile. 'Sides"—he looked at me furtively—"'Sides, we're already down, so we have no where to go but up!

"We're beat, Smith. They crippled the old U.S. of A., the greatest goddam power in the whole *friggin'* known universe, and they did it without even breakin' a sweat. They walked all over us, and we couldn't do a damn thing about it. And those machines up near San Rafael, hey, that was just an accident! We got lucky! And these're just the first wave. You know they'll keep coming. They've probably already got another fleet on its way. We're beat!"

I just stared into space, unable to counter his argument.

"This ain't a war," said the Guardsman. "It's a slaughter. The Martians are so far above us that we never even had a chance."

Suddenly I recalled that night in Mindon's observatory.

I mentioned this and added: "I only saw a few ships land."

"But you don't know what happened afterwards, you said so yourself. You don't have any idea how many ships they've sent. Look here"—he pointed to a nearby anthill—"These little buggers go right on building their cities, living their lives, waging their wars and revolutions, until man wants them out of his way, and then, *pfft!* They're gone! That's what we are to the Martians—just a bunch of ants. The only thing is—"

He swallowed hard.

"Yes," I said.

"We're the edible *ants!"*

We sat looking at each other in horror.

"What'll they do with us?" I said.

"Well, that's what I've been thinkin' about," he said, shaking his head again, "that's what I've been really thinkin' about, my friend. After what happened at San Rafael—you were there, you saw it—I headed south, and all the time I was thinkin'. I saw what was happenin'. Most people were squealin' like rabbits and pissin' all over themselves. But I'm not a squealer or a pisser. I've seen death and I've seen pain, and death is just death, you know. It's the thinkin' man who always comes through.

"Everyone was runnin' south towards San José. And there was a Martian camp there! Does that make any sense? *Does* it? So I says to myself, 'You know, the food won't last,' and I went back to the city. I headed there because I knew I couldn't outsmart the buggers. Down there"—he waved a hand at the southern horizon—"down there everyone's starvin' and runnin' and killin' and fightin' each other, all over scraps of bread. Not me, friend, not *me!* Mama Mayer didn't raise any stupid kids.

"The ones who had money, well, they all got away. I'm not

goin' to worry about them. The politicians, the businessmen, the big kahunas, they're all gone now. They left us in the lurch. Funny thing is there's plenty of food in the city. Plenty if you know where to look: canned goods in the stores, all kinds of packaged stuff, and lots of wine, beer, even mineral water, if you like that sorta thing. Well, what was I sayin'?"

"You were talking about your plans."

"Oh, yeah, I was tellin' you what I was thinkin'. 'There's these thingies,' I says to myself, 'these aliens, and they need our land and they need *us*, the people, for food. Well, first thing they did, they smashed us all to smithereens—the ships, the guns, the cities, the government, the police, the army, the stores, everything! All that's gone now, and it's not comin' back neither. If we were ants, well, we might pull through. But we're *not* ants. It's too much for any one person to stop.' That's the first thing."

I nodded my head.

"Well, I've thought it all out very carefully, *verrry* carefully. Right now they can catch us whenever they please. A Martian only has to go a few blocks to get a crowd movin'. The other day I saw one down around the 'Barcadero, rootin' through the warehouses, pickin' them to pieces and diggin' in the wreckage, lookin' for people and stuff. But they won't keep doin' that forever. They can't. As soon as they've finished destroyin' our shit—and it's pretty much over already, like I said—they'll start roundin' us up more systematic-like, picking out the fattest and the youngest and storing us in cages and stuff like that. That's what they'll start doin', and it won't take them long, neither. Shit! I've seen it already. You understand?"

"They haven't even begun!" I said.

"Everything that's happened so far is because we didn't have enough sense to keep our heads down. Every time we've tried to fight them, they've beaten us. Every time we've tried to run away, we've given them another quick source of food. There're no safe places anymore. They're still organizin' all their shit. They're still makin' their machine-thingies, puttin' together all that stuff they couldn't bring with them, gettin' things ready for the next batch. That's probably why the ships have stopped coming now, 'cause they have to make way for the new ones. So, instead of us rushin' about like fools, *without* thinkin', we've gotta stop and think for a change. We've gotta decide what to do. That's how I figure it, anyways. See, the cities, civilization, progress—hey, it's all over now. We've been played by someone who's better at the game."

"Yes, but what do we do to entertain ourselves?"

I was pulling his leg and he knew it. The Guardsman looked at me suspiciously.

"Hey, there won't be no more rock concerts for a million, gazilion years, so you can forget all about your game shows and your palm pilots and your IPODs and your computers and your bars. Starbucks ain't serving no raspberry *latté*; and every McDonalds in the world is closed. So if that's what you want, friend, you're just doomed. Hey, forget all your manners, the Martians ain't gonna pay any attention to them when they start suckin' the blood out of your veins. Forget it all, I say."

"You mean—"

"I mean, guys like me are goin' to go on livin', no matter what. I mean, I'm dead set on livin'. I mean, if you want to survive, you're gonna have to change your ways as well. The human race is *not* goin' to let itself be wiped out by a bunch of creepy-crawlies from outer space. And I don't intend to be caught neither, or tamed like some dumb goat, or fattened up like some whiny sheep, or bred like some stupid cow on the hoof. Christ! Save me from all the wishy-washy namby-pambies!

"I'm goin' to do it right under their stupid Martian noses"—I didn't bother pointing out that the Martians had no noses—"I got it all worked out. I've thought it out real careful like. I'm no lightweight, friend. Sure, we men were beat, fair and square. Sure, we don't know enough to fight back, at least right now. So, we've got to learn a lot more before we can send those buggers back to alien hell. But we will! We'll survive, we'll learn, and in the end we'll kick some Martian butt. Yeah. *Yeah!* We'll kill 'em all, every last one!"

I had to admit, this last part sounded pretty good to me.

"I'm right, ain't I?" he said, his eyes shining. "Right is right, and you know it when you hear it. I've thought it all out, haven't I?"

"Indeed you have," I said.

"Well, anyone who wants to escape has to start plannin' things right now. And I'm doing it! Sure, not all of us are going to make it, but some of us will, the smart ones will, see. That's why I was watchin' you, see. I had my doubts at first. You were putzin' around in the open too much. That's not smart: you can't do that any more. I didn't realize it was you, or I'd've said somethin' right away. The kinda people who live in the city, the damn clerks and paper-pushers, they're just no good at all. They're all goin' to die. They haven't got any spirit left in them—no dreams—and a man who hasn't got one or the other—shit! What the hell is he, anyway? Nothin', I tell you. Nothin'!

"These people, they just shuffled off to work everyday by the hundreds and thousands, stuffin' breakfast burritos in their bellies, runnin' to catch their bodacious BARTs and cabs and buses, all because they feared for their little jobbies, slavin' away in businesses they didn't even understand, skulkin' back home to their wifeys and hubbies and kiddies, hidin' indoors at night because 'it's dark out there!' for cryin' out loud! All because that was what was expected of them. Hell was built for rabbits!

"Well, the Martians'll be a godsend to them. Nice comfy cages, some food to fatten them up, a little careful breeding, jeez, not a worry in the world! After a week or so of chasin' 'round the countryside on empty bellies, they'll come right on home to mama. They'll be happy to do it, too. They'll wonder what people did before there were Martians to take care of them. And the bar hoppers, the performers, the singers—I can imagine them too. I can *really* imagine them," he said, with a sort of somber gratification, "singin' for their suppers. They'll be full of sloppy sentiment and religion, not that it'll do them any good. There's lots of things I saw with my own eyes that

I've only begun to understand these last few days. There's lots of folks who'll take things just as they are—fat and stupid people, all of them; and just a few who'll be bothered by the sort of feelin' that it's all gone wrong, that they ought to be doin' somethin' about it.

"Now, whenever things are so bad that a lot of people feel that they ought to be doin' somethin' about it, those who're weak and those who go weak with a lot of complicated thinkin', why they always head for religion, becomin' very pious and superior-like, and submitting 'emselves 'to persecution and the will of the Lord.' You've noticed it yourself, I know"—I thought of Reverend Lesley—"The Martian cages will be full of pretty psalms and hymns and pleas for mercy on high. And there'll be those who'll get down to basics, so to speak, tee hee, just to maintain the species.

"You know, I wouldn't be surprised if the Martians didn't make pets of some of them, train 'em to do tricks and the like, maybe even get sentimental over the 'boy' or 'girl' who grew up and finally had to be sacrificed for the tribe. And some, maybe, they'll train to hunt their own kind."

"No," I said, "Not that. That's impossible!"

"Is it? Why lie to ourselves?" the Guardsman said. "There're plenty of men who'd do it without any problem at all. *Plenty*, my friend!"

I just shook my head.

"Well, if they to try to come after me," he said, "I'll take care of them, yes I will, and I won't be taken alive, neither!"

I sat thinking on what he'd said. His reasoning was basically sound, so far as I could see. In the days before the war no one would have questioned my intellectual superiority—I am, after all, a published author, a Ph.D., a commentator on philosophy and the modern times, someone talked about in fashionable circles. Who was he, really? Just a common soldier. Just a rube. And yet he'd already formulated a philosophy to cope with the emergency.

"What are you going to do?" I asked.

He hesitated.

"Well, it's like this," he said. "We have to invent a way where men can survive, a place that's safe enough to raise our children. The tame ones are already dead: they're big, beautiful, rich, stupid—and dead! None of that means shit now. Problem is, those of us who're left could turn savage. So, we need to move underground where they can't find us. I've been thinkin' for weeks about the sewers. Of course, there're those who'll think that's a fate worse than death, so to speak, but right beneath our feet are hundreds and hundreds of miles of drainpipes, and just a few days' rain will wash Old 'Frisco clean, leavin' them sweet and empty and ready for use. The main sewers are big enough for all of us. Then there're the cellars, the vaults, even the BART tunnels. See? All we need are people like us: able-bodied, clean-minded, right-thinkin', hard-hittin' men. We're not going to include just anyone who drifts through the door, so to speak.

"Those who're chosen—and those who choose to remain—will have to follow orders. There's gotta be a structure if we're goin' to survive. I'll be one of the officers, of course. We also need able-bodied, clean-minded, good-lookin' women for mothers and teachers and wives. No silly sluts and 'socies' here. Life is becoming real again, and the useless ones will have to go, my friend, yes they will. They're all goin' to die anyways, don't you see? So they ought to be willin' to die for the rest of us. It's a sort of disloyalty, after all, to not help the human race survive. And they can't really be happy in this kind of world. Dyin's not so hard; anyone can do it. It's the whiners that make it look bad.

"We'll gather together in the underground places, the hidden places. Our headquarters will be 'Frisco. If we keep our eyes and ears open, we might even be able to come out in the open when the Martians are busy. Play baseball, maybe. That's how we'll save the human race. But savin' the race is nothing in itself. As I said, we have to save our knowledge and somehow add to it if we're going to live. That's where men like you come in. There're books that need to be preserved. We have to establish safe spots way, way down deep, and get all the good books moved there—not the novels or the poetry, but the how-to stuff, the technology books, the science books. That's where you come in, friend. You can help us. We have to go to the Public Library, even to Stanford and Berkeley, and pick out the good things, the ones we really need. We gotta keep it up, we gotta learn more. We gotta watch the Martians and their machines and learn from them.

"Some of us will be trained as spies. Hell, when it's all workin', maybe even *I'll* volunteer. And the thing is, we have to leave the Martians alone. We don't challenge them, we don't steal from them, we don't let them see us. If we get in their way, they'll clean us all out. We gotta show them we mean no harm. Yeah, yeah, I know, that's hard. But they're intelligent, and they won't hunt us down if they have everythin' they want, if they think we're just harmless rats."

The Guardsman paused and laid a brown-burnt hand on my arm, looking into my eyes.

"You know, we might be able to cheat a bit. Think about this: four or five of their fightin'-machines suddenly start off, sting-rays blazing right and left, and not a Martian among 'em. Not a Martian *in* them, either, but men, red-blooded men who've learned how to operate the things. Fancy drivin' one of those, firing its stinger everywhere! *Wow!* It wouldn't matter if you were smashed to smithereens yourself. I reckon the Martians'd open their big beautiful baby blues at that!"—Martian eyes were invariably black—"Can't you just see 'em? Can't you just see 'em scurryin' and hurryin' and puffin' and blowin' and hootin' to themselves? 'Something must be out of whack,' they'd yell. 'Somethin's gone screwy again!' And swish, swish, bang, bang, rattle, crash, boom, just as they're tryin' to get things going again, here comes the sting-ray mowin' 'em all down. Yeah, I can see it as clearly as night turns into day."

For awhile the imagination of the man, and the sense of certainty and courage he conveyed, completely dominated my reason. I believed in both his forecast of human destiny and in the practicality of his scheme; and anyone who thinks me overly susceptible or startlingly foolish should put himself in my position, crouching fearfully in the rose bushes and listening to this torrent of words, all the while being distracted by fear over our situation.

We talked like this through the early morning hours, and later crept out of the park and hurried as quickly as we could to the house on Nob Hill where he'd made his lair, not far from the hotel I'd stayed in the previous night. His hidey-hole was actually located in the basement of the place, and when I saw the work he'd supposedly expended—it was just a pit ten feet deep, through which he intended to access the main sewer—I had my first inkling of the gulf between his dreams and his abilities. I could have dug the damned thing myself in a day.

But I still believed in him enough to work with him all that morning until noon. We had a shovel and a garden rake, and we stashed the dirt we removed upstairs by the kitchen stove. Then we broke for lunch, washing down a can of vegetable soup with a bottle of Château Saint-Bérnardine Pinot Noir '77 filched from a neighbor's wine rack. As we resumed our work, I turned his project over again in my mind, and presently a few doubts began to rise; but I continued to labor all that morning, just because it felt good to have something to do. After an hour I began to speculate on the distance one had to go before the sewer was reached, and the possibility of missing it altogether. I suddenly wondered why we should have to dig this tunnel at all when we could have just opened one of the manholes in the street. Before I could pose the question, though, the Guardsman stopped working.

"We're doin' pretty well here," he noted, putting down his spade. "But I'm gettin' tired, so let's take a look-see upstairs."

I wanted to continue, so he picked up his shovel again, and then I had another thought.

"Where's the rest of your company?" I asked.

"Uh, uh, well, they're all, uh, out on patrol, yeah, they're out patrollin'. I'm expectin' one of them to report back before nightfall. Private Lambe. He should be here soon."

"Why were you up in the park, instead of working here?"

"Well, see, I was, uh, I just needed the air, 'cause it gets real hot and stuffy down in the basement, particularly when you've been workin' at it a long time. I was on my way back when I spotted you."

"But why isn't the hole any bigger?"

"Well, uh, you can't work all the time," he said—and then I saw him for what he was. He hesitated again, then put his spade aside. "You know, we really ought to check the roof," he said, "because if any of those damn machines are around, they might hear us workin' and catch us unawares."

I no longer bothered to object. So we went upstairs and stood on a ladder that loomed out of a trap door on the roof. No aliens were visible anywhere. We ventured out onto the tiles, and slipped down under the shelter of the chimney.

A tree obscured part of Nob Hill, but we could still see the Bay spread out below us, and on the shore a bubbly mass of red weed poking up its hair. Some of the red creeper had swarmed up the trees a few blocks away; the branches of the earthly growth were dying or dead, with brown, shriveled leaves poking out from amidst the purple flower clusters (I realized after the fact that some of the trees may have already dropped their leaves for the winter). Neither of the alien plants had gained much of a foothold on the hill. In the few places where there were open areas, I could see the usual complement of garden shrubs rising out of private patios and plots, green and brilliant in the evening light. In the distance smoke was rising; a blue haze hid the northern hills towards Marin County.

Mayer began telling me about the folks still living in the city.

"One night last week," he said, "some fools got the lights workin' again with a generator, and there was one block of Market Street all lit up, crowded with tattooed, ragged dopers and drunks, men and women dancin' and shoutin' till dawn. A guy who was there told me all about it. When the sun came up, they suddenly saw a fightin'-machine standin' over them. Christ knows how long it'd been there. Must've given them a real turn. The buggers came down the road, and picked up a hundred or more people who were too stoned or pissed to run away. Hope they made the Marshies sick."

Then he started back on his ideas again. He spoke so eloquently about the possibility of capturing a fighting-machine that I half-believed him. But I was beginning to understand something about the man. The emphasis that he placed on doing nothing defined his true spirit. I noted that there was now no question of him *personally* capturing and directing the great and glorious machinery that would save all mankind, oh no. He would just organize the effort. Sometimes he called himself "Captain" and once "Colonel." He'd been just a Private in the National Guard, but in his own mind, he'd advanced in rank through the deaths of his comrades-in-arms.

After a bit we retired to the basement again. Neither of us was disposed to resuming work, so when he suggested dinner, I readily agreed. He suddenly became very voluble, and when we'd feasted on some sardines and canned crab and asparagus, he fetched two bottles of excellent whiskey and a couple of cigars. I declined the latter, but shared the drinks, while his optimism continued to glow with the same fierce fire that highlighted the tip of his smoke whenever he puffed on it. A self-satisfied grin was etched in crimson on his face. He now regarded my appearance as a godsend.

"You know, I've got some pot down in the cellar," he said.

"'Candy's dandy, but liquor's quicker'."

"Well, I'm in charge today, so weed it is! We've a lot of work before us, my friend! So let's rest our feet and gather the roses while we may."

"Ye rosebuds," I said, making a circular motion with my hands.

"What?"

After he "liberated" his stash and lit up a hand-rolled toke, he pulled out a tarot deck and insisted on trying the cards. He taught me tarot poker, and after dividing San Francisco between us, I taking the northern side and he the south, we played for control of the neighborhoods, money no longer having any value here. I know this sounds foolish, but I found the game and the several others that we played quite refreshing. Perhaps they helped divert my mind from the trauma I'd experienced during the preceding month.

So, with our species dancing on the edge of extinction, and with no clear idea of what to do about it, we sat there all evening pursuing the chance shuffle of these painted pasteboards, playing the "joker" with absolutely unmitigated delight. Afterwards he showed me the meaning of the cards, and then I beat him three times in a row at chess. When darkness fell, we took the risk of lighting a candle.

Then we ate again, an unexpected luxury, dividing up a canned turkey. Mayer lit his second cigar. He was no longer the energetic utopian whom I'd encountered that morning. He was still optimistic, of course, but this was a more thoughtful optimism generated by a full stomach. I remember that he toasted my health in a gesture that moved me to tears. I realized then how much I'd missed ordinary human company. I went upstairs to look at the lights he'd mentioned earlier, the lights that blazed out so greenly in the west along the edge of Golden Gate Park.

I stared across the rolling hills of San Francisco, looking in vain for any sign of the Martians. The northern part of the city was already shrouded in ebon; the fires on the other side of the Bay glowed red, and now and then an orange-tinged tongue of flame flashed up into the deep, blue-black night. The rest of the city was dark. Then I perceived a strange, flickering light, a pale, violet-purple will-o'-the-wisp. For a time I couldn't imagine what it might be, before realizing that it had to be the red weed. My long dormant sense of wonder, my realization of the proportion of things, stirred once again. I glanced up at Mars itself, hanging red and ugly and mean in the night sky, glowing in the west, and then gazed long and earnestly into the darkness.

I remained there a very long time, looking out upon that eerie vista, wondering at the changes that I'd experienced. As I relived my recent days, suddenly I felt nauseated. I flung the dregs of my drink off the roof, and would have crashed the glass too if I hadn't been afraid of making a noise. I realized the utter folly of believing the Guardsman's nonsense. I'd been a traitor to my wife and to my own kind, and I was filled with remorse and despair. I resolved to leave this undisciplined dreamer of great things to his drink and gluttony, and to head towards downtown San Francisco. There, it seemed to me, I had the best chance of learning what the Martians and my fellow men were doing.

I was still standing on the roof when the moon began to rise, blinking its lone sullen eye at me, judging me for the fool that I'd become—and the fool that I still remain.

CHAPTER TWENTY-EIGHT
DEAD-FRANCISCO

Make no mistake, stranger:
San Francisco is West as all hell.
—Bernard De Voto

ALEX SMITH, 23 BI-JANUARY, MARS YEAR I
SAN FRANCISCO, CALIFORNIA, PLANET EARTH

I left the Guardsman at first light, despite his protestations, saying that I still had important things to do. The red weed now flourished everywhere, in the city drains and the sewers and the gardens and even in the streets, choking out the other vegetation wherever it spawned; but its fronds were already showing patches of gray-white, a sign of the disease that eventually destroyed most of it without any aid from mankind.

Near a BART station I found a man lying by the side of the street. He was covered with a dusting of the Black Death ash. He still lived, but was helplessly, hopelessly drunk. I could get nothing out of him but curses and inarticulate grunts. I would have helped him, but he didn't want my help. He didn't want anyone's help. He just wanted to die.

The inert dust also enshrouded Market Street from the Embarcadero to the Financial District. The city streets in downtown San Francisco were horribly still, particularly in contrast with what I remembered of them. I found some dinner rolls sealed in bags in a small bakery—sour, hard, and moldy, but still passable. As I walked through the downtown the roads became clearer, and then I passed a block of offices that were still smoldering. Maybe one of the refugees had overturned a candle or let a fire get out of control. The crackling sound was almost a relief against the utter silence of "Dead-Francisco." It was as if someone had draped the entire city in funereal shrouds.

The rust of the Black Death was everywhere, covering wrecked and abandoned automobiles, trolley and cable cars, trucks and vans, and hundreds of human bodies—corpses lying every which way in grotesque positions, all in various stages of decomposition. I finally learned to ignore the pervasive odor of death—I had to. I saw a dozen corpses strewn up a one-block side street; they'd obviously been dead for many days. I paid them no more attention than the buildings themselves. They made no difference anymore. The powder had softened their outlines, but it didn't keep off the flies. One or two of the bodies had been worked over by dogs, and several others had been picked clean by the all-pervasive murders of crows.

Where the dust was absent, it almost seemed as if the city had been closed for some public holiday, perhaps the Fourth of July or the Gay Pride Parade. Many of the stores had been locked before being abandoned. The houses and apartments and condominiums were also shut tight, and most places seemed utterly deserted, at least by any *living* people. If survivors were lurking there—and surely there *must* have been some—they were hiding themselves very well indeed. I realized then how much the underlying rumble of civilization means to us. The background noise is part of our modern world. Now it was gone, and the ruins of Dead-Francisco had become silent in tribute to those who'd fashioned them.

Scavengers had systematically gutted out the retailers, usually focusing on the food shops, delis, cafés, and liquor stores. I saw that a jeweler's glass front window had been broken into, but either the thief had been disturbed in the robbery or had thought better of his act, because a number of gold chains and a Rolex were scattered about on the pavement. I didn't bother with them:

they meant nothing to me in the new reality. Time and gold were no longer factors in my philosophy.

Further on I saw a tattered young woman slumped in a heap on a doorstep, one hand dangling idly over her knee, the wrist gashed open; it had bled a rusty brown stain down her rusty brown dress. A smashed crack pipe still blazed a trail of deceit across the pavement, pointing out the folly of her ways. She might have been asleep, but for the flies and ants and beetles already at work upon her flesh. I didn't bother with her either.

The further I penetrated into San Francisco, the worse the stillness became; it was not so much the emptiness of death and destruction that bothered me as the hush of suspense or expectation. At any time, now or in the near future, the destruction that had already singed and scarred and seared this great metropolis might fall again among these quaint old offices and houses and shops, leaving them naught but smoking ruins. This was a city condemned and derelict. This was Dead-Francisco in all its empty, ugly reality.

I lived here now.

Near the Civic Center the streets were miraculously clear again, both of dead bodies and of the Black Death. It was here that I heard the weird howling tune of the Martians. I became aware of it almost imperceptibly as I strolled through the streets, this sad, sobbing song of two long notes with a half-catch in the middle:

"Uol-lah, uol-lah, ool-lah, ooool-laaah-ha."

This mournful dirge repeated itself over and over again, as if God Himself was crying terrible tears over the ash heap of mankind. When I passed the streets that ran towards the west, it blared again, but the intervening houses and buildings seemed to deaden the sound, as it faded in and out, in and out. I continued down Market Street to the U.S. Mint, wondering why no one'd bothered to force open its doors. Food was a more valuable currency in Dead-Francisco.

"Ool-lah, ool-lah, ool-lah, ool-lah."

I stared southwest towards Twin Peaks, wondering at the

strange, remote wailing of the aliens, the expression of a million, million dead voices coming back to life again, the vocalization of thousands of vacant, staring window-holes moaning their collective distress at the overturning of the status quo. This seemed right to me somehow, this memorial dirge; it seemed a proper ending to it all.

"*Ool-lah, ool-lah, ool-lah, ool-lah.*"

The wailing of that superhuman double-aught note rose in great waves of sound that swept down and around the broad, sunlit streets of the city, echoing strangely between the tall buildings on each side, reverberating back and forth in unusual patterns. I turned north again, marveling at man's grand funeral service, striding towards the iron gates of the university. I had half a mind to break into the library there and find my way to the summit of the tower, in order to peer across Golden Gate Park.

But I decided to remain on ground level, where I could hide myself quickly if necessary, and so continued gradually easing west. All of the large buildings to either side were empty and still; the sound of my footsteps provided an eerie point-coun-terpoint to the mournful moaning emanating from the distance.

Near the Park I saw a strange sight: a bus had overturned, and the skeleton of a man was hanging halfway out its door, his bones picked clean. I puzzled over this weird, surrealistic architecture, and then crossed to the other side of the street. The noise waxed louder and louder as I gradually moved west, although I could see nothing above the housetops save for a haze of smoke drifting slowly in the breeze.

"*Ool-lah, ool-lah, ool-lah, ool-lah.*"

The voice cried out once again, blasting out its lazy lament from the area surrounding the Park. The desolate cry worked its way deep into my soul, impressing it with melancholy. The mood that had sustained me to this point had now passed. The incessant wailing took possession of my soul. I found that I was becoming intensely weary of everything, of the struggle and the battle and the clash of civilizations. I was hungry and thirsty again. My long procession seemed a futile gesture of defiance.

It was already past noon. Why was I wandering alone in this city of the dead? Why was I walking by myself when all of Dead-Francisco was lying in state in its black shroud, while the mourners were conducting the service for the dearly departed? I felt completely isolated. I remembered old friends whom I'd forgotten for years. I thought of little things, of food in the supermarkets, of fine wines in liquor stores. I only knew of two humans who shared this immense city of the dead. I suddenly wished they were there beside me.

Further down the road I spied more dead bodies. An evil smell percolated from the sewers and the homes. I'd grown very thirsty from my long walk. I managed to break a restaurant window and find something to eat and drink. The latter was better than the former. I was so very weary after lunch, just tired to death in body and soul, that I located a couch in a back room somewhere, where I laid down and slept the sleep of the dead. Even the sofa was black.

I awoke to that distant, dismal howling ringing in my ears again.

"Ool-lah, ool-lah, ool-lah, ool-lah."

'Twas now brillig, and after I'd rousted out some cookies and cheese in the bar—the meat in the fridge was covered with green slime—I wandered through the silent residential districts. Far away I saw the hood of the Martian machine from which this howling apparently emanated; it was poking just over the trees, outlined against the sunset. I wasn't at all afraid. Indeed, I was long past the point of fearing anything. Encountering the aliens now just seemed to me the "right" thing to do, as if I were destined for one final meeting with the invaders before finding my own end and my own peace. I watched the silent sentinel for quite some time, but it didn't move. It just stood there and cried its cry of despair, for no reason that I could discern.

I tried to formulate a plan of action, but that perpetual refrain of *"Ool-lah, ool-lah, ool-lah, ool-lah"* was getting on my nerves. Perhaps I was just too tired to think clearly anymore. Certainly

I was curious about the monotonous wailing. I turned into the park, creeping alongside the shelter of a nearby terrace. Again I could see the stationary, howling Martian in the distance, growing ever closer as I worked my way towards it.

Suddenly I spied a pack of dogs, the leader dangling a piece of raw, reddish meat from his jaws, followed madly by a dozen starving mongrels hot in pursuit. It bolted away from me, as if fearing some competitor for this luscious tidbit. As the yelping died away, the wailing sound reasserted itself.

I came upon the wreckage of the handling-machine not far from the Martian pit. At first I thought one of the buildings had fallen across the road. It was only when I clambered over the ruins of the structure that I realized that it was intertwined with the workings of an alien handler, which was lying with its tentacles bent and smashed and twisted among the debris that it had made. The front section of the thing was completely smashed in. It looked to me as if it had driven itself right into the side of the structure, and then been crushed when the building tumbled down around it. The driver in the cab must have lost control, but I couldn't get close enough to examine the damage personally. All I could see were the "earthly" remains of the creature itself: the tattered and gnawed gristle of the alien, and a seat smeared with blood or some other fluid.

What was going on here?

I pushed forward. Through a gap in the trees I spied a second Martian strider, standing as straight as the first somewhere over near the Zoo; it was as still and silent as a guardian of Hell. Patches of the red weed filled a nearby drainage ditch, making a spongy mass of dark-red vegetation splotched all over with sickly white flecks, as if it had been sprayed with acid. It looked like it was dying. Suddenly I glanced up: a giraffe was strolling by, red weed dangling from its lips. Someone must have released the animals from their cages.

As I crossed a small bridge, I again heard the wail—*"Ool-lah, ool-lah, ool-lah, ool-..."*—but it cut off suddenly in mid-syllable, as if someone had pulled the plug on a stadium sound system. The abrupt silence rolled over me like a thunderclap.

The nearby trees stood faint and tall and dim in the twilight, growing dark as the sun settled well below the horizon. All about me the red weed clambered among the ruins, writhing to reach the remains of that dim light. Night, the mother of fear and mystery, was rapidly approaching, just as it had drawn its cloak over all mankind.

But while that mournful voice had interrupted the solitude, the desolation had somehow seemed more endurable: Dead-Francisco had been alive to me again, even if that life was utterly alien; and the sense of life surging around me had bolstered my spirits. This abrupt change, this sudden absence of sound, this passing away of something ineffable—I didn't know what—left me with a stillness in my soul that was almost palpable. There was nothing remaining but the eerie quiet, the gaunt, gray, ghoulish quiet that just wouldn't go away.

I wanted to die.

Dead-Francisco gazed upon me with its empty, spectral eyes. The windows in the white houses of the city were like the sockets of bleached, barren skulls. Around me I imagined a thousand voiceless, noiseless enemies moving ever closer, surrounding my form. My paranoia seized me by the throat, exacerbating my horror of my own temerity. The Park became as pitch black as if it were tarred, and I saw a contorted shape lying prone across the pathway. I couldn't bring myself to go on. I turned around and ran headlong from the unendurable stillness. I hid from the night and the silence until long after midnight, crouching down in a nearby taxi stand, I don't know where.

Just before dawn my courage returned, and while the stars were still shining I crept back once again to Golden Gate Park. I missed my way somehow among the city's crazy-quilt streets, but presently saw the place revealed again in the half-light of the early dawn, down at the end of a long, long avenue. I knew then just where I was. On the right, reaching towards the fading stars, was a third Martian fighting-machine, erect and motionless and still, just like all the others.

An insane resolve suddenly possessed me. I would die here and now! I would just die and end it all. I would save myself the trouble even of killing myself. So I marched recklessly towards this giant behemoth, but as I drew nearer and nearer and the light became clearer, I saw that a flock of black birds was circling around the top of the machine, clustering on its hood. Suddenly my heart gave a little jump, and I began running down the road.

I hurried through the red weed, wading across a small stream of water that was oozing from a broken main towards the sea, and emerged into the open parkland just before sunrise. Great mounds of dirt had been heaped about the Martian pit, making a kind of fort. It was the last and greatest of the alien camps. A thin line of smoke rose into the sky. Against the skyline I could observe the outline of a dog, prancing and jumping and tugging at something. I felt no fear, only a wild, trembling exultation as I pelted up the hill towards the motionless monster. The cab was draped with dangling, stringy shreds of dull, red-brown flesh, which the hungry crows were fighting over.

It took just a moment to scramble up the rampart and stand on its crest. The interior of the structure was suddenly revealed to me. Gigantic machines, larger than any I'd ever seen before, were arrayed here in row after row amidst huge mounds of raw materials and strange, almost nest-like shelters. And scattered about them, some hanging from their war-machines, some in the now rigid handling-robots, some stark and silent and laid out in a formal line, I saw the Martians—all of them!—dead and damned and decaying.

They'd been murdered, I was later told, by a hidden killer for which they'd been completely unprepared: the earthly bacteria that had overwhelmed their defenseless internal systems. In essence, they were destroyed by their own feedings, slain as the red weed was being slain—killed, after man's efforts had failed to have any effect at all, by the humblest of things on this Earth.

We should have known. If our terror hadn't so blinded us, we *would* have known. Disease has taken its toll on mankind since the very beginning of our race, indeed, has taken its toll of all of our animal ancestors since life itself first began. But disease had apparently long since been eradicated on Mars, so long ago, in fact, that the invaders had completely forgotten the lessons of the past. As soon as the Martians began drinking our earthly water and feeding on earthly blood, our microscopic allies began their work of undermining the alien bodies. The invaders were irrevocably doomed, dying and rotting from within even as they went busily about destroying civilization.

It was inevitable. Man had bought his birthright upon this Earth through billions of deaths, and those who'd survived the onslaught of the unseen were fortified against future attacks. Even if the Martians had been ten times greater than they were, they would have perished anyway.

I saw the scattered bodies of at least fifty of the aliens, abruptly overtaken by a death that must have seemed as incomprehensible to them as any to us. Even I failed to understand the why and where of it. All I knew was that these "things" that had been so horribly alive a few days ago, so terribly destructive to mankind, were now all dead. For a moment I almost believed that the destruction of Sennacherib had been repeated, that God Himself had sent the Angel of Death to slay our enemies in the night.

I stood staring down upon that pestilent pit, and my heart suddenly brightened, even as the rising sun reignited the new world with bright, burning fire. The excavation was still layered within its darknesses; the mighty engines, so great and wonderful in their power and potency, so unearthly in their tortuous forms. They rose weirdly and vaguely and strangely out of the shadows towards the light—but ultimately had been overthrown by it. A pack of dogs was already fighting for the right to the bodies laid out in the depths of that awful camp.

Across the structure on its farther side, flat and vast and strange, was propped the great flying-machine with which the Martians had been experimenting when Death had suddenly announced his unmistakable presence. The sound of cawing caused me to look upwards at the huge strider that would fight no more, one of the tallest of the Martian fighting-machines that I had yet encountered. The tattered red shreds of flesh now dripped down to enrich the soil of Golden Gate Park.

Death creates life; life creates death.

The two other Martian machines that I'd observed earlier stood a little further off, just where doom had overtaken them. The one whose howl had been stopped in mid-blast might have been the final alien to perish upon the Earth; its voice had rung out until its energy was exhausted, pleading with its companions for an assistance that never came, in an awful parody of my own experiences of this past month. The machines just glittered now in the bright sunlight, harmless tripod towers of shining metal, seared and cleansed by the rays of the rising sun.

I turned around. The great Mother of Cities, the glorious metropolis of San Francisco, was like a phoenix destined to rise again from its ashes. Those who've only seen the town veiled in its somber robes of smoke can scarcely imagine the naked clarity and beauty of that silent wilderness of houses and offices and places of worship. My heart was suddenly caught up in its beauty.

Eastward, the sun blazed dazzlingly in the clear azure sky, and here and there some facet in the great wilderness of roofs caught the light and reflected it back at me with a white, pure, clean intensity.

As I gazed upon this wide expanse of buildings, silent and abandoned, I thought of the hopes and efforts, the hosts of lives that had gone into building this human reef, and the swift and terrible destruction that had been visited upon it. I realized then that the shadows had finally been rolled back, that man might again live in these streets. This dear, vast, dead city of mine was once more a living and powerful thing. I felt inside me a wave of emotion that nearly overwhelmed my soul. A tear rolled down one cheek.

Our long torment was over. The healing could now begin. The survivors of the people scattered over the countryside— leaderless, lawless, foodless, like sheep without a shepherd—

the thousands who'd fled by sea, would soon begin to return. The pulse of life, growing stronger and stronger, would beat again in the empty streets and pour across the vacant squares. The hand of the destroyer was finally stayed. The gaunt wrecks, the blackened skeletons of the houses that stared so dismally at the sunlit grass of the Park, would presently be echoing with the jackhammers of contractors and the tapping of carpenters. I extended my right hand towards the sky and thanked God for our deliverance. In a year, I thought, in just a year, it would all be remade anew.

Suddenly I was overwhelmed with the prospect of my old life restored again, something that I'd once thought was lost forever.

Was it really possible?

Could Becky still be alive?

CHAPTER TWENTY-NINE
THE WRECK OF MANKIND

In this wild, solitary girl I had at length discovered the mysterious warbler that so often followed me in the wood.

—W. H. Hudson

ALEX SMITH, 24 BI-JANUARY-11 BI-FEBRUARY, MARS YEAR I
SAN FRANCISCO, CALIFORNIA, PLANET EARTH

I come now to the strangest part of my story. I remember, clearly and coldly and vividly, all that I did on that day until the time that I stood weeping upon the summit of the Martian pit in Golden Gate Park. After that, though, I blanked out.

Of the next few days I can recall nothing. I've since learned that I was not the first person to stumble upon the Martians' destruction; several other wanderers had already discovered the deaths the previous night. One man—the very first—had gone back downtown at about the same time I'd been sheltering in the taxi stand, and had managed to signal someone through a satellite link. The news had flashed around the world on CNN and the other media. San Francisco and Los Angeles and their suburbs had been the most severely affected areas; the rest of the country, the rest of world, had gone on pretty much as usual—well, except for the knowledge that we were no longer alone in the universe.

When I regained my senses, refugees were already beginning to return to San Francisco by bus and train and automobile. Supplies were being brought from Sacramento by the National Guard. Within days life began flourishing once again in the silent streets of the city. The people found themselves overjoyed, even elated, at the sudden end of the war, despite the destruction that was everywhere visible. Men would suddenly embrace complete strangers, hugging them on public streets, just grateful to be alive.

The European Community sent ships to the major eastern and Gulf ports of the United States, while China and Japan and Australia dispatched supplies to Portland and Seattle and San Diego on the West Coast, which were serving as the major distribution centers until services could be restored to San Francisco Bay in the north and San Pedro in the south.

But I knew nothing of this until long after the fact. I drifted in and out of a world of my own. When I finally awoke, dazed and disoriented, I found myself surrounded by kindly people, a couple who'd found me wandering and raving in the streets of the city, somewhere near the upper reaches of Market. They said that I was singing some demented doggerel about "The Last Man Alive Can Scarcely Survive!" These people sheltered and bathed and fed me—and protected me from myself. They learned something of my story during the days of my recovery, when I was still rambling in my mind and uttering utter nonsense.

When I was restored again to some semblance of normalcy, they gently broke the news that the town of Sonoma had been destroyed during the invasion, together with most of its population. A strider had swept the place out of existence without any apparent provocation, as a boy might step on an anthill.

I was still a very lonely man, but they were gentle to me in my extremity. I was also sad, tremendously sad and morose, and still they nurtured me. I remained with them for four days after my recovery. During that time I felt a vague, growing need to revisit whatever remained of my previous life, an existence that now seemed so happy and untroubled in the warmth of my memories. They tried to keep me from leaving. They did all that they could to divert me. But at last I could resist the temptation no longer, and, promising faithfully to return, I left my new-found friends with tears and gratitude and thanks, and went out again into the streets that had lately been so dark and strange and empty to me.

Already the city was busy with people; in places even a few stores were open again, and I saw a drinking fountain spurting fresh running water. The remnants of the red weed were being systematically rooted out and cleared away.

I remember how mockingly bright the day seemed before I began my melancholy pilgrimage to my long-lost house in Novato, how busy the streets were, how vivid life seemed in New-Francisco. So many people, so many things to do: it seemed incredible now that any great number of them could have been killed. But then I noticed how yellow the people were, how gaunt, how shaggy their hair, how large and bright their eyes, how every other man still sported a set of dusty, dirty rags. Their faces seemed to hold one of two expressions: an exulta-tion at the work to be done, or a grim resolution to persevere in the face of adversity.

Otherwise, San Francisco seemed almost like a city of tramps. Charities were distributing free sacks of food arriving from other parts of the country. Haggard police (they wore white stars on their breasts to distinguish them from everyone else) stood at the corners of every street to maintain order (the power was still out). I saw little evidence of the Martian occupation until I reached the North Beach area, where I noticed fronds of the red weed still scaling the walls of a garden.

That was where I saw the single sheet of paper tacked to a power pole, the first issue of the *Chronicle* to be published since the fall of the city. It was the most primitive thing I've ever seen, obviously run off a laser printer that someone had managed to get working again. There were even a couple of ads at the bottom of the page, one for "clean water" and "good food," and the other from Madame Stavroula, who had miraculously risen from the dead and was back telling fortunes again—this time for a can of beans or some lentil soup!

That told me as much as anything about the spirit of the returnees: they now had a future to look forward to! But I learned nothing new about the Martian invasion from the paper, except that already, just a short time after the last of the aliens had perished, an examination of the alien machines was already yielding results in our laboratories. No details were forthcoming, however, and few have actually been published since.

Regular service on BART and flights to and from the San Francisco International Airport gradually resumed, albeit on a limited basis. Service to Oakland was promised within the week, once a makeshift bridge had been constructed by the Navy. A few buses were up and running free of charge. I took one north, wanting to see my home again and to find some trace of my wife. I wasn't in any mood for casual conversation, so I just got a seat to myself, and sat there with folded arms, looking out at the sunlit devastation flowing past the windows. The vehicle jolted over potholes that had been temporarily filled in; on either side of the road the houses were frequently just blackened ruins.

One lane of the Golden Gate Bridge had been cleared, with police directing traffic back and forth. No tolls were being collected. Part of Highway 101 was blocked just the other side of Fort Baker, however, so we had to detour over several rough side routes. Gangs of volunteer laborers were trying to remove the worst of the wreckage and restore basic travel. Many of the highways would obviously require repaving.

Everywhere the countryside seemed unfamiliar to me. San Rafael in particular had suffered grievously. The old mission there was completely demolished, and would have to be rebuilt from scratch. The little streams that we crossed were heaped with masses of red weed that had mottled leaves like pickled cabbage. The woods around here were too dry, however (those that still survived), to support the red climber.

Beyond the city, but within sight of the highway, I saw a

mound of earth that signaled where one of the great spaceships had initially landed. A number of people were standing around the open pit, and some National Guard troops were busy doing something (I couldn't see what) in the very center. Over the workings flew the Star Spangled Banner, flapping cheerfully in the morning breeze. The adjoining gardens were everywhere crimson with the weed, a wide expanse of livid color cut with purple shadows, very painful to the eye in the bright sunshine. My gaze shrank with relief from the scorched grays and sullen reds of the foreground to the ochre-brown softness of the northern hills.

The portion of the Redwood Highway that led north to Novato was still under repair, but I wanted to go to Sonoma anyway to check on Becky. I hitched a ride in the back of a pickup truck. The town of Sonoma was pretty much gone, as if a tornado had swept through its center, wiping out the businesses and most of the housing, including Anita's place. All that remained there was a concrete slab, a chimney, a driveway, and a bright green lawn.

One of the surviving neighbors pointed me north, so I walked a ways up Highway 12 before another kind soul gave me a lift to Glen Ellen. After much searching I located Berke Fernández at his Star Rover Lodge (named for a Jack London novel), and he told me that Becky and her relatives had been evacuated weeks earlier to Rohnert Park. He knew nothing of them after that. Somehow he and his family and motel had come through the war unscathed.

I went to Rohnert Park, but no one there could tell me anything except that refugees had been sent off every which way during the war, depending on the deployment of the fighting-machines, and that they had no records of who'd passed through the area or where they'd gone.

So eventually, after a week's searching with nothing to show for my efforts, I finally went back home.

I stopped by the pit where the first Martian machine had landed, and remembered Private Mayer, the National

Guardsman. The wrecks of the military vehicles still littered the landscape. I stood there for the longest time. I don't really know why. I just did.

Then I walked through the burned skeletons of the trees, neck-high at times in the red weed, only to find that Novato Boulevard was already being restored. I wandered around town for awhile, delaying the inevitable. I wanted to go home—but I didn't. I was afraid of what I might find—or what I wouldn't find! Finally I quit debating with myself, and turned up Olivet. A man was standing out in front of my house. He called me by name as I approached. I'd almost forgotten who I was in the past month; it seemed strange hearing my name spoken again by a former acquaintance.

"Alex," he yelled. "Alex Smith!"

Then I recognized Mindon, my dear old friend Min! Mindon lived! One of my friends had survived the war!

I rushed forward and embraced him.

"Man," he said, "man, I thought you were dead for sure. No one knew what'd happened to you."

"Where'd you go?" I managed to gasp out.

"They took us to Ukiah," he said. "The Martians never got that far. I worked as a civilian volunteer, trying to get supplies to the border areas. Hot damn, it's good to see you again."

"You too. Have you heard anything about Becky?"

He looked down. "Sorry, man. So many people are missing now, and there's just no news about any of them. She could be anywhere."

"Yeah," I said.

I looked over at my house. It seemed empty and forlorn. There wasn't any life left to it. I'd already known that, of course. The door was open, swinging in the light breeze.

"I was trying to clean the place up for you," he said, "just in case, you know. I kept hoping, even as the weeks went by. I guess it worked!"

The door slammed shut once again, jolting me out of my lethargy. Time to take stock, I thought. The curtains of my office fluttered in and out of the window from which the Guardsman and I had watched the coming of the dawn more than a month earlier. No one had closed it since. The bushes were just as I'd left them so many weeks earlier, and part of the garden was still trampled into the ground. Many of the plants had suffered from lack of water.

I stumbled into the downstairs hall, but the house felt completely bereft of spirit. The stairway carpet was discolored where I'd crouched on the night of the invasion. I could still see our muddy footsteps going up the stairs.

I followed the traces to my study. On my desk, with the meteorite paperweight still holding it down, was the sheet of paper that I'd left half-finished on the afternoon that the skies had opened wide. I reread my priceless prose with some amusement. This was intended to be a book on the probable evolution of *Man's Moral Ideas* with the development of civilization, *ad nauseam*, *ad nauseam*, all of which seemed perfect nonsense to me now; the last sentence was supposed to be the opening of a prophecy:

"In about two hundred years," I'd written, "we might expect—"

You betcha! I still remembered my inability to finish that sentence, a little more than a lifetime ago, and how I'd taken a break to read my newspaper and to get a cup of coffee to recast my stale thoughts. I'd gone into the garden, and there I'd heard the story of "The Men from Mars."

I went downstairs into the dining room. The spoiled food had been tossed, thanks to Mindon's efforts, as had the empty beer bottles. I was desolate. I'd been stupid to think that I'd find anything here worthwhile other than broken dreams and wishful thinking.

I went back outside to Mindon, and he suggested that we walk over to Zee's, which was open for business again.

"I don't have any money," I said.

"It's on me."

He pulled a pad of bright green paper out of his pocket, and wrote an "I.O.U" to Zee.

"Real money seems to be scarce these days," he said, "so the businessmen are accepting tokens."

Zee's was run by a veteran of Iraq, whose brain had been partially fried by the atrocities he'd witnessed there; he only seemed halfway normal when he was cooking. You never knew what was on the menu until you sat down, because he just fixed whatever sounded good to him that day; but he was an extraordinarily natural chef, and anything that he made was really, really good to eat.

"You, uh, you back?" he said, when he saw me sit down.

"I'm back," I said. "How've you been, Zee?"

"I, uh, I, uh, I…."

"Never mind, you look good."

"Thank, uh, you."

Then he turned back to the grill, where something truly scrumptious was in process.

"You know," I said, "this is really strange."

"Yeah, I know what you mean," Mindon said. "You turn towards Zee and everything seems, like, normal again. Then you look out the window and you realize you'll never, ever be normal again in your entire life."

"That's it!"

So we watched Zee. That seemed a more normal thing to do.

I paid no attention to the patrons, some of whom I knew, but who were wholly absorbed in the small communities of their tables or their food, or both. People came and people went, and we just talked idly between us. Mostly I told him what'd happened to me.

The door opened again behind us, and then a very strange thing happened, one that to this day seems nothing short of a miracle.

"Well, it's just no use, Auntie," a woman's voice whispered. "The house looks deserted. No one's been there for weeks. No one seems to have any news. Let's get a bite to eat before heading back."

The voice was familiar.

I turned around and gasped out loud. Standing there before me was my dear, dead wife, whose face had now gone completely white. She uttered a faint cry.

"You," she said. "I...I knew—"

She put her hands up and swayed. I rushed and caught her as she fell forward into my arms. In a moment my life had been restored to me. I felt so damned grateful that I cried. I just couldn't help myself. I just cried and cried and so did she. For once I couldn't say anything at all. The academic man was finally buried beneath the raw emotion of the moment.

I just knew that finally, finally, I had come home again, and that fact somehow made the whole trip worthwhile.

EPILOGUE
DEAD RECKONING

Knowledge enormous makes a God of me.
—John Keats

ALEX SMITH, 18 BI-NOVEMBER, MARS YEAR I
NOVATO, CALIFORNIA, PLANET EARTH

Now that I've reached the end of my story, I realize that I can actually add very little to the questions that remain about the invaders. My particular interest is speculative philosophy: what if, what might have been, what could be. My knowledge of comparative physiology is confined to having read a few popular books and essays. Even so, it seems to me that Martina Kosnick's conclusions regarding the sudden disappearance of the Martians are likely to remain unchallenged for the foreseeable future. I've assumed here that her rationale is absolutely correct.

No bacteria except terrestrial bugs were found in the bodies of the aliens—or in the Martian plant life. The fact that the aliens failed to bury any of their dead may point to their ignorance of bodily decay, which on Earth is caused by microbes; or it may just represent some peculiarity in their cultural heritage. So many questions like this have answers that are wholly based on supposition; the sad fact is, no one was ever able during those days to communicate with the Martians, either directly or indirectly, and much remains uncertain about their methods, motivations, and even the operation of their machines.

The composition of the Black Death, which the Martians employed with such deadly effect, also remains unknown, despite numerous attempts at synthesis; and the mechanism used to generate the sting-ray remains a puzzle, although the weapon appears to be based on some sort of laser technology. The terrible disasters at Alabaster Sands, Rancho Cucaracha, and Castle Rock have made experimenters somewhat wary of dissecting advanced Martian technology. The brown scum and dark dust that were a residue of the neutralized Black Death mostly vanished before it could be recovered, leaving just minute samples that have proven equally difficult to analyze.

The results of Professor Jarmann's multitudinous dissections of the Martian bodies, his cutting and sawing and probing, have already been discussed earlier in this narrative. Almost everyone is familiar with the magnificent, almost complete alien specimen on display in the Natural History Museum of the California Academy of Sciences, and the detailed videos and photographs of the Martians that have been posted on the Internet.

A question of more immediate concern is the possibility, even the probability, of another invasion by the Martians. In my estimation, not nearly enough attention is being given to this threat. With every orbit of Mars, with every opposition of the two planets, we can anticipate another attack. If Singletown is right, and the Martians were unable to communicate with their lost expeditionary force, then it may take years, even decades, for them to analyze exactly what went wrong. But the reasons why they attacked Earth in the first place, whatever those are, are still valid, and the likelihood of their return is without question. Sooner or later "they'll be back," to paraphrase a famous California governor who spent the entire invasion period raising funds in Europe.

But maybe the Martian home world *did* communicate with its outriders on Earth. Maybe they're already preparing a second strike force. If so, we must be ready. We have to keep watching the skies, and especially the Red Planet. We have to have defenses in place to fight the invaders wherever and whenever they land, immediately, before they can establish their bases and their war machines—and, if possible, even before they reach the Earth.

It does seem to me, though, that they've now lost one great advantage: the element of surprise. We now know they exist, and we now understand the threat that they pose to our species. Possibly they understand this and will be more cautious in any future attack. Possibly not.

No human being will ever be able to think about man's place in the universe in quite the same way again. We're not alone any longer. And our nearest neighbors, while they may be intelligent, are surely not our friends. Perhaps the only way that we'll ever be able to rest at night is to take the fight to Mars itself. Analyzing the cold equations in this light, I really think that we have no choice: it's us or them. Another war is surely inevitable.

We've learned a hard lesson here. We can never again regard our planet as a safe, secure hiding place for mankind. We can never again dismiss the unseen good or evil that may suddenly fall upon us from the depths of outer space. Maybe in the greater design of things the invasion from Mars was not without benefit: it's robbed us of that serene confidence in the future that is the most fruitful source of decadence; it's leveled our innocence. Human science has already benefited by the study of the Martian machines. The war has also done much to promote the community of man. We can only hope that the Martians have watched the ugly death of their pioneer settlers and have learned their lesson.

Before the alien ships landed, most of our scientists questioned the notion of intelligent life on other worlds. We simply had found no evidence to support the theory, despite the work of SETI and other such projects. Now we see things quite differently. If the Martians can travel through space, so can we. If the Martians exist, then others do as well, possible friends or possible foes, and we would be fools to ignore the opportunity they present.

It's time for man to spread his wings and cast his seed beyond the confines of just one planet or one solar system. But right now that's only a remote dream. The destruction of the Martian threat has to come first. To them, perhaps, and not to us, the future is ordained—unless we take the initiative, unless we carry the fight to the Red Planet.

For myself, I confess that the stress of my experience during the War of Two Worlds has left me with an abiding sense of insecurity. I sit in my office writing these words, and then suddenly I see again the red weed and the writhing flames, and I feel my house abandoned and desolate. I walk out to Novato Boulevard, and watch the vehicles passing by—an SUV filled with vacationers, a delivery van, a police car, a school bus—and suddenly I find myself escaping again with Mayer the Guardsman through the hot, brooding silence of a dark and dangerous night.

I suddenly come awake at three A.M., reliving my imprisonment with Reverend Lesley, and wondering what I could have done differently.

Why did I live while so many others died?

I see the Black Death darkening the silent streets of Dead-Francisco, and the contorted bodies scattered in its gutters; they rise up as one to accuse me, tattered and ragged and dog-bitten, they gibber at me and shake their fists, growling unintelligible mutterings of accusation. I know what they're saying: "You lived, Smith. You survived!"

Those pale, ugly, even insane distortions of humanity are all I have left in the dungeons of the night; and when I finally come to my senses, cold and wretched in the damp, tossing sea of my bed, my heart galloping (*ooh-lah, ooh-lah, ooh-lah*), my lungs gasping, I find my wife sleeping the sleep of the just right next to me. She doesn't understand these things. She doesn't know the terror of my dreams. She can't parse "*ooh-lah.*"

Then I go down to San Francisco and see the busy multitudes, the human ants, rebuilding their businesses in Market Street and the Embarcadero; and it seems to me that they're nothing more than the pale riders of the past, ghosts and goblins haunting the streets that I have walked silent and empty, phantasms and zombies perambulating through a dead city, mocking the lives of real folks.

It's strange, too, to stand on Mount Sutro, as I did the day before finishing this book, and see the great rows of townhouses, dim and blue through the haze of smoke and mist, vanishing at last into the vagueness of the sky; to view the people ambling to and fro among the flower beds in Golden Gate Park; to spy the sightseers gathering there about the stark Martian fighting-machine that still stands erect and silent by the empty Martian pit; to hear the tumult of playing children; and to recall the time when I saw it all bright and clear, hard and silent, under the dawn of that last great day, the day when I was preparing myself to die.

What really happened to me—and to us? All these questions that I have, and so very few answers. All I know is that my role in this great melodrama has yet to be concluded. Mindon, a wiser man than I, says that I spend way too much time contemplating my own navel, and he may be right.

Why did I live while so many others died, if not to bear witness to what happened to us?

Becky and I did decide on one possible answer, at least for ourselves—and one adopted by a great many others as well—to bring a new life into this world. Mélusine Elizabeth was born a few days ago, less than a year after the events recorded in this book. She's different somehow than I ever expected, with strange dark eyes and an understanding beyond her age.

But the strangest thing of all, the one thing that I could never account for, was my wife's unexpected reappearance in my life, and the miraculous fact that it happened to me twice. Most men only get one chance in life.

So I reach out and touch my Becky's face again, and I take her warm hand in mine, and I feel the beating of her heart—and I marvel to think that I counted her, and that she counted me, among the disassociated dead.

AFTERWORD
"H.G. AND ME"

It started in the Fall of 2004 with a phone call from Tim Underwood, Publisher of Underwood Books, whom I've known for thirty-five years or more. He was considering publishing an illustrated, coffee-table-style volume as a tie-in to the then forthcoming motion picture version of *War of the Worlds*— itself a very loose adaptation of the classic science-fiction novel by H. G. Wells—and wanted me to write the commentary. The project never developed, for a variety of reasons; and I've never viewed the Spielberg film, again for a variety of reasons.

Late in the Spring of 2005, Tim called me out of the blue, and asked me to do a quick rewrite of the second half of Wells's 1898 original novel, which Tim had already started recasting into a modern-day version set in the San Francisco Bay Area. I agreed, and quickly finished the job on a rush-rush basis. After seeing my work, he then asked me to revamp the entire book into one consistent, unified voice, and to use what I could of both his contribution and H. G.'s seminal work. Shortly thereafter, I proposed—and Tim agreed—that I pen two sequels to *War of Two Worlds*, as it was now called. These would be set some years after the action in the first novel, and would be entirely of my own devising.

The first two books in the sequence were announced for publication in the Fall of 2005. Covers were designed and orders solicited. I rewrote Volume One in its entirety, with an eye towards creating the sequels; and then promptly plunged into

Volume Two, *Operation Crimson Storm*, completing it at the end of July. The books were typeset and I approved the galleys. I also prepared a brief outline of Volume Three, which was due to be written and published the following year, depending on the sales of the first two.

Once again, however, fate intervened, and the titles never appeared as scheduled. Well, *c'est la vie*—I'd been paid an advance and I'd done the work, and my publisher *liked* my work, more to the point. Maybe the novels would eventually see the light of day in some other venue. Indeed, I've never yet penned a book that wasn't eventually released in some professional forum.

There the matter rested for several years. And then, early in 2007, I again heard from Tim, and he suggested that we do *all three novels* as an omnibus (mind you, *número tres* had yet to be written!). So, I reread and re-edited the first two books, to familiarize myself again with the material, and then wrote *The Martians Strike Back!* as the concluding volume to the trilogy. The books were published under a new title, *Invasion! Earth vs. the Aliens* later that year—to a resounding clap of silence from the critics.

When the three-in-one version was declared out-of-print in 2010, I asked Tim for a reversion of the rights, and decided to have the novels reissued in the way that they were originally intended to be published—as separate works. So here they are, released finally as individual fictions—but with the titles of the first novel and the series switched, at the urging of my publisher. I hope you enjoy their new incarnations.

* * * * * * *

Recasting a famous book by an equally famous deceased author presents the writer with an interesting set of challenges. On the one hand, you enter the forum knowing full well that some of the original creator's fans will never be reconciled to any tampering with sacred writ, and will either find fault with one's poor efforts, or dismiss them out-of-hand as being unworthy of the master. Then, too, the rewriter runs the risk of moving so far beyond the intent of the creator or the basic concept of his story as to warp it out of any semblance with the material that inspired it.

However, I had several things working in my favor. I really liked *War of the Worlds*, as well as many other of Wells's fictional prognostications; I not only felt that they were the *crème de la crème* of the science fiction stories of his era, but that they still remained highly readable more than a century later. In particular, H. G.'s early works possess a vividness, a fictional presence, if you will, matched by few writers of *any* period.

I was also well aware of his defects as a wordsmith. His female characters, particularly in these early creations, are mere stick-figures, having no personalities whatsoever. Even his strong-minded protagonists often display no personal identities (or names) beyond their professions.

Moreover, Wells is often so intent upon scoring points against his perceived enemies in society—the social ills and classes against which he railed in nonfiction form—that his fiction can easily descend into diatribe. This doesn't happen as frequently in these early fictions as in some of his later work—but it's there nonetheless.

Each writer carries with him- or herself certain prejudices, preconceived notions, favorite phrases, and personality traits that taint one's fiction, or perhaps make it distinctive, to use a kinder term. I am no more exempt from such authorial displays than H. G. was.

Still, it seemed to me entirely feasible to regarb the 1898 version of *War of the Worlds* with modern dress. Tim Underwood had already started the process in the first half of the new version, by setting it in a region that he personally knew quite well; and since I had at least visited the area on occasion, and had a general feel for the geography and layout there, I felt comfortable leaving the initial setting in the country just north of San Francisco—as well as in the city itself. I also maintained some of the character assignments that Tim had made in his initial rewrite of Part One, as a nod to my hidden collaborator.

As to how much of Tim's original contribution yet remains, I really can't be sure at this point. I rewrote the first half of the book (the section on which Tim worked) at least twice in its entirety, and later did some additional heavy edits of selected passages there; and I also inserted a new storyline set in the Inland Empire region of Southern California), and added several new characters, plus a new Prologue (the last piece to be created for the omnibus edition).

Similarly, I do recognize some of H. G.'s prose echoing in selected passages, but here again, much of what Wells wrote has been so altered that it's now very much a blend of "me and thee." The book *sounds* like one of my novels, at least to me; and it certainly shares the themes common to my other fictions, particularly the issue of communication. Alex Smith (the 1898 narrator has no name) is my Everyman, although he's not quite an "everyman" as most folks would define that term.

In rereading my version of Wells's vision again this past week, I was pleasantly surprised at how well it flowed, considering the choppy and occasionally chaotic history of its creation. *War of Two Worlds* is indeed the result of two worlds clashing, two cultures separated by a century of constant change. *My* world is wholly unlike H. G.'s in so many respects; but we at least share a common tongue and some common visions; and the resulting collaborative fiction is, I hope, a blend of the best of *both worlds*.

Well, that's something that you, the reader, will have to judge for yourself. I've made very few changes in the text for this new release—its first publication, I might add, as a separate work— because I felt that none were needed. I hope you agree.

Robert Reginald
San Bernardino, California
23 January 2011

ABOUT THE AUTHOR

ROBERT REGINALD started writing as a child, and penned his first book during his senior year in college. He's been infected with terminal logorrhea ever since, churning out more than twelve million words of professional fiction and nonfiction. He settled in Southern California in 1969, where he served as an academic librarian for 40 years. He currently edits the Borgo Press Imprint of Wildside Press, and has also penned more than 120 published books and 13,000 short pieces.

His recent works of fiction include four Nova Europa historical fantasy novels, *The Dark-Haired Man; or, The Hieromonk's Tale* (2004), *The Exiled Prince; or, The Archquisitor's Tale* (2004), *Quæstiones; or, The Protopresbyter's Tale* (2005), and *The Fourth Elephant's Egg; or, The Hypatomancer's Tale* (forthcoming); two science-fiction novels, *Invasion!: Earth vs. the Aliens* (2007; a trilogy comprising *The War of Two Worlds*, *Operation Crimson Storm*, and *The Martians Strike Back!*) and *Knack' Attack: A Tale of the Human-Knacker War* (2010); two Phantom Detective mysteries, *The Phantom's Phantom* (2007) and *The Nasty Gnomes* (2008); a comic mystery, *The Paperback Show Murders* (2011); and three story collections, *Katydid & Other Critters: Tales of Fantasy and Mystery* (2001), *The Elder of Days: Tales of the Elders* (2010), and *The Judgment of the Gods and Other Verdicts of History* (2011).

Recent nonfiction works include an anthology, *Choice Words: The Borgo Press Book of Writers Writing About Writing* (2010); two collections, *Xenograffiti: Essays on Fantastic*

Literature (1996 & 2005) and *Classics of Fantastic Literature; or, Les Épines Noires* (with Douglas Menville, 2005); three guides to the Deryni world, *Codex Derynianus I* and *II* and *III* (with Katherine Kurtz, 1998 & 2005 & forthcoming); four histories, *San Quentin* (ed. with Bonnie Petry, 2005), *¡Viva California!: Seven Accounts of Life in Early California* (ed. with Mary Burgess, 2006), *The Eastern Orthodox Churches* (2005), and *The Coyote Chronicles: A Chronological History of California State University, San Bernardino, 1960-2010* (2010); a short autobiography, *Trilobite Dreams; or, The Autodidact's Tale* (2006); a cookbook, *Cal State Cooks* (ed. with Johnnie Ralph, 2006); and several bibliographies: *BP 300* (2007), *CSUSB Faculty Authors* (2006), *Murder in Retrospect* (with Jill Vassilakos, 2005), and *Draqualian Silk* (with William Maltese, 2010). In 1993 he received the Pilgrim Award from the Science Fiction Research Association. You can find him at:

http://www.millefleurs.tv

www.ingramcontent.com/pod-product-compliance
Lightning Source LLC
Chambersburg PA
CBHW020757250626
47155CB00003B/1118